Fred Willard

DOWN ON PONCE

NO EXIT PRESS

D1355100

First published in Great Britain by No Exit Press, 1998.
18 Coleswood Road, Harpenden, Herts, AL5 1EQ, England.

http://www.noexitpress.demon.co.uk

A CIP catalogue record for this book is available from the British Library.

ISBN 1-901982-31-9 Down on Ponce pb

1 3 5 7 9 10 8 6 4 2

Composed in Bembo by Koinonia, Manchester
and printed and bound in Great Britain.

For Brianne, Rainbow and Margie

Acknowledgements

It is my fortune to have many friends and my regret that space does not permit me to acknowledge them all. This novel was written as I recovered from a period of disability accompanying the onset of arthritis. It was a difficult time and family and friends got me through it.

First and foremost, I'd like to thank Brianne and Rainbow Willard for their help then and now.

The Intown Atlanta Writers' Group gave me a place to listen, read, have potato salad thrown at my manuscripts, reconsider and rewrite. Its co-hosts, Bill Osher and Diane C. Thomas, deserve much public praise and compassion for having us in their home twice a month. They and the other members – Eric Allstrom, Jim Taylor, Anne Webster, Marilyn Staats, Gene Wright, Karla Jennings, Nora Harlow, David Darracott, Anne Gleaton, Donna and Jack Warner and Linda Clopton – have been able teachers of the writer's craft.

The following friends also lent advice and support: Randy Stinson, Jon Simmons, Missi McMorries, Howard Hursey, Carmen Gutierrez, Mike Marinello, Betsy Hall, Hart Ramm, Harry Resovsky, David Tice, Karl Brendel, Jean Dangler, Ainsley Beery, Marcus Calloway and Peter Henault.

I would like to thank John Yow, my editor, for his confidence in the book, his patience, and his sense of humor.

My agent, Frances Kuffel of the Jean V. Naggar Literary Agency, also deserves a tip of the hat.

Special thanks are due to Bill Diehl. When I was about to wave the white flag of literary surrender, his enthusiastic support of the manuscript gave me the resolve to continue.

Finally, a big secret handshake for the crew at Los Angeles and North Highland. You know who you are. Thanks.

Author's Note

Ponce de Leon Avenue, called "Ponce" by locals, is a haven for the homeless, the lawless and the restless located in Atlanta, Georgia – a city that may be too busy to hate, but isn't above taking a little time off to steal.

I LEANED BACK in a wobbly dinette chair with my feet propped on the table. No junk mail and one letter this week; it was from Lester "Bug" Raiford.

Bug was a funny guy whose problem with authority had gotten out of hand when he tooted too many lines of crank and became convinced his brain was haunted by the ghost of Sid Vicious.

The outside of the envelope bore the imprint of a rubber stamp: "Warning! The enclosed correspondence is from a prisoner at a Federal Mental Hospital and has not been censored."

The note was short, but more coherent than the last half-dozen had been.

> Good news. I finally got sane enough to convince them I was crazy. I like it much better here in the nut house because you don't have to do nothing to get drugs, they just give them to you, even when you don't want them.
>
> As far as I can tell, if I develop what they call remorse, I may be able to get out of here eventually. Remorse seems to mean that you cry when you talk about your past, so I have been like a weeping willow tree. You may see the tear stains on this letter.
>
> It's all bullshit because I enjoyed seeing the Federals jumping out of that burning car with their pants on fire.
>
> I have enclosed some artwork for your enjoyment.
>
> Your friend, Bug.

The second sheet was a heavy piece of construction paper

that held an awkward collage of cut-out magazine illustrations assembled to depict a grinning Dan Quayle about to be sodomized by Long Dong Silver.

Across the bottom there was a ransom note-style message which read: "Every cop is a criminal, and all you sinners are saints."

I selected a postcard with a picture of a Seminole Indian wrestling an alligator from a box on the table that held stamps, pens and paper and wrote a reply.

"Bug. Congratulations on your move. It sounds like you are doing much better. Take your medicine and cry as often as possible. Both may do you good."

Then I taped his collage on the wall above the dinette next to the jackalope. Invented by an anonymous Heironymus Bosch of the American Plains, the jackalope consists of a stuffed bunny head with pronghorn antelope antlers glued on top in order to confuse the tourists.

Lester had given it to me during the last stages of his methedrine psychosis. He said it illustrated a business plan to franchise surrealist open-casket funerals, where the deceased would have parts of various animals attached to their bodies. Needless to say the plan never went anywhere.

Shortly afterward, Bug was arrested for throwing a Molotov cocktail into a car full of ATF agents.

There was a tentative knock at the door. I imagined it was the neighbor trying to borrow money for his bad habits. Lately he had been sending his gaunt wife to ask.

Even though she always prefaced her conversations with a brief homily on the evils of drink and drugs, she'd been wiping her nose a lot lately, so I guessed she either had a perpetual cold or had been dipping into the snuff box with her old man.

She'd tell me a hard-luck story – God knows she has plenty to pick from – and I'd slip her a couple of bills, then she'd go home, and I'd hear his ragged Camaro race out the gravel drive of the trailer park.

I hoped she held back some for herself and the children, but I doubted it.

"Just a minute," I said.

I looked through the peephole. As near as I could tell through the distortion of the plastic fish-eye lens, my visitor was not the neighbor's wife with a sad tale or the neighbor with a baseball bat, but a clean-cut man standing in front of a shiny car.

I opened the door. He was well dressed, in his mid-thirties, freshly shaven, with a fashionable mop of blond hair. The car was a new Mercedes.

"I wonder if I could talk to you a minute?" he asked.

"What about."

"Could I come inside?"

"Why?" I asked.

"It's confidential."

"Are you sure you're talking to the right man? You might want to check on that if you're going to take me into your confidence."

I spoke in a fuck-you tone of voice. I didn't want to hear what he had to say. He didn't seem to want to say it either. He was shuffling around like he was going to propose marriage and was afraid I might accept.

"You're Samuel Fuller. My name is James Shirley. We have a mutual friend."

"And who might that be?" I asked.

"I'd rather not say." He avoided eye contact.

"I guess that's confidential," I said.

I could tell he knew I was making fun of him and was trying not to resent it. I let the silence linger until it became uncomfortable, then said, "OK. Come on in." I could always throw him out if he didn't have anything pleasant to say.

As he climbed up the steps of the trailer, I saw my neighbor eyeing the Mercedes from his kitchen window, and I wondered how long Shirley would have a radio.

He slumped into a worn easy chair.

"You follow the Braves?" he asked.

"You want my advice on baseball?"

He looked at his hands. "No, I want you to kill my wife."

I made my face go dead, nothing coming in or going out, like a happy-go-lucky psycho who would scratch his ear or cut your throat with equal conviction.

He tried not to show it but he was badly frightened. I liked that. It meant he would be easier to control.

"Wait here," I said.

I walked down the narrow hall. The trailer floor sank with a creak as I entered the bedroom. I'd been meaning to move. The place isn't worth fixing. It's a dump.

The closet door had slipped off its tracks, so I pushed it aside just enough to stick my hand in and pull out the pump shotgun. Then I walked back to the living room, worked the slide for effect like they do on television, dropping a perfectly good shell to the floor and pointed the muzzle at his face. I hoped it didn't go off by accident. It would be a mess.

"You can either go or stay. I don't give a fuck. But if you stay you got to take your clothes off."

"What?"

He blinked. I knew how a gun in your face can make your mind feel like an empty room with a bad echo.

"Clothes off," I repeated.

"Why?"

"I want to see if you got anything taped to your body."

"What do you mean?"

"Like a wireless mike or a tape recorder."

The idea finally caught up with him.

"That's smart," he said.

What a dumb shit.

He pulled off the hand-sewn loafers and socks, stood, dropped and stepped out of his khaki pants, unbuttoned the shirt and laid it on the sofa then took off the new striped boxer shorts.

"Turn around," I said.

He held his arms at shoulder height and did a 360. There was nothing on his body. He was trying to act casual, like, gee, I've been in the army and this doesn't bother me a bit, cause I'm used to being ordered to take my clothes off, but his genitals had shrunk to the point they looked like a goober balanced on two English peas. Luckily, they didn't share the same color scheme.

"See the picture on the wall of our former vice president about to get romantic?" I asked.

He nodded.

"A friend of mine did that. He's doing time at a federal institution for the criminally insane for fire bombing a car full of federal agents. Pretty interesting the way he's got all those pictures stuck together, isn't it?"

He tried to say, "Yes," but his voice cracked.

He was holding himself so tight that I imagined if he farted it would sound like he was playing the penny whistle.

"You can sit at the dinette," I said.

The trailer had an open living room–kitchen–dining area. He sat at the table like he was trying to touch it as little as possible.

I checked the shoes. Expensive. No swiveling heels with secret transmitters. No pockets on the shirt, nothing attached to it. A comb in one back pants pocket, his wallet in the other.

There were three hundred-dollar bills in the wallet; I took them out and stuck them in my jeans. The driver's license said he was James Shirley, like he claimed. According to an insurance card, the Mercedes out front was his. Nothing much else of interest. Keys in the right front pocket. He was clean.

"Go ahead and put them back on."

I pointed at his clothes, then put down the shotgun and sat

on the sofa. He dressed as we talked.

"Why should I want to kill your wife?" I asked.

"Ten thousand dollars," he said.

"That's the beginning of a reason," I agreed. "Why do you want her dead?"

"She makes my skin crawl."

"Ever thought of divorce?" I asked.

"No. Does it make a difference?"

"It could."

"Why would it make a difference? I don't understand."

"You could change your mind about a divorce. You can't change your mind once she's dead. I don't want some guy who knows my name mooning over his poor dead wife."

"I want her dead."

Aside from being a chickenshit, he was a cold-blooded little son of a bitch. I couldn't imagine him caring enough about anyone to want them dead. This had to be about money.

"All right. Let's talk about finances."

"How about five thousand before and five thousand after you do it?"

"And what am I supposed to do if you don't make the last payment? Sue you?"

"You can trust me," he said.

"Right. I see your point. People who hire people to kill people are generally trustworthy."

I thought about the best way to handle it, something he could manage, then said:

"You get yourself a box, you put thirty thousand dollars in used twenties in it, photographs that will show me what she looks like, and information about her schedule and habits. Deliver the box to the Sunnyland Marina on Lake Lanier, then just go about your business, don't do anything differently—only, without making a fuss be sure you can account for your time during the weekdays. OK?"

"Sure, sure."

He would probably fuck it up but it didn't make much difference. He hadn't blinked at my tripling the price. There was probably a lot of money involved.

"One other thing."

I didn't say anything until he looked at me, then I gave my imitation of Bug Raiford on the worst day of his life. I folded my arms together, let my jaw go slack and leaned toward him opening my eyes as wide as possible.

I hissed a little, and he leaned forward to hear what I was about to say.

I whispered, "I'm going to enjoy doing her. It's going to be fun. You know what that means?"

"Nuh no," he stammered.

"It means you don't want to fuck with me."

"You're right," he agreed quickly.

"I don't want to ever see you again," I said.

"No. You won't ever see me again. Don't worry," he said.

My neighbor's Camaro scratched gravel as he tore out of the trailer-court driveway.

"Leave."

Shirley walked briskly to the car without looking back. He didn't even stop when he realized the Mercedes' radio was missing.

What an idiot.

2

I WARNED JIMMY Cooley, the marina handyman, that I was expecting a package, then went about my normal business, mostly fishing and laying about listening to boats rock against their moorings.

Jimmy was an okay guy. He had done fifteen months at Jackson on a bullshit conviction for less than an ounce of marijuana. While he was doing time, he lost his family to a smooth-talking, purple-fire preacher named Melvin Keener who stamped out sin by fucking lonely women and selling cemetery lots. Jimmy's wife, Martha, should have been a Tantric Buddhist, 'cause she sure thought she found God in the middle of pitching a wang-dang-doodle.

What really pissed Jimmy was that when old Melvin got busted for selling the same lot 138 times Martha stood by him. She said nobody will need their graves on judgment day, anyway, and the preacher was just trying to raise money to do God's work. The few times Jimmy had seen his kids they called him Satan. Life can be a scream.

Jimmy felt real stupid for being the only man he ever met to do so much time for so little dope. He liked to hang out with other people who had plenty of reasons to feel stupid. As a result, he had a good picture of the general flow of your criminal elements.

When I first came to the area, I put out the story that I had sued somebody's pants off due to a construction accident and was living on the remains. Jimmy had understood the truth about me without being told and was too polite to ask for details.

If Shirley came up with the money, I would have to leave town till the ruckus faded, so it was possible I was saying goodbye for a while to some of my favorite people and places.

For days, it was like I was living one of those bittersweet Japanese poems which ached at the beauty of ripeness going to seed and the loss of one more of our allotted days. As I tied on to the dock, or used the marina's beat-up old bathroom where the paint had been worn from the toilet seat, I said to myself, "Well, I won't be doing this much longer," and then I felt sad.

I probably should abandon my life more often, because I never gave a shit about any of this until I decided to leave. Being in a poem isn't half bad.

I drifted in and out of the slip without attracting the attention of anyone but Jimmy. He would leave crazy post-cards of things like a 1959 Oldsmobile Super 88, or a mule wearing a hat and sunglasses for me to send to Bug.

The three of us, Jimmy, Bug and I, had become a sort of half-assed family, which was funny because we weren't at all alike. It had happened without us intending it. But it was fine that it had. It's nice to know that one person cares enough to go to your funeral and sort through your stuff after you're gone.

On the eleventh day, he waved to me as I throttled back the boat motor and glided to the dock.

"Sam, you got a package."

I followed him to the office and saw the box with big block letters on it: "Samuel Fuller, c/o Sunnyland Marina."

Jimmy lives at the marina in an old houseboat that looks like a travel trailer mounted on two silver torpedoes, and he lets me use it when I've got business to conduct out of sight of the curious and respectable.

In the cabin of the boat, I slit open the box. A brown manila envelope lay on top of the neat stacks of money. I cleared a space on the galley table and poured the contents out.

Two formal portraits of an attractive young woman, short dark hair, blue eyes, looking at the camera, more candid shots of her wearing a bikini, clowning on a beach with green water behind. From the color of the water it had to be the Keys, south of Islamorada.

There were four handwritten pages from a legal pad with headings like "Bio," "Friends" or "Regular Activities."

Maiden name: Anne Marie Quillman. She attended a large local high school, parents both deceased. Best friend: Mamie Berger, both go to a sports club three mornings a week for swimming and aerobics. Routine stuff. I didn't think he knew her very well.

On the last sheet of paper he had drawn heavy lines halfway down the page then written in block letters, "MAKE IT LOOK LIKE A SEX CRIME."

It was a good idea and would give the appearance of your basic random senseless act of violence instead of your basic planned senseless act of violence. Nice to know Shirley was thinking about the consequences of our project. Also nice to know he was playing a couple of beats behind.

Jimmy Cooley was hosing down a boat at the end of the dock. He waved with his fingers like a joke as I carried the box to my truck and threw it in the front seat.

I placed the call from the pay phone by the ice machine. A woman answered.

"Shirley residence."

"This is Roger Smith at Health Equipment Company. Will someone be there this afternoon for a delivery?"

"I didn't order anything," she said.

"James Shirley ordered a Nautilus."

"That's my husband. I didn't know he ordered anything."

"I don't know anything about that. I just need to know if you can accept delivery?"

"When can you be here?"

"Probably around three."

"OK yes, that will be fine."

She sounded excited at the prospect of being one more innocent lamb waiting for the slaughter.

3

I ONLY NEEDED to be believable enough to get inside the house, so I changed to a khaki shirt and slacks and put a large empty cardboard box about the size of a Nautilus machine in the back of the truck, weighting it with two cement blocks.

James Shirley lived in one of the expensive new subdivisions near the river with homes financed with stolen savings and loan money.

The older houses in the area, mostly sprawling ranches, were doing a good job of disappearing into the trees.

The Shirley residence, three stories of gingerbread in the middle of an enormous, cement drive, looked a lot like a dollhouse in a sandbox. There was something very crazy about buying a house this breathlessly romantic then paying to have your wife murdered in it.

I pulled next to a side entrance that looked like the logical place for a delivery and Anne Marie Shirley opened the door as I got out of the truck. Her dark hair was a little longer than in the picture but her eyes were still blue.

"Mrs Shirley?"

"Are you the man with the Nautilus machine?"

She was excited about getting it.

"Right. Before I unload it, do you mind showing where you want me to put it?"

"No. Come right in."

I followed her along a hall then down steps to a large basement room with a bar and pool table, holding the manila envelope under my arm.

"I think you'll want to pull your truck further to the side, then you can follow the walk to the basement door."

"Mrs Shirley, there's something important I need to tell you."

She looked at me like she was expecting to hear the machine's operating instructions. It was sad seeing her so clueless.

"I have something important to tell you about your husband. I'm sorry but there's no Nautilus. I apologize for misrepresenting myself, but I needed to make sure I could see you face to face, without James knowing what I was saying."

She steadied herself but didn't seem to want to leave.

"Could we sit down?" I asked.

"Yes." She gestured to the bar. We each took a stool.

"Is my husband in trouble?"

"Yes. He's in trouble."

Her expression was like a prolonged wince, face drawn, eyes narrowed in pain.

"Are you doing OK? What I have to tell you is going to be very hard to take."

"Oh God, is he dead?"

"No."

This was not getting any easier. I couldn't think of a painless way so I just said it.

"I'm afraid your husband hired me to kill you."

She laughed a little too hard and looked at me with disgust.

"What are you trying to do? Are you after money? My husband loves me. I'm going to call the police."

"Please, before you do, look at this."

I poured the contents of the manila envelope on the bar, spreading them out for her to see, the pictures of her, the schedule, and the note: MAKE IT LOOK LIKE A SEX CRIME.

"Can you recognize his handwriting?"

She looked, and I could tell she believed. Dumb at first, she began mumbling, "Oh God," over and over, then got control, obviously filled with terror, and asked, "And you're going to do it?"

"No, I've never killed anyone before, and I don't intend to start now."

"I don't understand."

"If someone offered you money to break the law you would probably get mad and tell them to go to hell. You're an honest person. I'm not. Your husband gave me a lot of money, and I took it without any intention of doing what he wanted. He needs to learn better business practices when he deals with people like me."

"But you told me about it."

"I'm happy to take your husband's money, but I don't care to see you dead. Your husband paid me thirty thousand dollars. Does being alive feel like it's worth that much?"

"Yes."

"Good. Then you're not going to mind my keeping the money?"

"No."

"Here's some expensive advice: Pack some things, go to a shelter. Don't try to understand him. No matter how much he whines, don't forgive him. The motherfucker wanted me to kill you."

4

WHEN I HAD told Anne Marie Shirley that I had never killed anyone, it wasn't exactly the truth. Back in the seventies, the dope trade had been pretty wild with rip-off gangs stalking dealers along the Mexican border and the Florida Coast. The ones that were good at it were invisible. They'd lie low, then swoop in at the deal and take both the drugs and the money at gunpoint. If you made this too hard for them, they'd settle for one or the other, whichever target opportunity put in their path.

We were going to move a stash of money, and were out on some God-forsaken crushed-shell back road inland from Boca Grande when these three guys in cut-offs came walking out of the palmettos, no shirts, no shoes, no service, each with a shotgun, beards and hair past their shoulders.

They were the headnecks of your nightmares, the Hatfields and McCoys after fifty hits of acid. Not much to do but hope for the best and do whatever it took to stay alive.

"This is a robbery, gentlemen."

The leader said this with a very heavy twang. It sounded rehearsed. His buddies grinned.

"Now we're going to do this real calm, and everyone's going to get through it fine. First thing, we're going to get your pieces."

"No problem, man. Nothing we got's worth getting wasted over," Mr Jim said.

No problem my ass. I thought there was a good chance these guys were going to kill us.

Sensing they had control, they backed off a little.

I didn't know I was going to do it. I felt very far from the Florida palmetto scrub on a cold, slow-motion planet covered with snow – no sound, no natural laws, no second thoughts or consequences.

I pulled the pistol from the waistband of my pants and shot the man closest to me in the center of his chest, and as he fell, the man next to him fired his shotgun. The shock wave ripped past my left ear, leaving it deaf and ringing. My hand jerked back from the recoil as I fired another round, and a hole appeared a little above his left eye, off to the side. He shuddered, and his head flew back before he crumpled. Blood and brains splattered onto the naked chest of the third man, who held the shotgun at his side and looked at the bloody mess as it slid down his front, like he couldn't figure if he had been shot or not.

I had done it so fast that it took a while for everyone, even me, to take it in. It seemed like a long time that nobody did anything. The guy was still looking at himself. It was probably less than a second. I don't know.

Somehow Tommy was behind him with his little .380 in his hand. It went pop, pop, pop real fast into the back of the guy's skull.

We looked at them for a while. They were sort of in a pile, with the white powdery sand caking to their wounds and their smeared blood. The bugs were already crawling on them.

Mr Jim said he would take care of the bodies, since he hadn't done any of the shooting. This surprised me, because Jim never did like using a shovel much, but afterward when he named them the gator-bait gang, I understood.

Things were different afterward. None of us talked about the incident, but it seemed that people were afraid of us. Maybe they saw what we had become more clearly than we did. We still thought of ourselves as Taoist pirates fighting the evil pigs who wouldn't let America's children get happy smoking flowers.

Twenty years later as I think of that time, the friends who died, the loss of my name and my past, it all joins together into one sadness, and I feel like a dung beetle rolling an ever-growing ball of shit through life. Warning Anne Marie Shirley had been a small payment on my karmic debt. I don't know if I will ever get off the hook.

COOP VOGEL WASN'T a bad sort. You could trust him if his hands were above the table and you didn't turn your back . He ran a little cement-block tavern on the highway between my trailer and the lake. It appealed mainly to scooter trash and country outlaws who lived their lives to a Waylon Jennings tune.

The place looked so unsavory that even a suicidal fool wouldn't start anything there, so you could drink a quiet brew and be left the fuck alone. Or if you wanted a little excitement you could play pool or buy crank in the back parking lot once you were established.

I hadn't asked James Shirley who had given him my name because he'd called me Samuel, and Vogel is the only one who does that – at least the only one who might also refer a hit man.

When you step through the door at Vogel's Shack, it takes a minute for your eyes to adjust to the darkness of the room, enough time if you're inside to dash to the bathroom and crawl through an open window if you are on the run from the law or a pissed-off husband.

The first thing you see is a lit bouncing-ball beer sign made in about 1963, and then Coop's shape lumbering behind the bar.

"Vogel."

"Yeah, man. What's up."

"Step outside into my office."

It's like Lord Baden-Powell once said, "The great out-of-doors will capture the heart of any true boy," particularly if he is prone to criminal activities and concerned about being caught on tape by the duly constituted authorities.

He threw a towel behind the bar then joined me in the front parking lot.

"What's going on, Samuel?"

"Don't bullshit a bullshitter, man."

"I'm not trying to bullshit you."

He looked at the ground and scuffed the gravel with his shoe and scratched his blond beard.

"So tell me about James Shirley."

"Don't know him."

"How about a man who's sick of his wife."

"That guy – OK, he came in and gave me five hundred bucks for a name."

"And you gave him mine?"

"Sure, I figured you could always tell him to fuck off."

"That's true."

"So, you going to do her?"

"No. I took the guy's money, and I told the wife."

Vogel laughed hard.

"You're cold, man. I mean a lot of people would have killed the bitch, but telling her is too fucking much."

"Yeah, Shirley's a piss-ant. I'm happy to do whatever I can to ruin his life."

I handed Coop a roll of bills.

"It's another five. That's for the referral and for your trouble if he comes back to complain."

"Like I give a shit. The guy doesn't have the balls to kill his own wife, he sure as shit isn't going to fuck with me."

"This guy is so clueless he might do anything. He doesn't seem to have any idea what he's getting into."

"OK, I appreciate the warning." He changed the subject. "So, what do you hear from Bug?"

"He said he thinks he might be able to get out if he shows remorse."

"Shit yes, that might work. Tell him he might try crying, too."

"He's already said he's going to cry."

"It's too bad he ain't in the county instead of that federal crazy place. There used to be a social worker that came down to county that would give you a blow job if you cried enough about how sorry you were for being a criminal."

"No shit, a blow job?"

"No shit, man. A damn good one too."

"Was this a man or a woman."

"Don't piss on me, Samuel. It was a woman. What the fuck do you think?"

"Just checking, man. Anyway I got to run, got to take care of business."

I walked to my truck across the gravel parking lot. Coop waved from the door of his shack. I didn't know if I believed him, but his story was probably close to the truth, or at least as close as I would know.

IF IT WERE a rational world, James Shirley would catch the drift, go to his room, sit down, and shut up. But I didn't think it would work that way.

Guys who are used to having things their way can get real pissed when a member of the lower orders gets the best of them. He could be a problem.

All of this called for a plan, and having been nearly killed being a devil-may-care man of action, I thought I might try something easier this time.

A vacation sounded safe enough. Maybe I would find one of those artsy communities around Tucson, look for a woman who wanted to paint all day and fuck me senseless all night, a place where I could go half naked and howl like a coyote without attracting much attention. Not a bad idea.

First, I had to execute step one: divest myself of immovable belongings.

Jimmy was stretched out on a nylon-web chaise longue on the afterdeck of his houseboat.

"Hey, Jimmy."

He opened his eyes and looked at me from under the brim of the beat-up straw hat pulled low on his face.

"Yeah, Sam. What can I do for you?"

"You ever want to live in a place where you don't get thrown out of bed every time a ski boat runs by?"

"Sure, but I get the slip rental for free. It's part of my pay. I can't really afford anything, you know."

"You can't beat the price. This place is free."

He sat up.

"What's the deal."

"I want to leave town for a while. I've decided to get rid

of my trailer. To tell you the truth, it isn't worth much, but it'll keep the rain off. I'd just as soon give it away as spend the time trying to sell it."

"I've seen your trailer, it's all right."

I knew Jimmy didn't have a car, so the trailer might seem like a booby prize. Here's a place to live, too bad you can't get there.

I threw him my keys.

"Here's the deal. You can use my truck till you get something else worked out. After that, make sure it has anti-freeze and oil and so on and drive it every once in a while. I need to borrow your boat for a week or two. I'll be out on the lake. But I'll let you know where you can pick it up."

"Sam, are you in trouble?"

"Trying to stay out of trouble," I said.

TOO LATE. ANOTHER two minutes and I would have been gone. Jimmy had helped me fill the gas tanks and carry the clean clothes, groceries and a big LP bottle to the houseboat, and then he had left in the truck to check out his new trailer.

I was squatting on the afterdeck listening to the outboard idle. He took good care of it, but I wanted to check it out before proceeding to the boondocks.

"You goddamn liar. You son of a bitch," Shirley screamed as he ran down the dock. I was sure he would hit me if I didn't hit him first, and since, as a policy, I never engage in a fair fight if there are better alternatives, I reached for the nearest blunt instrument, a boat hook Jimmy had made by duct-taping a bent rod from a TV antenna to a push broom handle. It was sort of flimsy, but, swung with enough authority, it could break a face.

He stopped about ten feet from the boat and slowly backed up. It looked like he might have stopped at Vogel's first. His hair and clothes were roughed up, and he had a mouse under one eye.

"We had an agreement," he yelled.

"Sorry, but I decided not to go through with it."

"I want my money back."

"I understand that."

"So, you're going to give it back." He sounded hopeful.

"No, I thought I might hold on to it and spend it on a good time."

"You son of a bitch. We had a contract."

"A contract?"

"You have a moral obligation."

"A moral obligation to murder your wife? You're a fucking idiot. Listen. I've done you a big favor. It's cost you some money, but now you can stop and think about what you are doing before you screw up the rest of your life. Stop and think about it. You don't really want to kill anybody."

I cast off the stern line.

"We can still work this out," he said.

I shook my head as much in disbelief as disagreement.

"I can give you more money, if that's the problem."

He was desperate, and nobody is that sick of their wife. There was something he hadn't admitted. I imagined the arrangement had really been about insurance money, or something like that. I had never believed he cared enough about her to want to kill her.

"As long as you're standing there with nothing to do, slip the bow line off that piling," I said.

He walked to the bow of the boat, and I wondered if he was going to climb aboard, but he obediently pulled the hawser from the piling and threw it to the foredeck.

From where I stood I backed the boat twenty feet from the dock by pulling the control cables with my hand, then, once clear, went into the cabin, took the wheel, and made a slow turn through the cove, heading north for open water.

This was step two of the plan: Get the fuck out of town.

I HAD THE dream again that night, for the first time in years. Maybe I've been thinking too much about the old days or maybe it was just sleeping on a boat, the gentle rocking in my berth, the creaking lines, and the hundred different little sounds as gear settled, rolled and clacked with each gentle swell.

I sat up and put my feet on the floor until my mind cleared and I remembered where I was. Then I walked to the afterdeck and sat on Jimmy's web lawn chair and replayed the dream in the safety of the wide-awake world.

It goes the same way every time. It's dark, and it's around midnight, and we are a mile or so off Boca Grande in the big cabin cruiser, nothing much happening, just drinking beers and passing a J. Alice is with us; by this time she is almost part of the crew. She's had about six beers too many and is not too steady on her feet.

"What I really worry about you boys," she says, "is that some day you're going to be as big of an asshole as you think you already are."

I'm stepping around the cockpit to get a cooler on the foredeck. Then a light too bright to see and a sound too loud to hear absorbed everything, and I was pushed toward the moon by air as hard as a column of marble. I looked down and saw the boat had exploded and what was left of it was on fire, and I still flew up toward the stars. I saw Florida's other coast, Key West, New Orleans, and over my shoulder, some businessmen I knew in Baranquilla grinning and licking their lips. And then it was daylight, and I crashed on a beach on Boca Grande, and there were five bodies on the edge of the surf being rolled back and forth by the waves, and from a distance I knew they were dead, because nothing living can be that limp.

I walked down the beach and saw their eyes staring in my direction but fixed on nothing, Tommy, Skeets, Alice, Mr. Jim. The fifth body was mine.

What really had happened that night wasn't nearly as poetic. I remember Alice talking. I went forward for more beer, then nothing else for a while. After the explosion, half conscious, I held onto a part of the deck that had been blown clear of the burning hull. As my mind defogged, I listened hard but heard nothing but the debris of the dead boat beating against itself as it rolled with the sea. I swam in circles and looked for survivors until I was exhausted, then headed for the light of shore.

What seemed like hours later, I rested my waterlogged hands and knees on a hard shell beach and puked saltwater through my nose.

I grabbed the hidden cash and the account books and got out, leaving everything else: my clothes, my car, and my dog. I figured that if they thought I drowned in the Gulf I might stand a chance.

A trucker gave me a ride to Tampa. As he sang Hank Williams, I was sure a Colombian angel of death was about to tap me for a dance.

In Ybor City, I paid cash for a clunker and drove to the Panhandle till I found a place where no one would look for me or find me, a funky little motel at Mexico Beach.

It was owned by a young widow. Her husband was a straight-arrow officer who had got his ass shot off in Vietnam, and she had used the insurance money to buy the motel. We spent most of our time fucking and drinking. It wasn't very sentimental but it felt better than grief.

I walked up and down the beach and wondered what I was going to do with the rest of my life, until it occurred to me that having inherited the entire proceeds of a major drug-smuggling enterprise, I didn't have to do anything at all.

It was then I searched the graveyards and found a boy born the same year as I who had died when he was less than a year old. His name was Samuel Fuller, and, with a copy of his birth certificate, I became him.

I read the newspapers. The boat explosion had been noted but the bodies were never found. I think they were eaten by sharks, but I guess there's a chance my friends are alive too, and I was just the first one to the money.

I walked back to my berth and stretched out. I was tired but didn't know if I could sleep now that I was thinking about the night the boat exploded. As always, I wondered who had wanted to kill us, or for that matter, if after all the fear and running, it had only been a leaking gas line.

THERE ARE ABOUT twenty pay telephones that I use to conduct business, mostly with off-shore banks that are sympathetic to depositors with unorthodox needs. Four of the phones are on the lake, one at Sunnyland, another at DJ's, a sort of half-assed boat dock and convenience store that's even further down the food chain.

I was proceeding to DJ's quietly just before dawn after having laid off and watched long enough to be satisfied there was nobody there. The sky was streaked orange, and I was moving at slow drift, the motor throttled back to almost nothing, just to give direction as a gentle breeze pushed the boat along. It was a beautiful morning and a great day to be alive and be a career criminal in the land of opportunity, the American Republic. Hallelujah.

The houseboat drifted to the dock sideways, two fenders over the starboard, my weight shifting to compensate for the slight jolt at contact. As I made fast, I checked out the dock and the back of the store. Not a creature was stirring, except for a half dozen fat Norwegian rats exploring a trash can without a lid.

I walked quickly up the dock toward the pay phone, but stopped when I glanced at the Atlanta Constitution paper box and saw the story above the fold.

"North Fulton couple slain in home. Real estate developer James Shirley and his wife, Anne Marie, were found dead from an evident execution-style slaying when a neighbor's dog wandered through the open door of their North Fulton home."

"Shit." I kicked the paper box three times before I noticed my foot hurt, fished some change from my pocket, put it in the machine, and got a couple copies of the Constitution, then walked back to the boat, cast off, and made for deep water.

Once I was far from shore, I killed the engine and sat at the galley table and read the newspaper.

The neighbor had followed his dog to the house and knocked at the open front door. Getting no response he had gone inside and found the couple in the living room sprawled next to each other. Both had their mouth sealed and their hands bound behind their backs with silver duct tape. Both had been shot in the face. It was the worst thing the neighbor had seen in his life, and he was frightened. The police had no immediate leads but agreed that it looked like an execution.

At this point, the story jumped to an inside page. I was folding the newspaper to hold it more easily when my eyes fixed on another headline.

"Man killed in trailer fire in hall. A Hall County man was burned to death in an explosive trailer fire Tuesday night. The man, identified as Sam Fuller, whom neighbors described as a local handyman, was killed when a defective space heater ignited a large volume of a flammable liquid he was storing in his living room, according to the Hall County fire marshall."

I had been living for so long in a world where emotions are not safe that I sat for ten minutes trying to convince myself that I didn't feel anything at all. It didn't work, but at least I got enough perspective to know that my rage was dangerous. If I wanted the satisfaction of revenge, and planned to live to enjoy it, I needed to cool off. I tried not to think about Jimmy, who had drifted to sleep thinking happy thoughts about his new home, never to wake again. I'd seen people who had been caught in fires. I didn't like thinking about him that way.

I tried to reason through the implications of the news. Nobody gave a rat's ass if some handyman in a Hall County trailer park got his butt shot off, but somebody had gone to great lengths to make my death look like an accident. On the other hand, the great unwashed were likely to become exercised over the murder of such a widely admired fellow as James Shirley and his lovely wife, and yet they had been obviously executed.

This said a lot. It suggested an organized group of some sort, one with the finesse to make a murder appear an accident and the confidence not to care about covering one up if the reason were good enough.

I tried to imagine the set-up. With a lot of accelerant they wouldn't have worried too much about the state of my body. My guess is that Jimmy was dead or unconscious when the fire started. Maybe he was chloroformed or someone bought him a doctored drink and tucked him in bed. The fire was as much to destroy any uncovered evidence of my connection.

It was hard to believe that Anne Marie Shirley had gone back to her husband. When I had left her, she seemed to be a believer.

The perpetrators probably wouldn't have wanted them together. It would have been easier to subdue them one at a time. There would have been at least two men, maybe three. They would have gone to Shirley first. Maybe they made him think they were killing his wife, letting him in on it, and this was his chance to get back in their good graces.

It was important that he believe long enough for them to get control and pick the time to take him, because struggles can get messy. So first they got his trust, not hard because he's an idiot. Then the tape goes over the mouth, the hands are secured behind the back in a matter of seconds and he is helpless.

Anne Marie would have been a different story. The approach would probably be made through someone she trusted since she was bound to be badly frightened. Maybe someone made an offer:

"Look, you had to leave in a hurry. Why don't I take you back to the house, you can go through the place and get what you really need. James won't be there, I promise it will be safe."

They would have moved on her as soon as she entered the door, mouth and hands taped quickly, forced to her knees next to her kneeling husband.

Then it would be time for death magic. A short pause for the couple's silent pleas to the man with the gun. She would look up at him, hoping he would see something in her eyes that would save her life. His only response was one shot through her upper forehead to scramble the brains. The mess would make it look like she was shot in the face.

He would give Shirley a few moments to fully realize it was really happening, then fire another round.

The killer would gain power from these deaths, because his accomplices would tell those who needed to know that he could stare into your eyes and kill without thought.

The message had been delivered, and if you were smart, you would be afraid.

JIMMY'S DEATH CREATED a problem. Unless I established a plausible reason both for him to be missing and for his body not to be found, there was a risk that some curious citizen would discover it was he and not I who had been incinerated in the trailer fire.

I spent the day inside the cabin of the houseboat avoiding other traffic and trying not to think about Jimmy's death. By nightfall I had a plan.

The boat had three alternate power systems: the refrigerator, the stove, the heater, and three mantel lamps were run by LP gas. Most of the interior lights and the water pressure pump were run by 12-volt DC. There were also several AC outlets.

Jimmy had rigged the boat so that when he was dockside the electrics all ran from a 110-power cord. He had also installed a power inverter so when he was under way he could use 110 devices like his old electric drill for a brief time from a 12-volt battery.

I went to the afterdeck and turned off the big LP bottle, then traced the gas line through the cabin wall, picking it up again on the inside. Almost flush to the wall, I rubbed the line with a file until the copper tube was thin on one side, then pushed the line upward until it ruptured. Given a cursory examination, I thought it might look like unnoticed wear.

I switched on the power inverter and tested his toaster. It worked. I unplugged it and after it cooled put a piece of paper next to one of its heating elements, then inserted two pieces of bread and pushed down the handle. I hooked the toaster to an old timer Jimmy used to turn the cabin lights on and off to give the impression that someone was at the marina when he was gone.

After quadruple-wrapping my nylon carry-all with garbage bags, I built a raft for it out of four flotation cushions, then tied together a couple cushions for myself.

If I wasn't careful I could get blown to shit because I wasn't sure of how accurate the timer was. I set it to turn the toaster on in twenty minutes, walked to the afterdeck and turned on the gas, then jumped overboard and swam like hell till I was a few hundred feet from shore.

The moon was bright enough to outline the houseboat as it bobbed and rocked with the same gentle swells that moved me back and forth as I rested with my chest on the cushions. The chances were probably even that the boat would burn after it blew. The explosion could consume all the oxygen, but the cabin was insulated with Styrofoam so if anything caught it would probably go.

I heard the low whoompf, and a minute later felt the shock wave. The roof lifted as if it were hinged on one end, then settled back on the twisted wall at an odd angle. A few flames flickered, then began to spread as small debris fell back to the water. I guessed the insulation had caught. It was possible that in a few minutes some boater would come to the rescue, so I swam the rest of the way toward shore. The boat was burning brightly.

I changed to dry clothes and spent the rest of the night in the woods. At daylight I thumbed a ride with a gaunt gypsy trucker with shoulder-length hair and a death's head earring. It was 6:30 and his eyes were open wide, and he was listening to a metal band sing about the highway to hell.

"I know that highway pretty good," I told him.

He grinned and handed me some crystal.

SOMEONE BEAT ON the door and called for Calhoun. I woke up. I had to pee.

I stirred and saw the dirty linoleum lit by the single light bulb and wondered how long I had been asleep. My body ached and I remembered where I was, but I didn't know the time or the day.

I sat on the edge of the bed, put my feet on the floor, and reached for my watch.

"Calhoun, man. I'm fucked up." The man called through the door, then retched loudly.

"If I have to clean up your puke, I'm going to beat your head in," I said.

"No problem, man. Where's Calhoun?"

"I just rented the room. I don't know Calhoun."

He retched again, not as loudly this time.

"Get out of here," I said.

"No problem, man, no problem. I just got fucked up. No problem."

I went into the bathroom and lifted the seat to the toilet. 1:30. It was dark outside. I looked out the bathroom window, and in the back parking lot in the half light two men sat on the fender of an old car. There was something about the way they held themselves that made me wonder if they were doing something illegal.

As I slipped on some clothes, vomit began to seep under the room door. I opened the door, but the man was gone. It looked like he had been drinking Ripple.

I stepped over the puddle and went down to the lobby.

The clerk was sitting behind the counter absorbed in reading a tattered copy of *The Metamorphosis* by Franz Kafka.

He looked up when I laid the key in front of him.

"Someone puked on my door. It's getting into the room."

He looked at me.

"I'm sorry. Do you know who it was?"

"He was looking for Calhoun."

"OK, yeah, I know who it was. I'll talk to him. He'll straighten up for a while, then, you know how it goes. Let me know if you have any more problems. I'm the only one on. If you could give me, like, a half hour I'll get it cleaned up."

"That's fine."

I looked around the lobby. There were about a dozen plastic-cushioned easy chairs arranged in random groups. Silver duct tape covered their rips. One man sat in the middle of the lobby. He wore a cheap black suit and tie. His dark hair was pushed back in a DA. He looked to be about thirty. If I had to guess his profession, I would have made him a rockabilly undertaker.

He held up a newspaper.

"Want a section?" he asked.

I sat next to him and tried not to look too interested in the front-page story: Double murder continues to baffle authorities. As long as they continued to be baffled, I was a happy man.

"Any place near here that might be open to eat at?" I asked.

"That would be the Majestic."

"Is it walking distance, or do I need to call a cab?"

"You could walk it, but I was going to go there myself, and I got wheels if you care to join me."

"Yeah, man, I'd appreciate that," I said.

"My name is Charley Shelnut," he said.

"I'm Sam Lam," I said. (As in Sam on the lam.)

"My ride's in the front," he said.

Then he spoke to the man at the desk. "You know, Harold, I bet you can get my men Stinky and Half-Moon to watch the desk while you clean up the mess that shit-ass made on my friend's front door."

"Good idea, Charley," the clerk said.

We walked to the front parking lot of the hotel and Charley stopped to look back at the building, five stories of aging dark brick with a miniature broadcast tower on top bearing the lit letters HOTEL FAIRMONT.

"Quite the place, ain't it?"

"Last stop before the street," I said.

"Yeah, well, if you ever been on the street, this old place can seem like heaven."

I am never ready for the manic energy of a city at night. Ponce de Leon Avenue smelled of car exhaust. Drivers drove frantically up and down the wide road, afraid they might be caught by a stoplight and forced to speak to members of the lower classes.

From what I could see of the foot traffic, the local residents seemed to be working overtime at life, trying to stay alive without much cooperation from the American dream.

They wandered from streetlight to streetlight trying not to get mugged, run over, or pissed on, all this while everyone else in town was fast asleep, having nightmares about losing their jobs and ending up down here. It's part of some plan they had a couple of administrations ago to make the country more efficient.

Two young girls sporting grunge chic walked past: cut-off jeans, stockings, combat boots, regulation black t-shirts and leather motorcycle jackets. One had short blonde hair, the other a fine purple cloud pouring across her face and shoulders.

"Hey there, Purple Haze! I'll take you for a ride in my deathmobile," Charley said.

The blonde looked at us and said, "Go fuck yourselves, assholes!"

"I think she likes you, man," I said.

"She just don't know it yet," he agreed.

I could hardly believe it. He was leading me toward a 1968 Cadillac hearse.

"That big ride yours, man?"

"Yeah. Actually, it's a company car. I work up at Cavanaugh's. Old man Cavanaugh lets me take it home. At one time this was the leading hearse in Atlanta, Georgia. Hop in."

He got in on his side, leaned over and unlocked the door, and I climbed in the front seat.

"They get these from the Cadillac plant, then a special coach shop does the custom work. This was the top of the line. When they start getting some age on them, you don't use them at the funerals anymore, you use them to pick up your stiffs at your hospitals or your nursing homes. Only this one started to break down, and old man Cavanaugh says the families would shit if they knew their loved ones were being pulled around by some tow truck.

"So now he lets me drive it as a fringe benefit to the job. He says I'm a good worker, wants to keep me around. It doesn't bother him that I did time."

"What's good at the Majestic?" I asked.

He thought about it.

"You might try their open-face roast beef."

We parked in front of the Plaza Theater and walked over to the diner. There was a counter, tables and booths, and the usual collection of people you find eating dinner in the middle of the night: shift workers, musicians with a night off, cops, citizens with an appetite, and various disoriented what-nots. They seemed better off than the people we had seen out on the street. I guessed the dividing line was between the folks who had the money to come inside and buy a meal and the folks that didn't.

I sat in a booth so I had a view of both the front door and

the street. Charley looked a little uncomfortable with my choice and sat down catty-cornered against the inside of the booth so he could see me and the door behind him out of the corner of his eye.

"You want to know if somebody is coming?" I asked.

"Could be," he said. "How about you?"

"Could be."

The waitress brought us our coffee, and we waited for the open-faced roast beef plates.

"You look like a guy that's been around," Charley said.

"I'm not sure if I'm supposed to take that like a compliment."

"Yeah, man, I meant it as one. The deal is this, I'm putting together a crew. You're looking at many opportunities that may develop for the right man."

"I got a full set of plans," I said.

He reached inside the breast pocket of his suit coat, took out a dollar-bill-sized document and laid it in front of me. It was a blank twenty-dollar traveler's check, both signature lines empty. I picked it up. The printing was good, offset, but it had gone through some sort of thermography process so the surface feel was close enough to right. I held it to the light. No watermark. The paper stock felt a little thick. It would probably pass, if you stuck to back roads where people weren't as familiar with what a traveler's check is supposed to look like, although, given the time and hassle of cashing it, I didn't know how much profit would be involved.

"These days, even though you sign with a matching signature, people like to see ID, so what you do is find some guy in a bar that looks sort of like you, get him drunk, get his ID. Use it for a few days, keep moving around."

"So how is it going so far?" I asked.

"Sort of slow. Me and the other members of my crew don't look like anybody else. So it's sort of hard to come up with good ID."

"I can see that would be a problem."

"I won't press you, but I want you to think about it. "

"OK, fine."

The waitress brought our dinners, and Charley played with his beef until she put my plate down and left.

"Another thing I have to warn you about."

"What's that?"

"You might want to get some sex sometimes, but you should know that not all of the ladies peddling it on Ponce are really ladies."

"Ladies?"

"I mean some of the women are really men. I found that out the hard way. I got one of your better blow jobs, but then I found out it wasn't a woman that gave it to me. Pissed me off. Not that I got anything against your homosexuals. My brother is one of the leading homosexuals in the tri-state area. I'm just not into fucking men, at least not unless I've been in the joint for a while, and that's different."

"Which three states?" I asked.

"Huh?"

"You said your brother was one of the leading homosexuals in the tri-state area. I wondered which three states that would include?"

"Alabama, Mississippi, and Tennessee."

"That's interesting. You don't usually see those three states clumped together like that."

"Yeah, well, you got too much competition in Atlanta and New Orleans, man. Who the hell could handle that? He decided to settle on those three states and let the other guys fight it out in Georgia and Louisiana."

"Good idea," I agreed.

"You want some pie, man?"

"Maybe so."

"Tomorrow, I'll introduce you to the rest of the crew."

12

I WOKE UP hungry five hours later and walked back to the Majestic for a stack of pancakes. The early morning light hadn't done Ponce any favors. The street full of mystery and threat the night before was lined with broken sidewalks, old men sleeping on patches of dying grass and empty half-pints of Mad Dog. It was like waking up in bed with a woman you met while drunk. You look her in the face and wonder what the hell you've gotten yourself into, all the while suspecting she's thinking the same thing.

The waitress smiled at me as I poured the syrup.

"You want anything else?" she asked.

"No ma'am."

It was time for soul searching. I had bought myself a few hours to think by going to earth, but soon I was going to have to do something, and I needed to figure out exactly what I wanted out of the situation because I didn't have a lot of slack or a lot of choices.

For years I had been preparing an escape hatch to Costa Rica. It was a beautiful country with democratic traditions and no extradition. I had friends there in banking. They played golf every day, drank piña coladas and talked about the old days of unscheduled air travel at 150 feet above the Gulf of Mexico. Yippee ki-yi-yo!

They would find me a nice bungalow and sponsor me for membership in their golf club. As lifestyles go, I thought it sucked, but it sure beat being dead or wearing orange coveralls for twenty years in the federal joint for racketeering.

I had to admit that my current identity was probably blown. Even if I was never connected with the Shirley murder, my sudden reappearance could create a curiosity that

I couldn't handle. That was too bad. I enjoyed my life. It might not fit everyone, but it fit me fine. It pissed me off that I was going to have to leave it like this. I had thought I might have to take a long vacation, but this was forever. That's the way it goes. I had taken a chance and lost.

I figured I would hang around as long as I could without taking stupid chances. If I could kill whoever had got Jimmy, I would; if not, I'd have to let it go for now.

After polishing off the pancakes, I walked over to the drugstore and bought a postcard and a stamp. Here's what I wrote:

> Bug:
> Once again the time for hardball is here. I'm feeling better than you'd think, but I'm afraid J.C. has left the team for good. We could use someone who knows how to swing a bat for our grudge match. Suggest you adopt a well-rounded sports program. Wrestling, pole vaulting, running are all reported to give a feeling of freedom. Try them out. You may find your sense of confinement disappears.
> I remain on the avenue,
> S Lam
>
> c/o Fairmont Hotel

I walked back to my room and lay down on my bed and turned the snowy black and white television on to "The Today Show." Katie Couric was interviewing a man who liked to use llamas for pack animals. The demonstration animal was spitting at her.

"What is Calvin doing?" she asked. Calvin was evidently the name of the llama.

"It's called expectorating," the man said. "They like to do that."

She looked at him like she thought it was sort of gross, and I could see her point.

"There's nothing wrong with it really. They're very clean animals. It's quite healthy," he said.

The llama spit again. It didn't seem to me that the llama craze was going to catch on very big, if their spit was healthy or not.

There was a knock on the door. I turned the sound off.

"It's Charley."

"Yeah, man. Come in, it's unlocked."

Charley Shelnut, still dressed in a dark suit, stepped into the room followed by two men. One had both legs amputated at mid-thigh, and was in a what looked like an army-surplus wheelchair. He was small and wiry, about fifty, had a gray, three-day growth, and a bald head with gray-brown shoulder-length fringe.

The other was an enormous bear-like man who was missing half of his face. Its left side looked as if it had been surgically removed. There was no brow ridge or cheek bone, most of the side of the jaw was missing, and smooth skin covered the place where the eye had been.

"This is my crew: Stinky Lloyd and Half-Moon Bob. Bob used to be called Full-Moon Bob, because he had a big round face until he got cancer from chewing a plug and dipping snoose, and they had to cut half of it off. You can see the part they cut off," he added, unnecessarily, since it was hard to miss.

The man in the wheelchair said, "Bob had his palate cut out and he can't talk too good, but I can understand most of what he says. The rest he can write on a pad."

"He likes to write poetry," he added.

"Oh-wree," Bob agreed. He held up a pad with big block letters which said "POETRY" and pointed to it.

"Man, I got to take a wicked crap and my shitter is broke. Mind if I use yours?" Charley said.

"Sure, go ahead."

Charley locked himself in the bathroom. I sat on the bed,

and the man in the wheelchair came closer and spoke in a low voice.

"My real name's Lloyd Nelson. But back when I was homeless I had a lot of trouble keeping clean so I got hung with the street name of Stinky. It was awful back then, Mister, 'cause if the street people think you smell bad, you really smell terrible."

"Charley ain't a bad kid. He's just a little crazy. He thinks we're some sort of gang. He tells us we're supposed to go into bars and find people who look like us, get 'em drunk and take their ID's, but shit, Mister, Bob and I could sit in a bar for the rest of our lives and never find two people who looked like us."

"I can see that might be a problem."

"Not only that, but Charley thinks everything is better than everything else. When he talks about anything, no matter what it is, it is always better than something else."

"I noticed that," I agreed. "I've never seen a camouflage wheelchair before. Where did you get it?"

"Somebody come up with this old heavy wheelchair. It originally was bright silver, but the seat and the back was torn out, so we found this old duck-blind seat somebody had thrown out 'cause the tubing went bad and we put the seat and back on my chair, and then I liked the colors so much we spray-painted the metal to match and now it sort of blends in."

"It's a one of a kind."

Lloyd spoke very loud.

"Like Charley says, it's one of your better wheelchairs."

"It is one of your better wheelchairs," Charley agreed from the bathroom.

"Bob wanted me to read you some of his poems," Lloyd said.

He retrieved several pieces of folded paper from the pocket of an army fatigue shirt, then put on what looked to be taped, drugstore reading glasses, cleared his throat, and began reading.

MY LIGHTNING BOLT IS BROKE

my addled brain confused
my hair and teeth have fallen out

and all about decry
my leering flatulence

Hey!
I got an idea!
Why not take me home to meet your parents!

"That's interesting," I said. "I can tell you've got a lot on your mind, Bob."

Bob was rocking back and forth with what looked like a smile on his face.

"Bob always says that it takes a while for people to figure out he's not just another pretty face. He used to teach English, had a family and everything. Then one day, he says, it felt like his clothes were on fire, and he had to take them off. He was teaching a class at the time and so everyone turned against him, and he lost everything."

"It's rough when that happens," I agreed.

"Here's another one," Lloyd said.

I HAVE FLED THE CITY

like a mouse
before a cat

built my simple home
of mud and hair from sleeping drunks

my radio is broken
so I make my own top 40

Song Number One
is the sound of the men working on the chain gang

Song Number Forty
is always hard to remember

"I like that," I said. "It seems to capture the essence of the absurdity of human effort, the bankruptcy of civilization, and the profound malaise that has gripped so many urban artists and intellectuals."

As Bob nodded in agreement, Charley stepped from the bathroom.

"That was one of your better craps," he announced.

"I'm gratified to hear it," I said.

"You enjoying Half-Moon's poetry?" he asked.

"Certainly."

"Good. As your master of ceremonies, I've arranged this poetry reading and now I'd like to ask you to join us on our field trip to see the fetus flingers."

Bob rocked back and forth on his heels and said, "Yeh, yeh, yeh," like he was excited.

Lloyd lifted himself up in the chair several times and let himself back down. "Ass gets sore sitting in this thing," he said.

"That's why we need to get this show on the road," Charley said.

13

"THEY'RE TRYING TO close down an abortion clinic up the street. Those folks are into some wild stuff, man. It's worth checking out."

"That what you mean by fetus flingers?"

"Yeah, man. If we luck out and they have one of their better demonstrations, they might be flinging them today. If not, at least we'll see some tongue-speaking and some limp-ass, drag-'em-across-the-asphalt busts. We might even see 'em bust some preachers, which as far as I'm concerned is the best thing to do with the sons of bitches."

I followed Charley to the front parking lot while Bob pushed Lloyd in his wheelchair behind us. As near as I could tell, they had developed a partnership based on Lloyd doing the talking and Bob doing the pushing.

"Got any spare change, Mister?"

A woman dressed in thrift-store dirty purple knit pants and a "PARTY TILL YOU PUKE" t-shirt stood next to Charley's hearse with her hand held out, daring me with angry eyes not to put something in it. She looked to be about forty-five with a sixty-five-year-old face.

"Janis, I want you to meet my man, Sam," Charley said.

"Hello Charley, hello Sam," she said. She looked at Charley like she thought he was the cat's whiskers.

"Sam, you know Janis is one of your better singers living on the street out here. You may have heard some of the songs she recorded with Big Brother and the Holding Company."

She beamed.

"That's right, Mister. I'm Janis Joplin."

"Holy shit," I said. "I'm pleased to meet you."

"Oh, Lord, won't you buy me a Mercedes-Benz," she sang.

"Which reminds me, Charley, when you going to take me for a ride in that deathmobile of yours?" she asked. "I think I might need to go to my funeral."

"It ain't time for your funeral yet, baby," Charley said. "Anyway, me and my crew have got important business to transact. What are you up to?"

"Trying to get the money up for a burrito across the street."

"How much you got?"

"Sixty-five cents."

"OK. Let's dig in our pockets and see if we can come up with a dollar fifty," Charley said.

I pulled two dollars out of my wallet and handed it to her.

"Thank you, Mister."

"Don't mention it," I said. "I've been an admirer of yours for years."

Bob opened the back of the hearse and lifted Lloyd so he sat on the floor, his head even with the back window, then Bob folded the wheelchair and slid it past him.

"I like to look back," Lloyd explained.

"Lloyd's a student of history," Charley explained. "How 'bout we let Sam ride shotgun, since he's the new guy."

Bob grunted in agreement, then slid into the center of the front seat. As I closed the door, the handle dug into my side as Bob's bulk pushed against me on the left. I tried to get comfortable by hanging my arm and shoulder out the window.

Lloyd spoke from the back.

"Janis's real name used to be Glenda Martin. She comes from a nice family. She's got a sister who's some sort of fancy lawyer. They tried to keep her at home, but she kept running off and coming down here because she said they called her by her wrong name and didn't know who she was. Finally the family just gave up; they couldn't get her committed no more and run out of money for hospitals, but the sister gave Charley her card and we sort of keep our eye on her. She comes down and checks on her, but I don't know exactly what we can do, Mister, because the street's tough on a woman, and she's going to get AIDS if she hadn't already got it, what with getting fucked by these winos all the time.

"The story on her is that when Janis Joplin died Glenda loved her so much that she became Janis so the singer lady could go on living. I guess she figured her own life wasn't worth much anyway. So now she is Janis Joplin."

"Thinks she is, anyway," Charley said. He edged the hearse into traffic and headed up Ponce toward Peachtree.

"She's the only one alive, at least the only one around here, so I guess she is her," Lloyd said.

"You make it sound like some sort of miracle instead of a nervous breakdown," Charley said.

"You seem to worry a lot about her starving to death, if you think she's so fucked up."

"Just because she ain't got one of your better lines of reasoning, doesn't mean I want to see her die in the street like a dog."

Bob grunted.

"That's right, Bob. See, Bob agrees with me," Lloyd said.

"Bob just agrees with you 'cause you cover each other's ass. When are you two going to get with the program and start covering my ass?" Charley said.

This seemed to be the way they carried on together. Now that I was part of the crew, party behavior was suspended.

We must have been near to the clinic because emergency vehicles crowded the curbside, mostly police black-and-whites with a sprinkling of unmarked vehicles, the plain, no-accessory American sedans with cop antennas that provoke laughter as they prowl the streets looking for the elusive criminal element.

"It's up there," Charley pointed ahead to the right.

As we drew closer, I saw a three-story white frame building separated from a milling crowd by a thin line of yellow saw horses. Cops were scattered through the no-man's land between the building and the crowd, which seemed to grow tighter and more organized nearer the police line. I imagined the ones up front were the serious limp-ass drag-'em-across-the-asphalt activists.

"Look up there, Mister. Look at the one with his arms in the air," Lloyd spoke from the back.

I saw the man he was taking about, in his fifties, gray wispy hair that stuck in odd directions, with a startling white pallor like a jailbird. He held his arms in the air and wiggled his fingers.

"When they move their hands around like that, it means they're possessed," Lloyd explained. "Only I don't think they call it that. I think they call it getting religion, or having the spirit or something. I'm not too clear on that because I got thrown out of Sunday school for smoking."

Charley said, "Look! He's moving his mouth. That's one of your better tonguers. We gotta find a place to park so we can listen to him."

Charley began scanning the curbside for a place to park. I didn't think it looked too hopeful, but a policeman saw him looking and waved him into a spot next to an ambulance. Then, after getting a closer take on the three of us in front and Lloyd in the back, he gave Charley a dubious look.

"Cavanaugh's," Charley explained.

The cop nodded knowingly, then directed his attention back to the building. "Nobody fucks with you when you're death's personal representative to the city of Atlanta," Charley said. "I can park anywhere, and nobody ever asks me what I'm doing, because they don't want to think about it. Hell, man, I could take their private parking space and be upstairs fucking their old lady, and they wouldn't want to know about it. Death's a hell of a dodge."

"You got that one right," I agreed.

I got out of the car and walked up the street a few feet while Bob got Lloyd's wheelchair from the back. The police quickly pulled four paddy wagons in front of the clinic, as if something was about to happen. After all the years I had spent trying to stay out of jail, it was hard for me to imagine what sort of nincompoop would go out of his way to be arrested. A lot of these people had traveled from out of town to get thrown in the Fulton County lockup and be surrounded by rapists with bad BO and shit-clogged latrines.

"We better get across the street fast, before our tongue talker gets hauled down to Decatur Street. Only problem is, if they start with the busts I need to pull back and watch from over here, because it probably wouldn't be a good idea for me to have to answer many questions from the cops," Charley said.

"Yeah, I got a similar status," I agreed.

"I figured you might," Charley said.

Charley and I walked across the street to the edge of the crowd. Lloyd and Bob were behind us, taking their time, Lloyd pushing himself in his chair, Bob flashing a toothy half grin at the people who gaped at him, then quickly turned away, pretending they hadn't seen anything out of the ordinary.

"It might be too packed to get up there to the tongue talker," Charley said.

A petite young woman in her twenties with short red hair was walking through the back of the crowd cradling a white cardboard box in her hand.

"What you got in that box?" Charley asked.

She looked up with sad green eyes and held the box toward us. It contained a dead fetus, one that looked nearly full term.

"How could anyone do this?" she asked.

"Do what? Curl up and die in a box? It ain't hard if it's cold enough," Charley said.

She shuddered and pulled back, not so much in distance, but her eyes grew further away and she spoke with exaggerated clarity.

"No. I meant to say how could anyone have an abortion."

"Lady, most of the people I know should have been abortions," Charley said.

"How can you say that?"

"I guess I just know a lot of assholes. You going to fling that thing?"

"Fling?"

"You know, throw it at someone?"

"There's nobody here to throw it at," she said.

"What do you mean? There's all sorts of people here," Charley said.

"There's nobody that we like to throw them at. Like abortionists or politicians."

"What about that guy over there." Charley pointed at Half-Moon Bob. "He's a man devoted to the abortion of everyone in the United States. He works at it day and night."

"I don't think so."

"You're just like everyone else. You don't want to throw a fetus at him because half his face is missing."

"No, that isn't the reason," she insisted.

Out of the corner of my eye, I saw a young black girl who looked about fifteen walking casually down Ponce, pretending not to notice the crowd. When she drew even with the walkway to the clinic she turned down it and began hauling ass toward the building.

"There's one." The voice from the crowd sounded like a gunshot.

A dozen people broke through the police line to block the entrance. One knocked the young black girl to the ground. Charley grabbed the fetus and sent it flying in a slow arc toward the center of the melee.

"Let's get the fuck outta here," he said.

We moved quickly across the street. The police lines were down near the building and people were lying on the walkway and steps in a single, immovable, interlocked mass.

We passed a red Corvette pulled behind a Grady Hospital wagon. Its driver, a man with an expensive haircut and even more expensive suit, watched the fracas with a weird look on his face, a combination of ecstasy and anger.

I spoke under my breath.

"Check out the dude in the 'Vette."

Charley glanced at him nonchalantly.

"Looks like he shot a load in his pants. I guess all this does something for him."

"If his hands weren't on the steering wheel, I'd think he was pulling his pecker."

"I swear, I've seen him someplace before," Charley said.

"Yeah, man, he's famous. I think he's got his own special room in the conservative psychos' hall of fame up in Cobb County," I said.

"Hey man, I like going around with you," Charley said. "You're good at spotting the better fuckheads."

14

WE ATE LUNCH at Tortillas, sitting in the suicide seat at the corner next to the driveway. Lloyd blocked the walk-through with his chair and scowled at everyone who tried to wriggle past.

"That was one of your better fetus flingings, even if I had to do it myself." Charley said.

"You did real good, Charley. That thing sailed through the air like a touchdown pass."

Bob nodded and held up his pad of paper.

"REAL GOOD!!!" it said.

"I figured out who the man in the 'Vette was, by the way," Charley said.

"What 'Vette?" Lloyd asked.

"You didn't see it. There was this guy, one very bent motherfucker, who looked like he was getting off watching the fetus flingers falling all over each other."

"You're telling the truth, now?"

"Yeah, man, Sam spotted him. This guy was one of your better lunatics. Anyway, the story is he used to be a district attorney out there in Cobb."

"What did I tell you." I said.

"I can't remember the name, but I remember the face and the story. I got this friend in your criminal element out there. He told me about this guy. He calls him the anti-Christ. Says the dude got in some trouble, and they didn't do anything about it because they didn't want the embarrassment, but the guy had to leave the DA's office. Now he makes a bunch of money working for himself.

"My friend says the people out there love him, but he can't figure out why 'cause the guy's pretty much a psycho with a taste for Colombian marching powder, anyway.

"Hell of a deal, isn't it? I fuck up, and I do time. This guy fucks up and they don't let him work at some shitty job anymore."

"You turning into a law-and-order man?" Lloyd asked.

"Only when it's assholes like that," Charley said.

"Being a prosecuting attorney isn't that bad a job anyway; you can get a lot of satisfaction out of putting people in jail."

"I guess it's OK if it suits you, but personally I'd rather carry corpses around for old man Cavanaugh. Why don't you go get a job as a county prosecutor if you think it'd be fun? You got the personality for it."

"Maybe I do, but I don't got the education. I got thrown out of high school for smoking."

"I thought that was Sunday school you were thrown out of," I said.

"I was thrown out of that, too. In my younger days, I cared more about tobacco than I did about my mental or spiritual improvement."

"I see."

"Then as I got older it was women and whiskey," he said.

"When you got even older the women wouldn't have anything to do with you so you got stuck with the bottle," Charley said.

Bob held up a piece of paper which said: "I THINK MY CLOTHES MAY BE CATCHING ON FIRE."

"I didn't know you still had this problem, Bob," I said.

He wrote again, "NO PROBLEM, I JUST TAKE MY CLOTHES OFF."

"I guess we'd better be getting back to our room," Lloyd said.

"Yeah, man. I'm going to take Sam down to the lounge. Come on down and join us once you get that fire put out. Maybe it will set your pants back on fire."

"I heard about the lounge. What's it like?"

"It's one of your more unusual places. It's a titty bar, but some of the strippers read their poetry and they got grunge guitar bands one night a week that bring in the girls with leather jackets and purple hair. So it's sort of a one-stop shop. You get your beer, your strippers, your lap dances, your poetry, your alternative music, and your girls who think you're a dumb shit-kicker if you didn't go to art school. Like you say, it's a great place to witness the profound malaise that has gripped so many urban artists and intellectuals."

We ambled up the street to the back of the hotel.

"Prepare yourself for an experience," Charley said. He nodded toward the door of the lounge. At that moment, two men walked outside, briefly squinted at the bright daylight, then their eyes fixed on Charley and they walked purposefully toward us.

They were both tall, over six feet, with black dreadlocks and white skin. I got the impression they planned to beat the shit out of both of us.

"This wasn't exactly the experience I had in mind," Charley mumbled.

15

ONE OF THE men stopped in front of me and reached back with his right hand to the small of his back. I thought he was going to pull a pistol, but instead he produced a knife, a Buck folding hunter – the Susan Atkins special. He flicked the blade open with his thumb and pointed it at my gut.

"Let's be real peaceful, now," he said.

"I'm all for peaceful," I agreed.

"Who's your little friend, Charley?" the one closest to Charley was speaking.

"Kiss my ass," Charley said.

He stepped into Charley with a hard punch to the solar plexus and Charley crumpled on the ground and rolled up to protect himself. My guess was that he knew how to survive a beating. The man kicked him twice in the ribs.

They had come on us so quickly that I was just beginning to sort out that there was something very odd about these two. They were so similar that they had to be identical twins, and while they acted black Jamaica their skin was white, and they talked white Bronx. I hadn't seen any signs of artillery, so I wasn't sure I was going to let this go on much longer before I ran over to the edge of the parking lot, picked up a two-by-four from the junk pile, and beat them both senseless.

"We ain't going to kill you, Charley. We just want our paper back. We don't make no money with you parading around in that pretty suit of yours. You got to move it. You got our paper?"

"Yeah, I got it."

"OK, now, you give it to me."

Charley unfolded a bit, reached into the inside breast

pocket of his suit coat, and handed him the traveler's checks.

"OK, Charley. They're all here, which means you didn't move jack shit, which means you still owe us money on rent for the paper."

"I don't got any money," Charley said.

"Well that's just too damn bad."

He nodded at me. The man standing next to me nudged me with the knife. "Let's see the wallet."

I thought, "What the hell. It's only money," and reached for it slowly and held it out for him. The man who had hit Charley grabbed it. There was about two hundred dollars in it, and when he saw it he grinned.

"Why don't you take the money and leave the wallet?" I asked.

"Why don't you suck my dick." He slid the wallet in his pocket.

This guy was pissing me off.

"You guys don't be around where we are looking for you," he said.

They smirked at each other, then ambled away, taking their time, flaunting their contempt.

When they were gone, Charley rolled slowly to his hands and knees.

"How are your ribs?"

"It hurts to breathe." He hit the pavement with the palm of his hand. "Damn. I hate this. I need a damn piece, man. I'm a fucking desperado; I'm not a funny-paper con man. Now I'm getting the shit kicked out of me by a couple of twin, white Rastafarians from Hoboken, New Jersey, and I can't even tell them apart. I'm sorry I got you in this. I need a gun so I can kill those fuckers.

"I feel like an idiot out here without a gun. I need to talk to Old Man Cavanaugh, get some money, get a piece, and hunt those simple fuckers down and kill them. I'll get your wallet back and get your money too. Don't worry about it."

I wasn't worried about it. The two hundred dollars was small change, and I had thirty more sets of identification. The main thing that concerned me was that if they took the ID they were probably going to use it in some scam, and I'd just as soon not have my face connected with it.

"I can help you out. Let's go to my room."

Charley stood slowly and looked over the suit he was so proud of.

"They tore a hole in the knee of my pants."

In my room, Charley washed up at the bathroom sink while I took off the back of the television with a butter knife.

"Who were those guys?" I asked.

"That was the Jackson twins. They don't have shit for brains, but they're connected with someone who makes all sorts of phony paper. I think the family may be from Jamaica, least they give that impression. They grew up in Hoboken. Talk weird, don't they?"

"Yes, they do. You still want to kill them?"

"No, man," Charley said. "I'm down off that one already. It isn't professional. What they did to me was just business. When they ripped you off in front of me, that went over the line into bullshit. They can't do that. I'm only going to kill them if that's what it takes to get your wallet and money back, only I know it won't take that, because they don't care enough about either of them to die over it.

"Look, they meet me, we do a little business, they just think of me as some funeral-home flunky. They need to be shown who they're dealing with. Then things might go a little more smoothly around here."

I pulled a bundle wrapped in a rag from the back of the television.

"Here's the answer to your prayers. It's a Smith & Wesson .38 special. Five shot, lightweight frame, two-inch barrel, and most important, it's completely clean. Can't be traced to nobody.

"So here's the deal, you use my pistol, there are some rules."

"OK, shoot. No, on second thought, don't shoot . . . just kidding. What's the deal?" he asked.

"If you have to bust a cap in one of them, ditch the gun, drop it down a storm sewer, and make sure they don't have my wallet on them if they're dead."

"Got ya."

"Also, I want to know what you did your time for."

"Armed robbery, but they only popped me for the one; the other eighty-five I got off scot free."

16

I PUT THE few things I didn't want to lose in a stash belt around my waist, then slipped on a loose sweatshirt and left. If Charley's adventure went badly, I didn't plan to be here.

I had already found a place where I could watch the front of the building if needed. The restaurant across the street had a wide window at the front. The dining room was deep enough that from a seat at the back you could see the street without being seen, and the hallway to the bathrooms ended at an exit that opened on a back parking lot that connected to an alley that led to the maze of little streets between Ponce de Leon and Virginia Avenue.

If I needed to run I could disappear among the constant foot traffic of ne'er-do-wells scuffling through the neighborhood. That was why I'd come to this area in the first place. The police here have got enough trouble seeing that the wild ones don't take off their pants in the street, throw up Muscatel, and cut their best friend in a fight over a plastic cup to care very much about questioning one more hillbilly who needs a shave.

I shared the place with a couple of depressed looking businessmen eating a late lunch. Their suits were crumpled, and occasionally they mumbled the secrets of going bankrupt to each other and nodded sadly. I drank tea for about thirty minutes and thought about a crazy plan that was forming involuntarily on the edges of my consciousness. Whether I wanted it or not.

It was based on my belief that quite a few of your basic head-banger criminals lead crazy reckless lives because they honestly don't care if they live or die, so if you really want to step on their dick the best thing to do is steal their money.

That will drive them crazy, then you can kill them and get the satisfaction of knowing that they were miserable when they died. It wouldn't make up for Jimmy Cooley, but it was as close as I was going to get.

The plan would require at least four, possibly five for a comfort factor. Charley, Lloyd, and Bob seemed like a crazy choice for accomplices, but the problem with crime is that it's insane to begin with. You don't usually pull jobs with people who drive Volvos and discuss the moral dimensions of American family life. Your partners have to be crazy enough to do the crime, but the catch is they can't be so out of touch that they end up busted.

A good example was Bug Raiford, currently of the federal nut hatch, who had been smart crazy, eccentric crazy, interesting crazy, and dangerous crazy until he had dipped into the old crank case a few too many times, at which point he just became fucking crazy. He became involved in a sloppily conceived and executed automatic weapons deal. Leading to the fateful close surveillance by the ATF.

Poor Bug, one of the ways he would keep people off balance was to pretend he was crazier than he was, so we all thought he was putting us on when he began spinning fantasies about ray guns hidden in the signs of pizza delivery trucks, occult symbols on dollar bills, and men following him around in government sedans. At least he was right about the last two.

He had forgotten rule one, which is don't use what you sell, and rule two, which is don't use what other people sell, and rule three, which is the regular use of crank, a.k.a. crystal methedrine, will make you psychotic.

If we'd known what was going on we would have locked him in a cabin in the woods until he dried out, then taken him to an understanding shrink.

As it was, the odds were excellent that he would recover his mind, in that methedrine psychosis usually subsides sometime after you have quit snorting the wonder drug. This was assuming he hadn't found a source on the inside.

In the meantime, there was no telling if he could find a way out of the mess he had gotten himself into either by using a legal chisel or by going over the wall. If he was sane enough to function, he would be a damned handy man to have around for what I had in mind.

I went over it in my mind again. As I saw it, we could use a wheel man, a lookout, and two or three guys with guns. A lot would depend on the set-up.

I was sure Lloyd and Bob could handle the supporting roles, and Charley was clearly willing to make his way in life with a gun.

I'd seen men in Charley's situation before. After doing time, they tried to stick to the straight and narrow by bullshitting themselves that they were making something of their life, when in fact they were not. More and more they would miss the adrenaline rush, as well as their romantic ambition to follow in the steps of the great highwaymen of the past – men like Cole Younger and Jesse James. Then they would begin choking to death under the water torture of respectability, and the weight of good citizenship would became intolerable.

At this point they'd cop to the ancient credo: "Live hard. Die young. Leave a bullet-riddled corpse."

If their social workers really gave a good fart about them, instead of finding them dead-end jobs lifting corpses for Irish funeral home magnates, they'd help them dream up a really good plan for their next criminal adventure, so they wouldn't end up as jailbirds or hamburger meat.

I was convinced Charley wasn't the sort of person whose personal emotional gravity kept drawing him into a sinkhole of jail time and hanging around waiting for his next bust. He simply lacked the experience to give him an important insight: if you want to make it as a career criminal, you can't work at it retail.

What his ambition lacked was a grandeur of scale. I was about to give that to him.

The businessmen drank enough coffee to keep them busy pissing for a week, paid their bill at the counter, and left without leaving a tip. Their plan evidently was to take as many people as possible with them into financial ruin.

I was the only person left in the dining room. I glanced at the proprietor to see if he was irritated that I was hanging around, but he only smiled. What the hell. I guess a customer drinking tea was better than no customer at all. It made the place look open.

Charley was walking down the sidewalk on the far side of the street like he didn't have a problem in the world. I put some money on the table and watched as he ambled in front of the hotel. He seemed to be checking out the street casually without making a big deal out of it. He walked toward the front door and stopped to lean against the wall, glancing casually back and forth, then he looked straight across the street at me and gave a thumbs up.

Since I hadn't told him I would be here, I was impressed.

When he saw me emerge from the restaurant, he nodded. I wove my way to the other side of the street, dodging four lanes of crazy drivers. He walked out to meet me at the curb.

"How did you know I was there?" I asked.

"Didn't know, but I figured you'd be checking the situation out from someplace and that seemed like the best place to do it. What the fuck, man, the worst that could happen is that I stand out here making a fool of myself giving a hand signal to a restaurant full of funny boys who think I want to stick my thumb up their ass, while you're up at the Plaza watching a movie."

"How did it go?" I asked.

"It was one of your smoother operations. Once I explained my feelings to the Jackson twins, they were very apologetic. Seems it's just a problem of they come from a different culture and don't know how we do things around here. I got your wallet. I'll give it to you up in the room. Didn't have to use the piece, although it is one of your better pistols, and it would have been a pleasure to blow out their fried Hoboken brains with it."

Back at the room he handed me the wallet. There were four hundred dollars inside of it.

"The extra two is their way of making up for their impolite behavior. They gave me the traveler's checks too. Said I could just go ahead and keep them."

I could imagine the conversation. Probably the one who hadn't had the pistol in his mouth had done most of the talking.

"Well, I got to go lift corpses for Cavanaugh. I was thinking that when I get off tonight we could go on a midnight tour in my deathmobile."

"Good plan, 'cause I got a proposition to make. We can drive around and talk about the Wheel of Fortune," I said.

"You got some way to make that wheel turn around for us?" he asked.

"Could have," I said. "Only problem is we might all get killed."

17

AFTER CHARLEY LEFT I fell asleep on top of the covers. I dreamt that I was lying on top of the covers with my clothes on, and I woke because I heard a man beating on the door and vomiting.

"Like Ghandi, I respect all living things," the man yelled.

"Good for you," I answered.

I opened the door, but he had gone. I walked down the hall, almost floated as I walked between pools of urine. I think this would have been a nightmare if I hadn't felt so detached. As it was, I simply took things in and felt nothing.

The man at the reception desk had a receding hairline and a Hawaiian shirt. He held up his copy of *The Metamorphosis* and pointed toward it.

"This is a great book," he said.

"What's it about?" I asked.

"It's a true account about what happened the day after Reagan got elected president."

I waited for him to tell me, but he didn't say anything.

"Well, what the fuck happened?" I asked after a long pause.

"Everyone in America turned into cockroaches."

"Well, if that's the case, why aren't we cockroaches?" I asked.

"Because we're the vermin."

As he said it, it sort of made sense, although I wasn't entirely sure what it was supposed to mean. As a criminal, I sort of liked Ronald Reagan because I figured that at last people like me had a man in the White House who had our interests at heart.

"Them bug people going to come and get us?" I asked.

"No, man, they don't give a shit about us as long as we

don't infest their houses."

"I had this weird dream this afternoon. I dreamed the whole country turned into bugs," I said.

"I have those bug dreams all the time," Lloyd said.

"Me too," Charley said. "It's because there's so many bugs around. Old Man Cavanaugh says there may be bugs all over the place, but one place you can't have any bugs is in a funeral home. He says the only thing that makes people lose it faster that thinking about their loved ones being hauled around in a tow truck is thinking about bugs in a funeral home."

"I can see their point," I agreed. "It's not the sort of thing I like to think about."

"There's only one way to take care of it, and that's to spray chemicals all over the place. Hell, man, we got so many chemicals in the air over at Cavanaugh's that you don't have to embalm anybody. You just leave them sitting out in the hall overnight. Work there long enough and they can't tell you from the corpses. Your skin looks like wax fruit."

We were driving with Bob and Lloyd on the back streets near Virginia Avenue in the deathmobile. It was dark. Charley had said he was going to take me to see "one of the better" views of Atlanta, and as we pulled up to the park next to a school building I saw that he hadn't been exaggerating.

The spot overlooked the central downtown skyline, a city of fire and ice that seemed to hover in the moonless night sky, vibrating as the heat from the sidewalks moved the cool night air. The buildings seemed too large for the tiny patch of earth that claimed them.

"Didn't have anything like this in Spuds, South Carolina," Charley said.

"Spuds ain't one of your better towns," Lloyd pointed out.

"Spuds sucked," Charley said. There was a bitterness in his voice that suggested he thought it sucked royally. "This park is closed at night, but if we don't kick up too much of a fuss nobody will mind. If they see the hearse they'll just figure it has something to do with death and won't want to know anything about it."

Bob was helping Lloyd with his chair over the uneven terrain. Across the field we sat under a tree, like the Buddha, waiting for enlightenment.

"What was life in Spuds like, Charley?" I asked.

"It sucked in more ways than one. They had this special school for bad boys there that they sent me and my brother to on account of our father was a drunk. They had this idea there that there aren't any bad boys, just boys that hadn't had enough love, so the way they figured they would solve this problem is by making us fuck the teachers. These were guys, or it might not have been so bad.

"In the dormitory everyone tried to rape my brother because he was a skinny kid, so I had to protect him. Man, I used to fight until my knuckles bled.

"Then one day he came to me and said, 'Charley, you don't have to fight for me no more because I'm getting married. Me and Fats are getting married. You got to understand. I'm not like you, Charley, it doesn't mean the same to me as it does to you.'

"Fats was this black fellow. He wasn't all that fat; he was just damned large. Anything he saw, he'd just beat the fuck out of you till he got it. Wasn't a bad guy really. Got shot up in a honky tonk. Never could adjust to the outside where some mean little shit with a gun can waste your ass as bad as a big man. He was standing at a jukebox listening to a song when this guy popped him in the back of the head."

"Wonder what song he was listening to," I asked.

Charley laughed. "I'm always interested in finding out the details like that myself. I asked at the time. He was listening to Wayne Newton sing 'Danke Schöne.'"

"That's a horrible thought. Having that as your last conscious memory," I said.

"I always liked that song," Lloyd said.

"That doesn't surprise me," Charley said.

"That comment would piss me off, if I hadn't heard the weeping and moaning you tap your feet to."

Bob laughed. Charley grumbled.

"OK, Mister. Charley told you why he doesn't like Spuds, South Carolina, so let me tell you what Bob and I don't like. We don't like doctors."

"A lot of people would agree with you," I said.

"Right. A lot of people sort a don't like doctors, but Bob and I really don't like doctors. This is because Bob was medically indignant so they made him go down to Augusta."

"Indigent," Charley said. "He was indigent."

"Yeah, he was that, too. Anyway the doctors down there treated him like he was stupid as a potato, like they didn't care about him being a former schoolteacher and poet and all. They acted like he couldn't understand why they were going to cut off his face, so they explained it to him like a baby, leaving out all the facts. And not only that, but it was a doctor that run over me in a Mercedes so I got both my legs cut off.

"He got up in court and said I jumped in front of him so he wouldn't have to pay me no money. It wasn't even his money, it was the insurance. He just couldn't stand to see me get anything. He had his friends who weren't even in the state that day say they saw me jump in front of his car. Like, sure . . . I'm walking down the road thinking, Gosh, it sure would be nice to get both my legs cut off, why don't I jump in front of a Mercedes-Benz automobile?

"It was bad enough the guy had to squash my legs, but why did he have to make fun of me like that? Why did he have to lie and say I jumped in front of his damned car that he couldn't even drive? Anyway, that's all I got to say."

Charley spoke gently, "That's what they mean by 'down by law' and 'law and order.' The swells that run things have the law to maintain order and the order they like to maintain says that they can use the law to fuck the white trash.

"The folks that think it's fair have got this juice they don't even know about. They go into court, a judge looks at them and thinks, 'Now, this is a bright young man with a promising future. Why should I mess things up for him.'

"But he looks at me and says, 'We better teach this bad boy a lesson.' By the time I was seventeen, I had done so much time for nothing, just status offender and having a drunk old man, I figured, what the fuck, if I'm going to do the time I might as well do the crime. That's when I decided to take crime as my career.

"Anyway, as long as we're having grudge-therapy night, is there anything you want to add, Bob?"

Bob held up his spiral notebook and turned the flashlight on it. It said:

"LLOYD EXPLAINED WHAT I DON'T LIKE … HAVING THE DOCTORS TREAT ME SO BADLY WHEN THEY CUT MY FACE. IT MADE ME FEEL BAD AND IT WAS A BAD THING TO DO."

"I agree with you, Bob," Charley said. "And now, I'd like to introduce you to a new member of our therapy group and outdoor outrage center. His name is Sam Lam, and I'm sure that like the rest of us, he's nursing a deeply felt grudge. Sam, could you tell us how you've been wronged and who you're mad at?"

"Sure, Charley. I'm not sure who I'm mad at yet, but I can tell you my story.

"The short version is that this guy came to me and offered me thirty thousand to kill his wife. I took the money and told the wife. I was planning on leaving town for a while, so I gave an old trailer I had to a friend and borrowed his houseboat for a while. I figured I'd drift around the lake until I got organized for my trip.

"Next thing I know the guy who hired me and his wife

are murdered and my friend is burned up in my trailer. I blew up the boat so nobody would realize it wasn't me that was dead, and I ran."

"Shit, Mister, I read about that one in the newspaper," Lloyd said.

"That's the couple that got popped in that big house up in North Fulton?" Charley asked.

"Right. James and Anne Marie Shirley."

"That was one of your bigger murders, covered in great detail by our Atlanta Urinal and Constipation. Man, still waters run deep, you got yourself involved in some serious shit. What's your plan?"

"No plan yet. Just the start of the idea. I think at first it was like when you got hit by the Jacksons. First thing you want to do is kill somebody, then after you calm down your instincts take over, and you realize that there may be other ways to fuck them up."

"So what's the set-up?" Charley asked.

"Don't really know that either. Let me ask you. They try to kill me, who nobody gives a shit about, so that nobody will know it's a murder, then they kill this couple like it's a fuck-you statement. What does that tell you?"

"It tells me they knew exactly what they were doing and they wanted to make a point," Charley said.

"Right, and Shirley was a real estate developer. Why would he be involved?"

"Someone's washing money."

"Right, and what does that suggest?"

"Drugs."

"Right."

"So why did they whack him?"

"They had a problem that killing would solve. Somebody was fucking somebody. Am I being too imaginative?" I asked.

"I don't think so."

"Wait a minute," Lloyd said. "Before you get too far out in

front of me. By washing, I guess you mean laundering money?"

"That's it. They take dirty money and clean it up so they can spend it above ground."

"How do they do that?" Lloyd asked.

"Different ways. Let's say you want to show some source of legal income. You could open up a little restaurant and shove money in the till, then report it as income. This way you've got a visible means of support. Nobody ever knows about the cash you spend on vacation. You can diddle your books to make it look like a very profitable operation. Who's going to complain? The IRS is worried about people who are trying to hide income, not trying to show it.

"Of course, once you get to be a big enough operation you'd have to own a whole chain of restaurants, so what do you do? These days a favorite dodge is to mule the money to the Netherlands Antilles, set up a dummy corporation, put the money in a NA Bank, then invest it over here.

"Let's say you buy a small office building around the perimeter, you incorporate a Georgia affiliate of the Netherlands Antilles Corporation, then borrow money on the office building and use it to pay operating expenses like salaries. All of a sudden you've got major financial leverage and enough cut-outs that people who worry about their reputations can deny they had any idea you were dirty.

"The way the Georgia laws are set up, nobody is going to know who's behind the deal if they look, and most people aren't going to look. In a very short time, you can go from wholesaling crack rock to major respectable wealth."

"That's slicker than snot," Lloyd said.

"Damn right it is," Charley said. "I know you've got an angle on this, Sam. What you got cooking?"

"The mule isn't going to be running over there every day; he's going to be making regular trips with big packets of cash."

"How much you think that would be?"

"Quarter of a million, anyway."

"And you're going to hit the mule?"

"Yes."

"Shit, Mister, what's going to keep them from coming over here and killing you if you do that?" Lloyd asked.

"First place, they think I'm dead; second, I think they might be too busy killing each other."

"You got a way to find out who they are?" Charley asked.

"I think so."

"How you going to take it from there?"

"Look for a connection to an airplane."

"That sounds like one of your better plans."

"You guys want to go along for the ride?"

"Hell yes," Charley said. "I wouldn't miss it."

Bob nodded and said, "Yaah!"

"How 'bout you, Lloyd?" Charley asked. "What do you think?"

Lloyd pointed toward the skyline. "I think there's at least a billion dollars' worth of pussy in that building over there, and on the top floor sits a man who's sort of like God, only instead of making sure the birds fly right side up and that it rains on time, he's fucking his secretary in the conference room."

"That's sort of an unusual answer to the question: do you want to pull a job," Charley pointed out.

"We all got our own motivations, and mine is that I'd like to find out what it feels like to be him. I knew the only way I could get the money is by doing something crazy. I just could never think of anything crazy that would make any money. Now this sounds like a hell of a plan. What do we do next?"

"First thing," I said, "is we got to get more guns."

18

We WERE SITTING on a narrow dirt road in the woods watching the gravel parking lot slowly empty.

"We don't want to kill this guy or he can't tell us a thing and the whole deal is blown. On the other hand, it would be pretty easy to get killed by him."

"You're saying he's dangerous," Charley said.

"Very. He keeps a piece behind the bar. After everyone leaves, he'll lock the door and put the money in a safe, then carry the gun in a clip-on holster when he goes to the car. He hasn't run a place like this for ten years without getting robbed by being careless. What do you want to do? I figure you're the expert on this stuff," I said.

"Okay, it's pretty dark out, so you and me will go down there on foot and hide behind his car. I'll carry the .38 special and a sap; you take the pump. Bob and Lloyd will stay up here and watch, when he gets close to the car you guys yell and scream, honk the horn, gun the engine.

"He'll look up here to see what the hell is going on, then you and I break around either side of the car. We'll both yell, 'Freeze.'

"If he doesn't want to cooperate, I'll hit him with the sap. If that doesn't stop him and it looks like he's going to make a real move with his gun, then you blow his shit away with the twelve gauge and we'll piss on him and the money. At least we'll be alive. Just do me a favor, and if you got to shoot, make sure it's him and not me."

"Sounds like one of your better plans," I said.

In the green dashboard light I saw Charley give me a thoughtful look of appraisal. "You ever had to whack somebody?" he asked.

"Yes. I never shot any of my partners in the process either," I said.

He laughed.

"Guess we better get a move on."

We crept down the hill through the scrub, then low-crawled the last hundred feet to the far side of the car, resting low on our haunches. We pulled the stockings over our heads, and Charley was right, we looked like monsters.

"You got to wear a mask or stocking," Charley had said. "They're a pain in the butt, make it hard to breath and they cut your vision, but you need to wear them. It isn't so much to hide your identity as to make you look inhuman. People can't read your face. It scares the shit out of them more than a gun."

We were in the dark shadow of the building's outside lights, but the light looked like it was passing through one of those gauzy portrait lenses photographers use to convince people they are beautiful. My eyelids felt like they were glued to my cheek. I moved the mask around to make my face more comfortable, and I could see a little better.

Charley held his hand up to show he was coming. I started counting seconds and got to seventy-two before the horn of the hearse started blaring.

We both broke from either side of the car yelling "Freeze," but he didn't freeze. Instead he went for Charley, pulling his gun. Charley swung the sap but hit him in the left shoulder. I saw the gun in his hand, but couldn't get a shot. I didn't even want a shot. Instead I gave him a hard stroke to the back side of his head with the stock of the shotgun. I saw his knees wobble, but he didn't go down. Charley made another pass with the sap. This time he crumpled.

"That's one tough motherfucker," Charley said.

"We're lucky he didn't shoot both of us," I said.

"We're lucky we didn't shoot each other."

It seemed like two minutes later that Vogel started to stir. I pointed the shotgun at his face, close enough so he wouldn't have any problem seeing it. Bob pulled the hearse into the parking lot, got the stretcher out of the back, and handed Charley the body bag.

Charley threw it on the ground next to Vogel.

"Okay, buddy, we need you to slip into that thing."

"Oh, man, we don't need to do that. I hadn't talked to nobody. I don't know why we got a problem, man. We can talk this thing over."

Coop was feeling good enough to plead for his life.

"What the fuck did I say?" Charley hissed.

"No problem. No problem." Vogel spoke quickly and slid into the body bag.

Charley zipped it shut and he and Bob lifted it onto the stretcher, then rolled the stretcher into the back of the hearse.

We drove down the highway a few miles then turned down an overgrown dirt back road that led to an abandoned saw mill. Bob was fidgeting badly as he drove.

"You having a problem, man?" I asked him.

Lloyd spoke quietly, "I think his clothes are catching on fire again. He's going to be real uncomfortable unless he takes them off."

"It's deserted up here. Shouldn't be a problem."

Bob stopped the hearse next to a ten-foot-high sawdust pile. He turned the headlights off but left the parking lights on so the front of the car glowed soft yellow, the back soft red.

As soon we stopped, Bob jumped out and stripped off his clothes. Then he joined Charley at the tailgate and they slid out the stretcher. Bob lifted Lloyd forward and was holding him, getting ready to find him a comfortable spot to watch the action, when Charley unzipped the body bag.

The first thing Vogel saw was a huge naked man with a stocking on his head, but half his face obviously missing, standing in the red light holding another man with a stocking on his head with amputated legs.

He screamed in total primal terror, then fell silent.

"Shit, Mister, I think our informer just had a heart attack," Lloyd said as Bob set him down.

Charley bent over and looked at him.

"I think he just passed out," he said.

Vogel woke up screaming. "Don't worship Satan on me, don't cut me up, man."

"We ain't going to cut your ass up. We just want some questions answered," Charley said.

I pulled off my stocking and leaned forward so Coop could see me.

"Goddamn! You're scaring the shit out of me. Fuck, Sam, you're supposed to be dead."

"They burned up Jimmy," I said.

"Oh, man. That was him in the trailer?" He was getting calmer.

"Right."

"So you blew up his boat?"

"Right."

"Does Bug know?"

"Yes."

"Oh, man . . ."

"We need you to tell us the whole deal, Coop," I said.

"Yeh, I know, man, only you got to help me out."

"How?"

"You got to tell Bug I didn't have anything to do with Jimmy. Bug listens to you."

"He listens to me because I don't tell him any bullshit. If I told him you didn't have anything to do with Jimmy it would be bullshit, because I don't know that one way or the other," I said.

"You know how I felt about Jimmy. He was like my brother, man," Coop said.

"People kill their brothers," I said. "I always thought we were pretty square, then you got me mired in this mess."

Charley pulled the stocking off his head. Lloyd and Bob saw him and did it themselves.

"Neither of us saw this coming," he said. "I'm on your side, Sam. I know I had a hand in getting you into this. I'll do whatever I can to help you out."

"When Shirley came to see you and you gave him my name, he must have given you a reference, somebody you would have known well enough to give him a name."

"Yeah, man, he gave me some names."

I could see he didn't want to tell me almost as bad as he wanted to tell me.

After waiting a few seconds, Charley said, "You going to tell us or we going to play twenty questions?"

"No, man, it was Dong."

"Chandler?" I asked.

I looked at Charley for a reaction and got just a little arching of the eyebrows.

"And that lawyer of his, Donald Weatherby," Coop said.

"Weatherby," Charley said.

"Right, Donald Weatherby."

"OK, Coop, I got a question. If Dong Chandler asks you if I'm alive, what are you going to tell him?"

"I'm trying to be straight with you, Sam. Dong scares the fuck out of me. I don't know what I'm going to do."

"Who scares you worse, Dong Chandler or Bug Raiford?

"You're not leaving me much of a choice," Coop said.

"One choice, get out of town till this is over," I said.

"I was putting that on my agenda."

"I thought you might be," I said. "When you get back, I'll give you a taste."

"Thanks, man."

"Give this man his gun back, he may need it," I said. Charley handed it to him.

"I'm not taking this personal," Coop said.

"Me neither," I said. "It's just business. The only thing I take personally is Jimmy, and I know you didn't see that coming.

"I thought I was doing you a favor," Coop said.

"I know that. One other thing, you got any money on you?"

"Couple hundred bucks," Coop said.

"My friend here needs to cash some traveler's checks."

19

"YOU FEEL ANY different about it now that you know that Dong is involved?"

We were driving down I-75 toward town.

"No, man. If you're going to get killed, you might as well get killed by somebody important, and if you're going to rob somebody, it might as well be somebody with a lot of money," Charley said.

"Who is this Dong?" Lloyd asked.

"You never heard of him?" Charley said.

"Why would I ask who he was if I already knew?" Lloyd asked.

"One of your better points," Charley agreed. "Billy Chandler is Dixie mob. The handle comes from donkey dong. They say his dick is about two feet long. I did time with a couple people who worked for him. Knew one named Eldo Justus pretty good. He's a good old boy."

"You'd heard of the lawyer?" I asked.

"Right. It was the name I couldn't remember at lunch. The one my friend calls the anti-Christ. He's one of your bigger lunatics. The people up here love him because he has so many nice suits."

"The news that Dong's involved brings up another possibility," I said. "I wonder if he has a bank?"

"What do you mean by a bank?" Lloyd asked. "You ain't planning on robbing a bank, are you, Mister?"

"Not that kind of bank. I mean a place where he keeps the ready money he turns around in his drug business, lots of cash from street sales and for big buys."

"How much you figure he'd have in a place like that?" Lloyd asked.

"At least two to three million," I said. "Maybe more."

"I like that number," Lloyd said.

"Yeh, yeh, yeh," Bob said.

"You're going to have to put your clothes back on before we get to town," Charley said.

"What do you think, Charley?"

"I think you're crazy as ever-living-shit wanting to knock over Dong Chandler's bank. You got to be the biggest lunatic in the tri-state area."

"What three states would that be?"

"Georgia, California, and Puerto Rico," Charley said.

"Puerto Rico ain't a state," Lloyd said.

"Fuck you."

"You don't want to do it?" I asked.

"I didn't say that. I'm pretty crazy myself. I think we ought to have a two-way plan. Look for the mule. Look for the bank. When the time comes, we'll know what we want to hit."

When we walked into the lobby of the hotel the man with the Hawaiian shirt began waving his copy of Kafka's *The Metamorphosis*.

"Charley, you got to come over here. I got to talk to you."

"What's happening, my man?"

"The Jackson brothers were in here a little while ago, Charley. They looked like they'd been smoking rock, waving a gun all over the place, said they were going to kill you. I called the cops, but they split. I don't know if I'd go out there tonight. You better be careful, Charley. They would have done it."

20

"WE'RE LUCKY WE didn't get our asses shot off last night," I said.

"It wasn't one of your better jobs," Charley agreed.

We were gathered in my room early in the morning. Lloyd had wheeled his chair next to the bathroom door. Bob was sitting on the bed against the headboard, Charley straddled the straight chair backwards with his arms folded against the top of the chair back, and I was leaning against the chest of drawers.

"Some parts of it went smooth," Lloyd said.

"Some just ain't good enough," Charley said.

Bob wrote, "SOME SUCKS," on his note pad and held it up.

"See, he's agreeing with me now," Charley said.

"OK, Mister, What exactly have you got in mind. How are we going to get smooth?"

"I'm glad you asked that because I want to make a little speech, we can have an organizational meeting, then I'll buy breakfast. As I see it, last night Vogel could have shot Charley and me, and we could have shot ourselves and each other, Bob's clothes caught on fire, we got two crazy white rasta baseheads from Hoboken trying to smoke Charley, and we're talking about ripping off Dong Chandler. Does this sound like a rational arrangement to anyone?"

"Fuck no." Charley pulled a toothpick from the inside pocket of his suit coat and held it against his lower lip with his tongue, a gesture to show that he not only had said, "Fuck no," but he profoundly felt, "Fuck no."

"OK. Here's a little story I want everyone to pay attention to, even you Charley. Years ago, I was a principal in a dope mob in southwest Florida," I said.

"I suspected it was something like that," Charley said.

"Anyway, one day these three guys tried to rip us off for one of our stashes of operating money."

"What happened?" Lloyd asked.

"We blew them away and fed them to the gators," I said.

"FAR OUT," Bob wrote.

Charley nodded knowingly.

"These guys made one big mistake. They never considered the possibility that the people they were robbing were crazier than they were. They may have been competent stick-up men, good at knocking over gas stations and convenience stores, but they didn't understand the psychology of the situation. A shopkeeper just wants to live through the robbery like it's a bad dream. A serious criminal may not care, or else he may figure fighting is the only way he's going to make it. Maybe he's done a lot of time. Charley, tell us how you survive in the joint?"

"First thing, when somebody tries to mess with you, you hit first and keep hitting until you're unconscious; then after they figure you for a serious person, you got to find yourself a crew," Charley said.

"So let's keep that in mind," I said. "You don't get a season in the minors in this business, you got to jump right into the bigs. As a result, figuring out where everybody stands is very important. None of us are psycho-killers, right?"

Everyone shook their heads to say no.

"No, man," Charley said. "When I pulled a job, if people did what I told them, I wouldn't bother with them. In the long run people don't mind much if you take their money. Might be pissed off at first, but they get used to it after a while. It's when you kill them that they get their ass up."

"I'm not a psycho either," I said, "and it's too bad, 'cause that way we could just waste everybody and get out of town with their money. As it is, we got to do some planning.

"How about shooting somebody if you had to?" I asked. "Lloyd, how about you?"

"I don't know if I could," Lloyd admitted.

"No problem with that. There's a place for people with different thresholds. We just got to find out what they are so we can put you in the right place. How about you, Bob?"

"ONLY IF I HAD TO," he wrote.

"Charley?"

"Already have done," he said.

"Same here," I said. "Now there's a point I want to make real clear. I'd have a lot of trouble killing somebody as part of a business deal unless it just happened to come down, but the person who burnt up Jimmy Cooley ain't business, it's personal. And I'm going to kill that fuck deader than an oak plank if I get the chance. But that's a side issue. It doesn't have anything to do with this job, and I'm not going to let it interfere. Understood?"

"I'll kill him for you if I get the chance," Charley said.

"I think we need to devote all our time to this enterprise. Can you get off work, Charley?"

"I got some time coming," he said.

"It isn't going to set off any bells with your parole officer?"

"No, I'm cool on that."

"I'm going to bankroll this with the cash I got from James Shirley. Since it's high risk, I want a hundred percent back on my money. Any objections?"

They shook their heads.

"I don't think we should have to grub around while this is happening, so everyone gets a draw. In exchange for that … nothing on the side, no funny paper, no nothing. Understood?"

They nodded.

"Now another brief object lesson. I was going up to Sarasota years ago on a shopping trip. On the way, I passed the homes of mullet fishermen I knew in Osprey and Vamo who were making a fortune bringing dope ashore, but you could never tell it by looking. They led very simple lives.

"I stopped at this Italian restaurant south of town. No customers, great-looking menu, low prices, a table full of wise-guys in tropical-issue wise-guy uniforms. Their girlfriends had spent a lot of money so they could look like they gave five-buck blow jobs. The guy at the head of the table was ordering for everyone and generally being treated like the Emperor of the Known Universe. He didn't seem to mind it.

"I made them as serious assholes, and the place as their laundry, a full fifteen seconds after entering the door. As it turns out, I wasn't the only one. They got busted for racketeering a week later. The mullet fishermen are still at large. Anyone care to draw any conclusions from this?" I asked.

"Don't flash your cash," Charley said.

"You tell a good story, Mister. I think you made your point real good."

"EVERYTHING SAME-SAME," Bob wrote.

"So let's get down to details. Lloyd, could you drive if we got a van with hand controls?"

"Yes sir, sure could."

"Why don't you check on rentals? Bob, what are we going to do about your clothes catching on fire. How often does it happen?"

"SOMETIMES EVERY THREE OR FOUR MONTHS OR SOMETIMES TWICE A DAY," he wrote.

"Anything you can do about it?"

"POUR WATER ON THEM."

"So if you got some canteens or water jugs and poured them all over yourself, it would put the fire out?"

"RIGHT."

"OK, you better get some. Charley, we need to get more artillery, Kevlar vests, mace, handcuffs, radios. You need to make a list. I'm putting you in charge of the arrangements. Make sure we can communicate with clicks or tones on the radios. I don't like people talking when we're supposed to be quiet. I got a simple code I can teach everyone. OK, next point. Anybody got a lawyer?"

"Janis's sister, the one I was telling you about, she owes me a few favors," Charley said.

"Why don't you make an appointment. Tell her we want her to check out a few people's assets. We'll pay. And while we're at it, we got to do something about the Jacksons."

"One of your better points," Charley agreed. "I got to find them first. Trick is to find them without getting shot."

"So let me run the final breakdown by you," I said. "I see Lloyd and Bob being lookouts and wheelmen and Charley and me doing the heavy lifting. As I see it, we need one more man with a gun."

"You got somebody in mind?" Lloyd asked. "We got sort of a cozy group here. Hate to see somebody that isn't too comfortable join up with us and not fit in."

"I got somebody in mind," I said.

"IS HE BAD?" Bob wrote.

"He's a good friend, but on his best day he's worse than you can imagine."

Charley held the top and leaned back in the straight chair.

"So this is one bad sucker?" he asked.

"Remember the guy who fire-bombed all those ATF agents?"

"You weren't joking. He's got to be one of your crazier earth people. If I were going to rip off Dong Chandler, I'd love to have him along for the ride. I didn't know he was still on the loose."

"Yeah, well, that's a small complication. He isn't. He's in this medium-security crazy hospital."

There was a knock at the door.

"Sam."

I opened it and saw the clerk with the Hawaiian shirt.

"You got a phone call. At least I think it's for you. The guy's loaded on some weird juice. It's got him locked in the slow lane. He says his name is something like Boog or Boo-hoo-wug or something."

"Speak of the devil," I said.

21

ONCE I HAD a broken tape player in an old '71 Ford that ran so slow that lyrics became inarticulate growls and moans. It could make the Vienna Boys' Choir sound like the Muddy Waters Blues Band. I felt like I was listening to that tape player again.

"Saaaaaammmm?" the voice rumbled. Dragging every vowel and consonant over loose lips that could easily sink ships.

"Bug?"

"Yo. Everything is . . . slow. Slow . . . and echo."

"They got you on some serious drugs?"

"Druuuggugs zzz?"

"You drugged?"

"Too slow. Everything is slow. Whoa. Go. Go fast."

"You want me to talk fast?"

"Fast. Assed . . . as the wind," he said.

I started talking as fast as I possibly could. The desk clerk put down his copy of Kafka and arched his eyebrow. I imagine it took a lot to convince him you were nuts, but I seemed to be doing a grade-A job of it.

"I'm talking as fast as I can does this help? Can you understand me now?"

"Yes, man, better. I'm, uh, trying to talk fast too. I, uh . . . I, uh got your card about Jimmy."

"It's the pits, isn't it?" I said.

"The pits . . . yes, it is."

Bug hadn't communicated much information since being sent to the mental institution. In fact, the letter about developing remorse was the first one that had made any sense at all. This was the first I had talked to him. My guess that he had been incapacitated by drugs was correct. The big question was whether he was coherent enough to tell me about his situation.

"Good to hear you, man."

"Just got phone privilege," he said.

"I've been worried about your spiritual development," I said.

"Don't worry. I've been reading the Bible."

"Good. I hope it's the King James version."

"Yes, King James."

"That's the best," I said.

Good. Bug was drugged but coherent. The Bible thing established that he had some information to pass on and that we could use the King James version for a chapter, verse, and word-number book code.

"Have you talked to your lawyer?" I asked.

"Yeah, I told him I wanted to throw a barbecue for his family."

"I understand. You have a lot of warm feelings for him after all you been through together."

"Very warm."

"What did he say?"

"I don't understand what he said. I'm too strung out. Things are so slow I don't always get them."

"Let's give it a try," I said.

"He said he writ down something about rabies and corpses."

"Hmm. That doesn't ring any bells." I thought about it a moment. "Wait a minute. It's *habeas corpus*."

"That's what I said. Rabies and corpses. That doesn't make sense. You understand that?"

"Yes."

Silence.

Well, I guess Bug was sort of coherent.

"So you got a new ball team together?" he asked.

"Right. They're one in a million. But I sure do miss your big bat."

"When's your first game?"

"I'm hoping to schedule one in a couple weeks."

"I wish I could catch it."

"I wish you could be here," I said.

"Is it against the crosstown rivals?" he asked.

"That's the way it looks," I said.

"I'd really like to be there."

"So, what's it like where you are?"

"Real pretty. They got a nice green lawn, and you got a good view, 'cause they don't have any walls, just a chain-link fence. Mostly the drugs are the walls. It's just easier to take the drugs and go along. So we just cruise on a cloud. Half the people are in here for something they did on dope, so why would they want to get out?"

"So I guess they don't have any breakouts."

"Oh, sometimes they'll be a breakout. But they just find the breakout wandering around in circles in the woods, and they bring them back."

"I see what you're saying. As long as you take your medication, you can't break out."

"Right. Thinking is too complicated. You just drift along with the program."

"Would you like me to come visit you?" I asked.

"No. That's OK. But I'd like it if you could get me some supplies."

"You want to write me and tell me what's the best way to do it."

"Yes. I'll write you and tell you the best way."

I took this to mean that Bug was planning on breaking out, thought he could do it, didn't need any active help, but could probably use a cache of supplies – clothes, money, maps, IDs, and so forth – hidden outside the fence on his route. That way the rest of us could be far from the scene in case the break went badly. We would work the details out through the book code. The fact that Bug was thinking this clearly was a good sign.

"Sam."

"Yeah, man."

"There's something I need to tell you."

"What is it, man?"

"It's what I've thought about since I got your card about JC."

"What's that, Bug?"

"The monkey gods are going to laugh when I bowl with the skulls of those guys that burnt JC."

"If that's what it takes to make the gods laugh, Bug, I'm all for it," I said.

"You got to understand, Sam; I am big-footed Shiva, and I'm coming down from the mountains to stomp the world flat. Tell them I am the destroyer of worlds, and I have no mercy. Tell them I'm coming."

Coherent my ass. Bug was in much worse shape that I had imagined was possible.

"Bug. I hear what you're saying, but I don't think we need to mention this to the other guys. Most of them may be a little antisocial, but I don't think they're into destroying things on that level."

"No, man. I wouldn't mention it," Bug said. "I don't want them to think I'm crazy."

22

THE DESK CLERK took the phone back.

"I never heard anybody talk that fast or that slow in my life," he said.

"Boo–Hoo Wug and I have a friendship based on extremes," I said. At the moment the greatest extreme was that Bug was extremely nuts.

The clerk picked up his tattered copy of *The Metamorphosis* and pointed to it. "This is a great book. It tells about how the day after Reagan was elected, the whole country turned into roaches," he said.

After talking to Bug, I felt almost like I was in a dream. Now I really wondered. I looked around for Charley. He had crept behind me and was grinning.

"I told him about that dream of yours," he said.

"If you told him about the dream, maybe you can explain why we aren't roaches?" I said.

"'Cause we're the vermin, and proud of it," he said. "I already made that call from the pay unit on the street. Elizabeth Martin, Attorney at Law, at 4:30 p.m. Got to go talk to Old Man Cavanaugh about the time off. Might have to work tonight. Depends on if we have a big time croakfest or not."

"Be careful, buddy. This is one of your better days to get shot by your Jackson twins." Damn, I was starting to talk like him.

"I'm going to check it out pretty good. Not planning on spending a lot of time in the great out-of-doors."

I followed him to the front door and took eight hundred dollars from my pocket.

"Why don't you pick up a vest. You should be able to get

a good one for that. Just keep everything in an account book."

I slipped the money in his suit coat pocket and felt a hard lump at the waistband.

"I got your little friend from the back of the television. Hope you don't mind," Charley said.

"It's the best plan."

There was a copy of the King James Bible in the peeling veneer bedside-table drawer in my room, thoughtfully provided by the ladies of the Temperance Union of a local church. I knew this because a rubber stamp inside told me not only their name and address but that God was only a phone call away. I was tempted to try the number to see what God sounded like but figured the way my plan was playing out I was more likely to meet Him through a gunfire exchange than the telephone variety.

Bug was definitely over the edge if he was convinced he was the destroyer of world. The question was whether he was manageable. If you're going to knock over Dong Chandler, having at least one homicidal maniac as a part of the crew isn't a bad idea. The ladies from the Temperance Union weren't going to make much of an impression on old Dong even if they had a phone line to God. But I was going to have to get Bug to lay aside the surrealist open-casket funerals, the ghost of Sid Vicious, and the collages of our former vice president dancing the Huckle Buck with Long Dong Silver, and get him connected back to his old mind, which was as effective as it was dangerous.

After going over the Bible for two hours, I took the bus to a shop on Peachtree that did desktop publishing and rented computer time by the hour. A sign on the window said: Let us publish your organization's newsletter!

It was an interesting thought. Perhaps Charley could have

a column called Corpse Kicker's Korner, in which he listed
the murder attempts against him that week.

A woman with short dark hair sat behind a generic blond-
wood counter. She was as young as she was sincere.

"Could I help you?"

"I hope so. I wanted to put together a pamphlet," I said.

"Do you have any word-processing experience?" she asked.

"No."

"We have a program that's very easy to use. It's sort of slow
this morning so I can give you some help."

I must have had a dubious look.

"I go to Tech. I know about these things," she said
defensively.

"It's not you I'm worried about."

After an hour filled with a thousand typos and losing something she called my file several times, I began to get the hang
of the machine, and she left me alone so she could talk on
the phone to someone named Alan. She seemed to be having
a hard time with Alan, and she didn't care who knew it.

Here is what I typed:

THE GOSPEL PRISON MINISTRY WARNS

SATAN is loose in the land.

Idle hands and idle minds are the breeding ground
of SIN.

Mindless repetition is the only path to SALVATION.

We at the Gospel Prison Ministry believe that the
godlessness of men in prison is so absolute that praying,
engaging in self-denial, practicing the mortification of
the flesh, and the reading of Scripture may not be
enough to insure salvation.

The only path to salvation for men who have fallen into
sin and done the work of the devil is to keep their mind

pure from devil-inspired thoughts and their life free from devil-inspired actions through the constant spoken repetition of Scripture. The following is the first lesson in our course for the repetition of Scripture. Please use the King James Bible, as all others are incorrect. Repeat the passages out loud the specified number of times. Use this brochure as your spiritual guide until lesson 2 arrives in the mail.

1. Question whether your life is on the right path and repeat Matthew 23:33 ten times and Matthew 19:26 twenty times.
2. Understand the gift of spiritual freedom and repeat John 14:18 two times, Mark 5:24 four times, John 2:25 two times, Mark 7:4 seventeen times, Matthew 23:26 sixteen times, and Luke 3:20 twelve times.
3. State your spiritual needs and repeat Luke 1:5 twenty-three times and Mark 13:7 twenty times.
4. State your spiritual goals and repeat Mark 5:9 eight times and Luke 23:33 eight times.

The Gospel Prison Ministry recognizes that there may be times when it isn't possible to speak out loud either because of prison rules or because you have lost your voice from the constant repetitions of Scripture. Under those circumstances it is suggested that you make yourself as uncomfortable as possible. Some suggestions include sitting on a straight chair with a broken leg, sleeping with your arms tied behind your back, and wearing your clothes inside out.

MAY YOU FIND PEACE THROUGH THE CONSTANT REPETITION OF THE GOSPELS.

As codes went, there wasn't much to it. I was reasonably sure that it would pass a cursory look from a prison security guard, and that it would be broken immediately by the NSA.

In plain text, it translated to: "Escape possible? Will leave needed things outside prison. Name needs. Name place."

Having dispatched Alan to the forgotten void of former boyfriends and typed a paper for her English class, the young woman returned to look over my shoulder.

"I'm ready to print it," I said. "I'd like to get an envelope with a return address that says Prison Gospel Ministries."

"Oh, you're working with prisoners. How nice."

She looked at the copy on the screen, and I could see she thought it might not be so nice after all. In fact, I would bet she was wondering if she wanted to be alone in the same room with me.

"That's a very unusual approach," she said after scanning down the lines.

"I'm not all that religious," I pointed out.

"Oh?"

"It's just that they won't let these guys have a ping pong table, and they need something to occupy their time."

"You're doing this because they can't have a ping pong table?" She was incredulous.

"It's part of my theology," I explained. "Our ministry is based on the belief that in spite of His infinite scope, it is much easier to fit God into a prison cell than a ping pong table."

She walked quickly behind the counter.

"I'll get this printed for you right away," she said. Her tone implied that an hour ago wouldn't be soon enough.

23

I DREW FIVE thousand from an account at a bank branch on Peachtree, then took the bus back to the hotel. The deathmobile was parked in front of the building, which meant that Charley Shelnut, a.k.a. Death's Personal Representative to the City of Atlanta, was probably in his room and receiving visitors.

His door was ajar, and I heard the murmur of voices inside.

"Come in, Sam my man. I was just helping Stinky and Half-Moon with a list. Give him the rundown, Lloyd."

"Here's the deal, Mister. We found a place to rent a van. Charley wants us to park it away from here so folks won't connect it with us. He says we need to find a garage to rent, maybe over in Little Five Points. Then we got to work on a van disguise. Find some magnetic signs. Get ourselves some of that one-way plastic for the windows from Pep Boys and get one of them cardboard sun things so people can't see in too good when we're checking them out."

"Sounds like you're working on a good plan." I handed him some cash. "Just keep track of it."

He pulled a little spiral book out of his shirt pocket.

"Already got me a notebook. I'm going to keep accounts on the money for Bob and me."

"I talked to Cavanaugh, and he gave me two weeks off," Charley said. "Had a vacation coming. I told him I had a family problem. He said I could take more off if I needed but he could only pay me for the two. He's going to cover with my PO. He said he'd have a hard time finding someone who moved the dead around with as much enthusiasm as I do."

"Good. Let's gas up that big ride of yours. We need to take a little trip after we see the lawyer."

The office of Elizabeth Martin, Attorney at Law, was in a piece-of-pie shaped building across from Woodruff Park.

"This is the building where Matlock had his office on the television," Charley said.

"The rooms look a lot bigger on TV," I pointed out.

"That's because even though the building is in Atlanta, all its rooms are in Los Angeles."

"So does that mean that this waiting room is in Los Angeles?"

"No, that's my point. Because the waiting room is so small, that means it's in Atlanta. If we go into one of your bigger conference rooms, we better check because we could be slipping toward Los Angeles."

"It doesn't look to me like the building is wide enough for one of your bigger conference rooms," I said.

We'd been cooling our heels in the tiny waiting room for nearly an hour. That and the casual attitude of the secretary gave Charley and me the impression that we were not highly regarded clients. As a result, we didn't mind that our conversation was driving the secretary batty.

"When I was a kid I always wanted everything on television," Charley said.

"You mean all the toys?" I asked.

"No. I mean like Mr Ed. I always wanted a talking horse that would solve all your personal problems for you. I had a lot of personal problems on account of my old man was a hopeless drunk, and so I used to do things like set fire to the Sunday school building. It would have been nice to have a talking horse to straighten out the problems for me, instead of a shitty court-appointed lawyer who got me sent to the school where you had to fuck the men teachers."

The secretary picked up the phone with a look of desperation and spoke quietly. I saw her say "please" several times, then she slammed down the receiver.

"Ms Martin is still busy," she said.

"Then, of course, there was the show where the guy had the bottle with the woman inside of it. He would rub on the bottle and then this woman would get real big and come out of the bottle. She had to do everything he said. I always wanted to have me one of them bottles with a woman inside of it."

The secretary stood abruptly.

"Follow me," she said.

She led us into a small office. A woman in a dressed-for-success suit sat with her feet on her desk talking on the telephone. She glared at the secretary and quickly pulled her legs down.

"Your 4:30 appointment," the secretary said. She looked pointedly at her watch. "It's 5:30."

"I'll call back later," Elizabeth Martin said to the person on the phone. As she straightened up the papers on her desk, she asked, "How can I help you, Charley?"

She was an attractive woman in her middle thirties. She had to be Janis's younger sister. It was hard to see any family resemblance.

"We want you to do asset searches on several gentlemen," Charley said.

"Look, Charley, I appreciate what you've done for my sister, and all, but something like this could run into some money."

"How much?"

"How many counties?"

"Metro."

"Two or three hundred dollars."

"We got it covered."

"I know that's a lot of money for you, Charley. If I could do it myself, I'd do it for nothing, but I'm going to have to call freelancers in each of the counties. They are going to cost me money I don't have. I haven't been in practice for long, Charley. I don't want to get the phone turned off."

"Money's not a problem," I said. I put five hundred on her desk. "Let me know when you need more."

She looked at me closely for the first time. "And who might you be?" she asked.

"Just call me Mr Money Bags," I said.

"All right, Mr Money Bags, who do you want the asset searches done on?"

I nodded to Charley, and he spoke. "We want a William Alvin Chandler, also known as Billy, and a Donald Weatherby."

She was writing on a note pad but threw the pen down on her desk.

"OK. What have you boys got on your mind? I know who Dong Chandler is, and Weatherby is a widely respected member of the bar. What's the connection?"

"They do some business together," Charley said.

"And what does it have to do with you?"

"We might do some business with them. We want to find out if they are men of substance with strong financial ties to the community."

"Don't bullshit me, Charley. Before I get even marginally involved with some goofy scheme you boys have dreamed up, I want your assurance that it isn't anything illegal."

Charley didn't say anything. He looked at the floor, then looked at me. It may seem odd, but it made me trust him more. We all have some personal morality, even if it may not be apparent on the surface. I understood, now, that Charley could steal without qualm from somebody he didn't know, but he couldn't lie to a friend.

"I can assure you that an asset search on Donnie and Dong isn't illegal," I said. "I can also assure you that if this enterprise screws up, we are going to need a lawyer very badly."

She flashed the smile of a born cynic.

"Then you've got a lawyer," she said.

24

I DIRECTED CHARLEY out the Buford Highway to a rental storage business, a small village of squat sheet-metal buildings. As we pulled through the gate, the manager was closing the door to his office. He looked at the hearse and gave us a hard look until he recognized me.

"How you doing, Glenn," he shouted.

"Just fine, Frank."

"Mr Money Bags, Sam on the Lam, Glenn, you're a man of many identities," Charley said.

"In some parts of town they call me Glenda," I said.

"Yeoow, take a walk on the wild side."

"My storage locker is 10C." I pointed toward the C building.

"These are one of your better dodges," Charley said. "Imagine all the merchandise that must be stuffed away in these things. Out in Seattle, they found the bones of this guy's family. I bet half these rentals are filled with things that were ripped off."

"I'm doing my part to add to that problem," I said.

I unfastened the padlock, opened the garage door, and turned on the light. It was a small enclosure, about eight by twelve with unpainted drywall. Charley followed me in and we closed the door behind us.

I pointed to one of three footlockers.

"That one's empty," I said. "Why don't you move it over here?"

He slid it next to me, and I unlocked another footlocker and began transferring some of the contents to the empty one. There was a gym bag with ten thousand dollars in it, an envelope containing three complete sets of identification papers, including driver's licenses, credit cards, and passports, two rolls of Krugerrands, shotgun shells, other ammunition, and three pistols, one small .38 special and two 9-mms with high-capacity magazines.

"The pistols are Brazilian knock-offs but still high-quality weapons; there are two 12-gauge pumps in that case in the corner, if you want to grab them."

"This is one of your better storage lockers. I could go for a room like this. You got more of them?" Charley asked.

"Yes, I do."

"You ought to leave a treasure map in your shoe, in case you get your ass shot off," he said.

"I already took care of that," I said.

We carried the footlocker to the hearse and slid it in the back. On the way out Frank waved us down.

"I wanted to give you your bill," he said. "What the hell, why not save the postage."

"Thanks. I'll get it back to you. By the way, I want you to meet my friend, Dullard."

He seemed a little taken back by the name, but said, "Hi there, Dullard."

"It's a family name," Charley explained. "Pretty common over in the part of the country where I hail from."

"Where might that be?" Frank asked.

"South Carolina piedmont," Charley said.

Frank thought for a moment. "Seems like I've heard about some Dullards from over there," he agreed.

"Place is full of them," I said.

Charley pulled on to the highway heading north. We had one more stop to make.

"Now you got another identity," I said.

He slipped Jerry Lee Lewis's greatest hits into the tape deck and cranked it up.

"You don't often see a hearse with a tape player," I said.

"It's a sort of a tradition among us Dullards. We don't think death should be a somber thing; in fact, we're happy when people die, 'cause we don't have much use for them when they're alive."

We stopped at a huge supermarket-sized store that sold firearms, taxidermy supplies, live crickets, cowboy boots, and anything else you might want if you thought you were the Marlboro Man or were still waiting for World War III. Charley stopped at the first aisle to look at a cardboard kiosk with taxidermy videotapes and a picture of a man with bug eyes and a waist-length beard standing in a forest of stuffed black bears, deer heads, foxes with chipmunks in their mouths, pheasants, boars, and for some inexplicable reason a green parrot and a miniature poodle.

"Sam, finally I see a reason to get me one of those VCRs. I'm going back home with a whole new appreciation for the folks that live there. I used to think all the crazy people in the United States must have been dumped on Ponce, but now I see all those people are perfectly normal. The real lunatics are living up here."

"The people up here just cover it up better by always staying indoors," I said.

It was a slow time, just before dinner, and there wasn't anybody in the gun department except a solitary neurotic young salesman with darting eyes. The top button of his shirt was fastened, the collar was too tight, and he wore the polyester tie with a smug certainty, like it was a religious medal. I was about to make his day.

"We need to buy some weapons," I said. "We need two 12-gauge pumps, improved cylinder with extended magazines. Three lightweight five-shot .38 specials, you know, good ankle guns, and while you're at it four nylon ankle holsters, five belt clips too, three high-capacity 9-mms, five shoulder holsters for those, and four Kevlar vests.

"What sort of pistols you got in Spanish or Brazilian?" I asked.

"We've got Taurus and Llama."

"Give me whatever is cheaper. Don't bother trying to sell me on it, just wrap it up. And give me your federal firearms crap that they're trying to take our rights away with, and I'll fill it out," I said.

"So you're another firm supporter of the Constitution," he said.

"Damn right, I'm a firm believer in law and order, except when they use that law and order to further the worship of communism or Satan, and then I think everyone needs to take the law in their own hands."

Charley was gathering up pepper gas sprays.

The clerk spoke in a low voice. "It looks like you guys are outfitting a small army."

"How could you tell?" I asked.

"Well, actually, it happens here fairly often. There's more of that going on than you'd think."

I was filling out the federal gun-purchase forms indicating that I was not a convicted felon, which was true, that I was not insane, which was debatable, and that I was Carter Sams, which was an outright lie, but the easiest to prove due to some exquisite forged documents.

"Listen, buddy, sometimes you got to fight for your race," Charley said.

"You won't have any argument from me on that. I'm committed to the concept of race struggle," the clerk said sharply.

"You got to fight for your race, even if it sucks," Charley said.

"I don't think the white race sucks," the clerk said.

"Then you haven't opened your eyes. The white race is completely fucked up. Too damned many cousins marrying each other. Now all we can do is drool and bankrupt savings institutions, but you want to know something, buddy? It doesn't make any difference that the white race is fucked up, because that was the club you were born in. You get my meaning. You think you can go and join up with the soul brothers at this late date? Hell no. In case you haven't noticed, you got the wrong complexion.

"Guys like you need to wake up. And guess what, I'm your wake-up call. You think the white race isn't fucked up, and I say get some standards. Look at the morons you sell guns to all day long. If you think they're better than anyone at all, you aren't the bright, articulate person I take you for. They are a bunch of human slugs that like to taxidermy their poodles.

"But let me tell you something, Mister. It doesn't make any difference that they're morons, because they're white, so that means they are just like you and me. We ruin everything we touch. It's our destiny. And because of that we need to go ruin everything in the world before your Asians, your Espanols, and all the various black factions get their hands on it and can attract all the white women."

"I think I see your point. It's sort of like my country right or wrong," the clerk said.

"Exactly, the country is another thing that is totally fucked up."

The clerk handed Charley a card. "I'm not saying I agree with everything you say, but I think you make some important points on the subject of race loyalty. I know some people you might want to talk to. Give me a call."

"I'd be pleased to."

Charley shook the clerk's hand as I handed back the forms and showed him my ID.

"The name's Dullard," Charley said. "It's a family name from over in the South Carolina piedmont."

Charley hadn't seen how good the fake ID was, so he didn't know he didn't need to provide a distraction. Still, it was fun watching him work.

25

"I'VE GOT TO use a telephone. Why don't we drive over to that one by the supermarket?"

"Looks like it might work. Don't see any dangling cords," Charley said.

"If anyone wants to use it while I'm talking, you can tell them you're next in line and maybe drool a little bit so they leave."

"I'll ask them if they got any idea how to cure the crabs."

We slipped the guns and other supplies into a body bag in the back of the hearse then drove across the parking lot.

"I'm going to check on a couple things. First thing I want to find out is how tight our buddy Dong is with the gentlemen from Colombia. My suspicion is that he makes a bunch of money selling his product in every nightclub, pool hall, shot house, and shooting gallery from Kennesaw to Covington, but I don't think he rates very high on your rock and powder food chain. He's a big fish to us and a little fish to them," I said.

"And not protected," Charley said.

"Exactly. The other point being that at some time we are probably going to want to sit down and talk with some of these people in order to find out as much as we can about them, so we need to have something to talk about," I said.

"Sounds like one of your better points. What exactly you got in mind?"

"I thought we might get in touch with the folks that are running the money laundry first. My guess is they've got a lot of ambition, and like to think they are tough. We can be sort of mysterious, say they have come to the attention of some guys …"

"I know those guys," Charley said.

"Right, maybe they want to get in bed with us, maybe they don't, we're just checking the situation out because we heard they been moving money real good. Main thing they are going to be worried about is that we're narcs, so we need to come up with some credentials."

There wasn't anyone around the phone, so I placed a credit card call to Costa Rica, the private line of a public person.

"Hello?" he answered.

"Jean-Paul?"

"Sam. Are you enjoying your vacation yet?"

"There's been a change of plans. I could use some help."

"How?"

"I'm going to do a number on some gentlemen. I need a reference."

"What do you need?"

"For you to say that I represent some interests who need to move money discreetly. You can be mysterious about it," I said.

"Are the objects of your attention anyone I know?"

"I don't think so. Local distributor and laundry."

"Names?"

"Billy Chandler, a.k.a Dong, and his attorney, Donald Weatherby."

"Dong, you say."

"He's supposed to have a big one."

"And you're planning on stepping on it."

"Right."

"And these gentlemen are going to be mad afterward?" he asked.

"Either very mad or beyond caring."

"I see." He paused for a moment, absorbing the implication. "What name are you using?"

"Carter Sams."

"Very well. If anyone calls, I will tell them Carter Sams is indeed who he claims he is. Give me a call once it comes down so I can change my story, and discover that I, too, have been conned by the notorious Mr Sams."

"I'll do that."

"Does this mean you are coming out of retirement?" he asked.

"I think so."

"When this is over, we need to talk. I might have some things you're interested in. Keep in mind, there are easier ways to make money these days. We aren't the bad guys standing on the outside anymore. We're the establishment."

As I hung up the phone Charley asked, "What did he say?"

"He's covering for us, Dong is fair game, and we should join the chamber of commerce."

26

BACK AT THE hotel, we put the footlocker and the body bag on the stretcher and rolled it toward my room.

"Making deliveries, Charley?" the desk clerk asked.

"Hell yes, Corpses for Cannibals. Dial 1-800-EAT-SHIT."

Bob and Lloyd were waiting for us. Both looked excited.

"Good news, Mister. We got that van and got a garage to put it in over in Little Five Points. It's a big double garage that a band used to practice in," Lloyd said.

"Good choice. As long as we don't burn the place down, the neighbors will probably like us," I said.

"I was thinking along those lines," he said. "We got that one-way plastic for the windows, but we haven't put it on yet. We came back over here so we could find you guys. What you got on the stretcher?"

"More goodies. Maybe we ought to take the stuff over to the garage."

"Let's take a look at it first," Lloyd suggested.

Charley unzipped the body bag and pulled back the flap.

"Here's your Kevlar vests and here's some of your better artillery." Charley handed Lloyd one of the 9-mms in a buff-colored box with a gold coat of arms on the front.

"It does look like one of your better handguns," Lloyd agreed.

He took it from the box, held it gingerly at first, and then seemed to take to it, pointing it at the television and out the window with growing enthusiasm.

"Pow. Pow."

"We're going to make a desperado out of you yet," Charley said.

"I like this thing," Lloyd said.

"Just think of that doctor that ran you down and got your legs cut off," Charley said.

"After we kill all them other boys, you think we can kill him too?"

"That's the spirit, man. You just keep working on that attitude."

Charley took the magazine from the box and began stuffing shells in it, then slipped it in Lloyd's pistol.

"Nothing will get you killed faster than an unloaded gun. Just work the slide and make sure the safety is off, and you're ready to rock and roll."

It was dark outside, but you couldn't hardly tell it because the street and parking lot lights were so bright. I didn't see the car coming, mainly because I wasn't paying attention. There was plenty of light. Charley was opening the back of the deathmobile, and the first thing that seemed odd was the heavy rhythmic thump from the amp of this raggedy-ass Oldsmobile as it paused in front of the parking lot on Ponce.

Traffic was moving so I glanced up to see why this car was stopping, and the first thing I saw was one of the Jackson brothers, hanging out of the car window, his body sticking out as far as his waist, holding a pistol in each hand, one of them pointed at me.

"Down," I screamed.

Charley hit the pavement, Bob knocked Lloyd out of his chair and threw himself on the ground. As I landed on the asphalt I heard the pistols fire at least a dozen times and the crackling of bullets ripping the air above my head.

My knees and elbow hurt as I crawled frantically behind the hearse. Charley, Bob, and Lloyd followed.

"Fuck you, Charley," the Jackson yelled as he pointed the gun in Charley's direction and fired one last time. The car sped up.

Out of the corner of my eye I saw Lloyd working the slide of his pistol. I turned to watch as he took careful aim and fired. The gun jumped back in his hand. He sighted down the barrel to survey the damage he had wrought, but didn't fire again.

The Oldsmobile went out of control and careened head-on into a power pole. I thought at first he had killed the driver, but he had hit the right front tire instead. The Jackson who was leaning out the window was thrown from the car and was lying in a bloody heap, the driver was slumped at the wheel.

"Any of us dead?" Charley asked.

We all answered no.

"Let's get out of here," Charley said.

"Shit, Charley, your vehicle looks like the Bonnie and Clyde death car," Lloyd said.

"Don't worry about it. We got to get out of here. We can't be here with all these guns when the cops show up."

Charley jumped in the front seat and started the hearse. Bob and I pushed the stretcher with the footlocker and body bag in the back, threw Lloyd's chair in after it, then Bob lifted Lloyd in, jumped in after him, and pulled the door shut. I jumped in the front and we were off.

Charley headed west on Ponce toward Barnett and the back way into Little Five Points. As we glided past the Jackson's car he stopped.

"Roll down the window," he said.

I rolled it down. The Jackson driver had partially regained consciousness and looked at us stupidly. Charley pointed my little Smith and Wesson at him and the Jackson began a panic blinking.

"Charley, if you shoot that gun, none of us will be able to hear for the next month. Not only that but the cops are going to be all over our ass. Let it go," I said.

"If I ever see your ugly ass again I'm going to kill you. You understand that, you dumb piece of shit?" Charley yelled, then he hit the accelerator.

The Jackson continued blinking. As we drove away, I saw him wobbling from the car to his brother and the two of them holding each other and walking away from the scene with a sideways jerky walk, like a dying crab.

"Those boys needed killing bad, but you were right, Sam, we don't need the heat with this job in the works."

"I got a question, Lloyd. What exactly were you shooting at?" I asked.

"Car's front tire," he said.

"That was one of your better shots," Charley said.

"I'm impressed," I agreed.

"I'm very impressed," Charley said.

Lloyd held the gun like it was his new friend. "I could like shooting this thing," he said.

As we turned on to Barnett, there was still no sign of the cops.

27

"LOOKS LIKE THE main casualty was the deathmobile."
Charley was pacing beside it in the garage, looking at the
bullet holes. "Better get some spray paint and some Bondo.
Old Man Cavanaugh is going to shit."

"It wasn't your fault, Charley. The Jacksons just shot the
piss out of it because they're crazy," Lloyd said.

"Good thing they weren't better shots," I said. "I think I
pulled about half my muscles jumping under the hearse."

I was feeling shaky so I sat on the open back door of the
rental van. Now that the run was over and we were safe, the
fear began to catch up.

"I need to get rid of those sorry fucks for good," Charley
said. "All this getting punched out, diving on the ground.
They've come close to destroying my suit."

Bob handed me a photocopied flier, which read "Gregor
and the Roaches – nasty men, nasty guitars, nasty music."

"I think that was the band that was renting the Garage,"
Lloyd said. "Call themselves the Roaches. I figured that out
'cause this girl with green hair came by here this afternoon
asking if I knew where the Roaches had gone to. I thought
she was crazy, what with the green hair and everything, but
afterward I figured out she was looking for the band and not
the insects."

"Maybe after we do this job, I ought to buy myself a
guitar," Charley said. "I could take some lessons, get up on
stage, and wiggle my butt and sob. That way I might finally
get some pussy."

"It might work," I agreed.

"Good thing we didn't put on them bullet-proof vests we
got. Wouldn't want to feel like I wasn't living a life of

danger," Lloyd said.

He started wheeling around the garage, giving us a tour.

"You notice we got plenty of room to store things in addition to the van and the big ride. The only windows are up high and they've been painted and got bars. We got a good hasp on the front door and we bought a stout padlock; the electricity is part of the rent. We even got art." He pointed to the garage walls which were covered with graffiti.

"I think you and Bob did real good," Charley said.

"Let's get this stuff organized," I said.

Charley and Bob moved the footlocker and body bag to an open space next to the back wall, then spread a sheet and began unpacking the equipment.

"Here's how I got it figured. Everyone is going to be responsible for their own firearms. Charley's going to show you how to take care of them; after that it's up to you.

"Since we aren't going to use all of them all the time, let's talk about when you might want to use what. We can say situations are hot, warm, and cold. OK?

"What this means is, hot is when the shit is definitely going to hit the fan, warm it may hit it, cold is very safe, like we are here. To put it another way, hot is when we are going to take the money away from the assholes, and warm is when we are in danger but not initiating anything. Understood?"

They all nodded.

"Okay, we just moved into a situation where we are warm with the Jacksons until we get them put away, and we just saw how crazy they are. Soon we may attract the attention of the guys we're going to knock over, and we may become warm with them without knowing it. So what does that mean?"

"It means we got to get paranoid about everything," Charley said. "Going out for milk becomes an adventure."

"And how do we feel about that?" I asked. "Resentful? Are we going to fuck up because we don't like it?"

"Hell no," Charley said. "We just got relieved of the

greatest burden a man can face, absolute boredom. It's why I love this business."

"Everyone else see it this way?"

"NO MORE BOREDOM," wrote Bob.

"I liked shooting that gun," Lloyd said.

"Good. So here's the rules. When we are in a hot situation everyone wears vests, carries a pump shotgun, and has at least one pistol. Everyone except Lloyd here. Since he's the wheels, the shotgun won't do him any good."

"I like that handle better than Stinky," Lloyd said. "From now on, everybody call me Lloyd or Wheels."

"Okay, Wheels," Charley said.

"You'll notice we got three firearms for everyone but Wheels, and that's a 12-gauge pump, a high capacity 9-mm, and the little five shot .38 specials. The little .38s are mostly for back-up, but you might also want to think about how easy they are to conceal.

"We aren't going to initiate anything and go into a hot situation if we care about how we look carrying all this artillery, but warm situations are different. They are pretty much a matter of just walking around out there and trying to stay alive and trying not to come to the attention of the authorities. So you see what I'm driving at?" I asked.

"DON'T GET NOTICED," Bob wrote.

"Right."

"So we just pack what we can without being obvious, and if we take a trip to the swimming hole, we don't wear the vests with our trunks," Lloyd said.

"You got it. Now, the main thing about the cold situations is that they got to remain cold. That means absolute caution coming to this place both from the hotel and from anyplace else. That also means we got to work out some security at the hotel. We need to change rooms. What's the clerk's name?" I asked.

"Harold," Charley said.

"We got to get with Harold and make sure he doesn't give out our room numbers. Shouldn't be a problem since he knows about the Jacksons. We need to find some way to secure the doors. We need to be very careful not to be traced back to the hotel. Once we get rid of the Jacksons, the hotel should be safe, as long as we're careful."

"We only keep the van here; we never take it over to the hotel since we don't want to connect it with us or that place. Anything we buy connected with the job needs to be kept here. Tomorrow we're all going to have to pick up some clothes. We all need some coveralls so we can blend in and look like a work crew when we are checking places out.

"Lloyd needs to put his hair in a ponytail and stick it under a cap. Sitting down in the van, you shouldn't stick out. Bob, you can get one of those hard hats with a plastic protective mask and maybe carry a weed whacker.

"Charley, you're going to love this next part. You and me need to go buy a little wardrobe so we can pass ourselves off as a couple of drug swells."

"Hot damn! If my momma could only see me now," he said.

"I think we ought to rack out here tonight. Even if it isn't comfortable, we won't have the cops crawling up our back."

"I think we can agree on that," Charley said.

"Next point. I need you to make two phone calls, Charley."

"Shoot," he said.

"Call up Harold. Ask him what happened. Tell him we left just before the shooting, but somebody over here told us about it. Keep insisting we left just before the shooting. You know how jumbled eyewitness testimony is. There wasn't anyone anywhere around us to see what actually happened. Could be if we stick to that story we may convince everyone it's what happened."

"After I repair the deathmobile," Charley pointed out.

"Yes, there is that. Second phone call you aren't going to like making. You got to call the cops, be an anonymous witness and give up the Jacksons."

"I've never given anybody up in my life," he said.

"I understand. I'm not asking you to like it. Just to see the logic of it. This game we're playing is about ninety percent brains and ten percent guns. Some of it isn't going to feel good."

Charley picked up one of the 9-mms and looked at it like it was an oracle, waiting for an answer.

"I think I'm learning," he said. "In order to pull myself up in the world, I got to change my ways."

"You got to be willing to do whatever is necessary."

28

WE ALL HAD trouble getting our bodies moving when
we woke. Bob and I had slept on a carpet in the back of the
van. He had tried not to take up most of the space, but once
he was asleep his enormous frame spread until I was left
with only a corner.

Lloyd spent the night on his side on the front seat of the
hearse. Several times during the night I heard him cussing
because he had hit his head on the steering wheel.

Charley had gone for the narrow stretcher.

"Every time I turned over last night, I fell off the damn
thing," he said. "This suit's about had it."

He had slept in it, and it looked like it. Cement dust was
ground into his shoulder where he had hit the floor.

"I don't know which was worse, getting shot at by those
Jacksons or sleeping here," Lloyd said.

"We ought to get some sleeping bags and pads in case we
do it again," I said. "First thing, we need to find out what the
situation is at the hotel, see if they bought our version of
events. Then, since Charley saw the light and made that call,
we got to see if the cops have picked up the Jacksons."

"Yeah, man. After thinking about it awhile I realized it was
one of your better ideas, getting the cops to do our work for
us, take the Jacksons out of circulation, so we can pull a job.
Pretty neat."

We walked a few blocks to the Baker's Cafe for breakfast. I
was surprised at the number of people who were wandering
around at this hour. A few looked even more disheveled than
we did – like maybe they had been thrown by the big bull at
the drug rodeo.

The regulars on Ponce had gotten used to Bob's face, but here we were dealing with a new crowd which responded with the predictable shocked incredulity. He always reacted with what appeared to be a smile. Aside from the fact that his clothes occasionally felt like they were catching on fire, and who knew what caused that, he seemed to possess a remarkable degree of sanity for one who continually got such extreme reactions to something as personal as his face.

After we ordered, Charley went up the street to a pay telephone, returning a few minutes later with the news.

"Cops bought it. Harold says as far as he knows they haven't picked up the Jacksons yet. He gave me the name of this police detective who wants to talk to me. I called him up, ended up speaking to his partner. Told him as far as I could tell we left just before the shooting, but we didn't see nothing. Told him Lloyd and Bob were with me, but didn't mention you."

"Hope you're good with the Bondo," Lloyd said.

"Harold kept his mouth shut about them looking for me, but I told the detective that they jumped me by the lounge entrance and that I heard they were just crazy and had been running around waving guns. I figure I can use an insanity defense, their insanity, if they start talking about my little visit with the handgun."

I saw a paper on an empty table and picked it up. On the front of the local section there was a brief article that basically stated that the authorities had no leads under a headline, "Shoot-out on Ponce de Leon." There was nothing about the Shirleys.

I threw it on the table.

"Check it out. I'm going to make a few phone calls myself."

"I always wanted to be in the newspaper," Lloyd said.

"In your criminal professions it isn't one of your better developments," Charley said.

My intuition had told me the easiest way to find the courier with the money was to look for a connection between the principals and a private airplane, and the easiest place to begin the search was at the pay phone in front of me.

"Weatherby, Carmichael and Mudd," the voice said.

"Hullo, uh, can you hear me?" I tried to act as if using a phone was a new experience for me.

"Yes, I can hear you. Who would you like to speak with?" she said.

"Uh, I guess I need that lawyer fella, Weatherby," I said.

"Mr Weatherby?"

"Yes, that's the fella."

"And what might this be in reference to?"

"This is Ralph out at the airport, and there was some kids out here messing around with his airplane. I think it's okay, but I think he better get out here and check it."

"Mr Weatherby doesn't own an airplane," she said.

"I thought it belonged to the lawyer fella."

"No, a lot of people make that mistake because he flies it a lot. The plane actually belongs to Mr Bice."

"Mr Lice?"

"No, Mr Bice, Henry Bice, the real estate developer. I can give you his number." She did, bless her heart.

"Now let me make sure of this," I said. "Just so I can make sure I got the right buck. What sort of plane does he have?"

"I don't know the exact type. I know it's a Cessna and it has two engines."

"That sounds like the plane. What airport is it at?"

"Surely, you know the airport you're at."

"Look, lady. I may not have all the fancy degrees of your lawyers all strutting around in their suits and ties, but there ain't nothing wrong with my brain. No matter what everybody says, I ain't stupid. I know which airport I'm at; I just want to make sure what airport he's at, because I don't know on a factual basis whether his airport and my airport are the same airport, and it would be damn hard for it to be his plane if it were at the wrong airport."

"I believe it is at Peachtree-Dekalb," she said. "Thank you ever so much for calling."

I hung up and put another quarter in the box.

"Bice Properties."

"Bice there?"

"No, I'm afraid he's not available, but I can take a message if you'd like."

"This is Ralph out here at Peachtree-Dekalb. Some damn kids was messing around with a plane I think might belong to Bice."

"When was this?" she asked.

"Last evening."

"I'm afraid it couldn't have been Mr Bice's plane, but thank you for calling."

"You sure about that?"

"Yes, quite sure. Mr Bice has taken the plane on an out-of-town trip."

"Out of town?"

"That's correct. He's visiting Winward. That's a property he's developing in the Netherlands Antilles."

29

CHARLEY KNEW A place near the Atlanta Federal Pen that sold jeans and work clothes. Lloyd drove the van.

"Bob and me come down here when the Cubans was burning down the place," Lloyd said. "It was a real good show. They were jumping up and down on top of the buildings, setting everything on fire. TV people were running around like Jesus Christ had come again."

"BUNCH OF IDIOTS," Bob wrote.

"Would that be your Cubans or your TV people?" Charley asked.

"TV."

"Never thought I might be in one of those places," Lloyd said. "What's it like, Charley?"

"You having second thoughts, Lloyd?" Charley asked.

"No, I just want to know the worst case."

"I guess your worst case would be getting gut shot and dying a slow and horrible death."

"Well, then what about the second worst case."

"Then you're talking about going to the joint, and what it's like depends on where you go. Some are a lot worse than being dead, others are a lot like being in the army. You get three hots and a cot, and you got to do what the man says."

"Sounds like the nursing homes. I did some time in them after I got my legs cut off."

The store was a big open room with concrete floors and rows of long dining-hall tables piled high with clothes. Among the jeans, work shirts, and denim jackets we found ten pairs of zipper-front coveralls in dark blue. Each of us, including Bug, had a pair to wear while the other was in the laundry. That way, as Charley pointed out, we could observe the approved standards of hygiene while we robbed, blew up, killed, and otherwise inconvenienced Dong Chandler and his friends.

Next we drove across town on beyond Buckhead to the Chattahoochee Industrial Area. Lloyd and Bob dropped Charley and me off at a large warehouse that sold men's suits, then left to buy sleeping bags and other equipment. The suits probably retailed for six hundred dollars or more and would pass for slick if we dressed them up with a few flashy accessories.

Charley was in heaven. He walked up and down the rows looking overwhelmed.

"I could get used to this," he said.

"If things go well, you'll be able to afford to get used to it," I said. "It's probably going to take Bob and Lloyd an hour. I figure we need to get at least three outfits. They're going to think we're traveling so they won't be surprised if we're dressed in the same clothes a few times.

"Guys like we're impersonating might not wear ties very much. We probably should get a couple of rayon or silk t-shirts or collar knits, get a couple of dress shirts. We need to get the ties someplace else. They need to look very expensive. Same with belts. Bennie's has deals on Bally slip-ons. It's the details that are hard to fake and that get noticed.

"These guys are always flashing fancy watches. That's going to be the difficult part. Yuppies have made Rolexes so common that they'll spot a fake by looking to see if the second hand sweeps. Believe me, they check too. That's a big issue with these people, seeing who's got the real and who's got the fake Rolexes. We could probably get by with believable knock-offs of something they weren't too familiar with."

"No need to. I got some connections among your better hot watch dealers. Your basic gold and stainless Rolex is

pretty easy to come up with. That be good enough?" Charley
asked.

"Sure. It's just a question of attitude. Wear it like it's not a
big deal, like your real expensive watch is back home."

Charley wandered off, and we both began to seriously
shop the merchandise. Ten minutes later he tapped me on the
shoulder.

"Check it out, man."

He was wearing an Oxford gray single-breasted with a
subtle blue pinstripe. I was beginning to think my plan might
work. With the exception of the rolled-up legs of the
unaltered trousers, he looked like a drug swell in town to do
business.

30

"PEACHTREE-DEKALB AIRPORT used to be a naval air station back in the days of propeller aircraft. When they started flying the faster jets the runways were too short, so the government gave it up. They made it into a field for private planes.

"Eventually the runway was extended and the county put a landfill at the end of it. One day a Lear jet took off, scared the ever-loving bird shit out of the dump's winged residents, who flew skyward and were immediately sucked into the jet's engines," I said.

"What happened?" Lloyd asked.

"It fell down along Buford Highway. Blew up, killed everybody on board, the passengers and crew . . . burnt up some people on the ground, gave some others good reasons for nightmares," I said.

"It's amazing what politicians can get away with – one of your more interesting features of life. They can steal money and kill people in broad daylight and get away with it. If any of us did that we'd have the bloodhounds on our trail," Charley said.

"If I had it to do over again I probably would go into politics and own a couple of S&Ls," I said. "If you get busted, you do what? Maybe fourteen months in a country club prison, and in the meantime all the businessmen are lining up crying for you. These are the same guys who are always whining about law and order. I love it."

"You've got me to doing a lot of thinking about this," Charley said. "At that school I went to there was this teacher who used to tell us the pen is mightier than the sword. I used to think he was a dickhead, but I'm beginning to think he might have known what he was talking about. He'd put people on discipline who wouldn't be his fancy boy. One little pencil mark in his book and your life was hell. Thing about that shitass is, he put himself in the position of getting plenty of what he wanted. All he had to do was juggle the paperwork."

"A lesson to us all," I agreed.

We pulled into the gateway of the airport. There was an array of buildings: low wood-frame leftovers from the navy days, newer brick offices, hangars with yellow aluminum siding, and a control tower. A half dozen large concrete pads held one- and two-engine prop planes, larger business planes, and several Lears. It had been awhile since I had been here. I was surprised at how busy it had become.

A workman was sitting on a cement block to our right next to a twenty-foot-long silver tank which bore the stenciled lettering, "Warning AVGAS."

"Why don't we ask him where the Bice plane is kept? Looks like he might work here," I said.

"I'll ask," Charley said.

He lay down on the floor of the van and slipped into one of the blue coveralls, then pulled a baseball cap on with the bill low on his face, slid the door open, and jogged over to the seated man. As the two talked, Charley nodded and pointed toward the hangar that was farthest to our left.

"Looks like he's getting somewhere," Lloyd said.

Charley jogged back and hopped in the van. "We're in luck," he said. "Bice's plane stays on the far side of that hangar over there on the left. It's right up against the hangar. It ain't exactly isolated, but it's about as far from the center of activity as you could get around here."

"I imagine that's what he liked about it too," I said. "Let's check out our vantage points."

Lloyd drove the van slowly toward the hangar.

"This is one of your better venues for watching without being seen. There are places everywhere. Of course, that works both ways. On the big day we got to make sure nobody is watching us," Charley said.

"An important point. That's why we're going to have Bob and Lloyd watch the airport until they know every nook and cranny and can spot anybody we need to know about. That includes airport security, workers, anyone connected with Bice, Dong, and Weatherby, and citizens who might be likely to wander in by accident."

"We can cover that fine," Lloyd said.

"You seen enough to get started on a plan, Charley?"

"Seen plenty for starters. Lloyd and Bob can draw a map. I need to spend some time riding the roads around here so I can get a feel for the best escape route. I figure we need to rip off two or three cars. Take one to the job, drive it away, then park and trade it for the other one, then get to a third location where Lloyd can pick us up. We'll have fall-backs in case the deal doesn't go down too smooth.

"Thing that's real different about this situation is that it ain't the cops that are going to be looking for us. Dong isn't exactly going to be calling a press conference to announce he was ripped off. He isn't going to do a house-to-house search.

"Of course, if it was the cops that were looking for us instead of Dong, we wouldn't have to worry about getting cut into small pieces with a filet knife and fed to his pit bull."

"You paint a pretty picture, Charley," Lloyd said.

31

WE STOPPED AT Pep Boys for Bondo and paint, then Bennie's for shoes. We took the suits next door to an alteration shop, wandered around, bought maps, drove to the garage, unpacked and organized the equipment, and then hoofed it to the hotel. It was quite a walk.

"Where the hell is easy street?" Charley asked.

"Police were here looking for you, Charley," Harold the Hawaiian-shirted Kafka fan said.

"They just want to torture me since I did time. That's the way they relax after a hard day busting the soul brothers. They get themselves a cracker and knock his teeth out."

"I think they just wanted to ask you if you remember seeing anything. Didn't look like they wanted to torture anybody. Anyway, you got a visitor, a nice lady. She's been waiting a while."

Elizabeth Martin, Attorney-At-Law, was sitting in the lobby. Perched on one of the ragged plastic chairs, her shapely legs crossed, she wore another blue suit, this one cut to show her figure.

"All right boys, we need to talk. What say we adjourn to a less public place."

"That would be my room," Charley said.

Charley had obviously been living in the place for some time. Unlike mine, which was totally bare, he had accumulated a few comforts, including an old easy chair which he offered to Elizabeth Martin. She unfolded a copy of the Journal and began reading an article.

"Suspects sought in Ponce de Leon shoot-out," she read. "Police are seeking two men who sprayed the front of the

Fairmont Hotel on Ponce de Leon Avenue with pistol fire last night. According to Detective Mark Webber, 'It appears that two individuals fired six to ten shots at the front of the hotel. We don't have any theories as to why they may have done it. There were no eye-witnesses, but we've come up with a couple of names from the street.' Police sources would not speculate if the shooting was gang related. The Fairmont, a Ponce de Leon landmark, is an SRO hotel."

She put down the paper. "You boys wouldn't happen to know anything about this incident would you?"

Charley looked at me, and I nodded. She noticed the exchange and raised an eyebrow.

"Seeing as how you're our lawyer, I guess I can clue you in," Charley said.

"I wish you would."

"Those guys were shooting at us, but it doesn't have anything to do with what we got you working on. These guys are a couple baseheads. They jumped me behind the hotel. After that, things sort of got out of hand."

"How many ways can you boys get in trouble at one time?" she asked.

"I don't know. Maybe we're going for the record."

"Think you might be a little less ambitious?" she asked.

"No guts, no glory," Charley said.

She gave me a hard look and unfolded a sheaf of typescript she had rolled in the newspaper.

"Here's what I've turned up so far in your asset search. There wasn't much to Mr Dong Chandler. Whatever he's got isn't tucked away in real property. He's got a house in East Point and owns the dirt and the building out on Stewart Avenue where his barbecue palace is located.

"Donald Weatherby is another matter. It seems he has a taste for real estate. He has the house in Cobb, along with a big piece of property along the Cobb County side of the river. There's a small house on it. I don't know if it's habitable or not. He owns the building where his practice is located and two other medium-sized office buildings, all in Cobb. There's also a lot of property he's holding for development.

"He seems to be involved with a lot of people in shuffling property back and forth, but three main names keep coming up over and over again: Henry Bice, Jerome Winkler, and James Shirley. That last name mean anything to you?"

Charley didn't answer at first; instead he folded his arms and looked at the ceiling with a studied casualness.

"That would be one of your major murder victims of the last week," he said.

"And you don't have any more to say about it?" she asked.

"No, I guess I don't feel the need to talk about it."

"When you want to express yourself, you might give me a call," she said.

"It might be better if I didn't."

"So it's going to be like that."

"Yes, ma'am. You're pretty good at giving advice. Feel like taking some?"

"Try me."

"If you are going to work as a lawyer for your criminal elements, you might want to consider that knowing some things can make you into a criminal too."

I waited for her reaction. I expected her to be mad or frightened or both, but instead she was amused.

"I get your point, Charley. Keep your information to yourself. Just don't end up like James Shirley and his wife. If you get in trouble with the law, I can help you out, but I can't do a thing for you with Dong Chandler."

32

"BICE PROPERTIES," THE woman said.

"Hello, could I speak with whoever schedules appointments for Mr Bice," I said.

"That would be his secretary. Hold, please,"

The phone played horrible soft rock while I held. I couldn't imagine why, since a dead line would have been far preferable.

"Mr Bice's office. How could I help you?"

"My name is Carter Sams. I'd like to set up an appointment with Mr Bice."

"I'm afraid Mr Bice is out of town. Would someone else do?"

"No, I'm afraid not. Is it possible I could get something when he comes back? I apologize for such short notice. Let me explain my situation. I represent a number of offshore investors. I was in the area transacting business for them when they called and asked me to meet with Mr Bice and see if we could explore a possible business relationship. As I'm from out of town, I'd like to meet with him as soon as possible."

"I'm sure he'd like to meet with you. I could set something up when he calls. Do you have a number where you can be reached?"

"My most reliable number is in Costa Rica, so why don't I call back? When is he getting back?"

"Friday morning he will be back at work. His schedule is very light that day."

"Why don't we tentatively set something up for Friday at 10:00 a.m.? I can call to see if it will work for him. That will allow me to hold my schedule in New York beforehand, then come back here on my return to Costa Rica."

"I'm sure Mr Bice will looking forward to meeting with you. I should know if that is a good time by noon tomorrow. Let me make sure I have your name right."

"My name is Carter Sams."

"And your firm, Mr Sams?"

"I have a number of firms. Just tell him I live in Costa Rica and represent several Latin American investors. He'll understand."

I walked back to Charley's room from the pay phone in the lobby. Elizabeth Martin was gone. The rest of us were making plans.

"Bice is going to be at his office Friday morning. My bet is he'll be coming in Thursday. That means we're going to have to get busy. I want Lloyd and Bob to be at the airport and see who gets off the plane with him," I said.

"Bob and I were talking about that, and figured it might make sense if we could get one of them television tape cameras so we could get pictures of everyone who was hanging around," Lloyd said.

"Good plan. Why don't you get one of the small ones so it will be easier to conceal. Get one that has a real good zoom."

"I think it's a good idea, too," Charley said. "Only thing to remember is you're also making evidence that will hang you. Be real careful about what happens to those tapes. Get yourself some way to destroy them all real quick if you have to, so they won't fall into the hands of the bad guys."

"I thought we were the bad guys," Lloyd said.

"We are the bad guys. They are the worse guys," I said.

33

CHARLEY AND I were waiting for a taxi at a MARTA station on our way to eat at Chandler's Bar-B-Cue. We didn't think it likely that anyone would trace a taxi, but if they did we didn't want the trail to lead back to the hotel.

"We need to rent another car for a week or two," I said, "something to make a good appearance, but not be too flashy. Let's think about what we need."

"Right, if we show up driving a Ferrari we're going to look like narcs. We aren't going to want to have a limo driver know what we're doing. I wouldn't want to have to run in one of those anyway. I'd say look for something comfortable on your average car rental lot, like a Chrysler New Yorker."

"Good choice. We'll be intentionally vague about how we got here, just say, 'We have our own resources,' if they ask how we flew. We may want to check into the Ritz-Carlton for a few days for cover."

"One of your better covers," Charley agreed.

"You been thinking about hitting Dong's bank?"

"Thinking about it. It's one of your crazier ideas. He ain't going to be too thrilled about the courier. But I figure we're going to be able to get away clean, and he'll have to lump it. If my share is, say, fifty grand, that ain't too bad for a couple weeks' work, but it's not a lot of money if you're on the run.

"I'd like to try for his bank, but I want to see the way our first run goes. Could be it queers the deal."

"Could be it makes it easier," I said.

"I thought about that too. They might panic and start moving money around, and that could make it easier to find. We should wait and see," Charley said.

"That's about where I stand on it too," I said.

The cab driver didn't seem to have any idea where Stewart Avenue was located. He was dressed in African clothing and got mad and waved his arms in the air and yelled something that sounded like "Bah-Boo" every time Charley told him you couldn't get there by heading north. The trip took about forty minutes longer than it should.

Chandler's Bar-B-Cue was a long pseudo-log cabin with an animated neon sign out front featuring a dancing pig. I imagined it as redneck Valhalla, a place where the gods of pig sacrifice could gather in their long hall, drink mead, and tell tales of rape and pillage like the Vikings of old.

"I looked at that driver's cabby license," Charley said. "His name was Leroy Jerkins and in his picture he didn't look like no African. Just looked like one of your regulars on Auburn Avenue."

"That's a new one on me, the I-don't-know-where-I'm-going-because-I'm-a-foreign-cabby scam. You think we got taken for a ride?"

"Twice. Once on the road, once on the meter."

The hostess was dressed in a square-dance dress. She knew she was cute.

"Two for dinner?" she asked.

"We'd like to eat in the lounge," Charley said.

"We don't seat in the lounge," she said. "You can just go back there and find a place and your waitress will be with you."

The main dining room was a large open hall with hillbilly caricatures on the wall showing barefoot good old boys passed out next to liquor stills, standing in line at the outhouse, chasing women through a swamp, and either dancing or having a seizure, I couldn't tell which. I looked for a picture with grinning country bumpkins having sex with barnyard animals, but they didn't seem to have that one, even though it would have complemented the rest of the collection nicely.

If Atlanta's residents were really as moronic as the drawing suggested, Billy Sherman burning the town to the ground was an act of kindness.

Booths lined the walls, and picnic tables covered with checkered plastic tablecloths were scattered through the center. Most of the customers seemed to be your average lower-middle-class solid citizens and their families.

"Dong's crew hangs out in the back," Charley said.

There was a hand-lettered sign on the wall that read, "Buck 'n Wing Bar, NO MINERS." Hopefully there weren't any members of the UMW trying to get a drink on this part of Stewart Avenue. We followed the arrow at the bottom of the sign down a long hall, which took a right-angle turn, then opened to the barroom.

The light was low so everyone could drink with the confidence that they looked much younger and thinner than they were. We sat in a booth across from the bar. It gave us a good view of the room. A framed picture of dogs playing poker hung on the wall above us.

"Judging from the art, Dong likes his dogs smart and his people stupid," I said.

"That's about the size of it," Charley said.

The waitress was dressed in a square-dance dress, just like the hostess. She may not have thought she was as cute, but she knew how to wear that dress.

"Would you like to see a menu or do you know what you want?" she asked.

"I guess I want a sliced pork plate with Brunswick stew, okra, cornbread, and a beer," Charley said.

"I'll have the same, but with iced tea," I said.

"We'll get that out to you right away," she said. "I know you're hungry, and Mr Chandler don't let his meat loaf."

"I feel the same way about mine," Charley said. She smiled at him like she thought he might be something special, then went to the kitchen with the order.

"Of course, it don't do me any good," he said. "You picked out Dong yet?"

"Big man leaning on his elbow at the end of the bar. White t-shirt, in his fifties, sort of pudgy babyface?"

"That's him. What do you think of him?"

"He's frightening," I said.

"Why's that?"

"He doesn't scare you?" I asked.

"No, he scares me too. I just wanted to hear what you thought about him," Charley said.

Thirty years ago Chandler might have had the boyish good looks that made old ladies only too happy to let him in their house so he could steal their grocery money. I imagined *The Portrait of Dorian Gray* in reverse. Somewhere, maybe tucked away in his mother's room, was a photograph of that pretty young boy's face yet untouched while life's coarse brush had painted Chandler with progressive layers of corruption.

"He looks like he doesn't feel anything and he feels everything," I said. "Like he could kill with the same passion as he picks his nose, but there's also a rage just beneath the surface."

"Just looking at him makes me shiver," Charley said. "What's your impression of the situation here?"

"They're hunkered down."

"Look's like they got their defensive seating chart out tonight. Bartender sticking next to Dong, man sitting to his right, obvious body-guard type, guy over near the door, two guys each in two booths, all some of your tougher-looking customers. Every way you've read this has been right so far, Sambo. I'm impressed. They're definitely in the middle of something."

Chandler leaned over and whispered something to the man standing to his right. The man nodded then walked toward us.

"Incoming," I said.

He stood stiffly next to our booth. "Mr Chandler wants to know if you got some business with him. He seen you looking at him and wonders if you got something you want to say?"

"No. I just recognized him. A guy I done time with over in South Carolina used to work for him."

"What buck might that be?" he asked.

"Eldo Justus," Charley said.

"Yeah, I knew old Eldo, he was a good old boy. Just a minute."

He ambled back to the bar, with this stiff-legged walk sort of like Frankenstein. I wondered if he had a rash. He whispered to Dong, who put down his beer and walked toward our table himself.

He shook hands with Charley, then with me. He and Stiff Legs stood close enough to the booth to block our exit.

"Billy Chandler," he said.

"Dullard Gooch."

"Carter Sams."

"I hear you done time with old Eldo," Chandler said.

"Yes sir. We was over in South Carolina together. That's when Eldo was in for that little problem over on the coast," Charley said.

"With the shrimp boat?" Chandler said.

"Yes sir."

"Damn government planted that weed."

"They like to do that."

"So what were you in for?"

"Armed robbery. They only popped me for the one, though; the other eighty-five, they never connected me to."

"What about your buddy here?"

"I'm doing a spot of work for Mr Sams. He's up here representing some Spanish-speaking gentlemen from the Southern portion of our hemisphere."

Chandler dropped his eyelids like a reptile and studied me through the slit. I returned the look with a blank stare. You're not much of a smuggler if people can tell when you're frightened.

"What end of their business might you be in?" he asked.

"Used to work in the salt-water end of things. Now, it's mostly banking and investments."

"You in Atlanta on business?"

"Could be, but not tonight."

"Just came for the pig-cue. Eldo said it was great," Charley said.

"Eldo didn't kid you," Chandler said. The waitress came from the kitchen door balancing our food on her arms. Dong stepped aside so she could put it on the table.

"These boys' money ain't no good tonight," he said. He handed Charley a business card. "You want to talk, give me a call. Jarvis, here, will take care of you."

"We appreciate it, Mr Chandler. Is old Eldo still on the scene?"

"'Fraid not. Old Eldo got himself dead."

"I'm sorry to hear that."

"Yeah. Eldo was a good old boy. I hated to see him go. 'Bout six months ago he got himself burnt up in a house."

There seemed to be a lot of that going around.

34

I SLEPT IN the next day for the first time since I read of Jimmy Cooley's death. I heard people walking in the halls, trash cans banging out back, and the local dogs howling as a fire engine passed. I stirred each time and went back to sleep.

I had changed rooms, jammed the door shut with a two-by-four under the handle, and hung a 9-mm from the headboard, but I thought the real reason I had felt safe enough to relax was that our plan seemed to actually be working out. The most important part was the crew seemed to be falling into place.

Lloyd and Bob were happy as clams and were proving to be real assets, but Charley was something else.

When I had first met him, he had seemed delusional, convinced he was running a paper-passing ring with Bob and Lloyd, but as I had suspected, it was all part of his inability to cope with doing the right thing by society. He was a criminal at heart, he couldn't face the reality that he was actually supporting himself at a shitty job, so he told himself a lie to make life bearable.

Now that he was in the middle of a caper, it was as if he had blossomed into his best self – knowledgeable, self-confident, and competent.

His transformation made me wonder if I was on to something. Maybe I should write self-help books for criminals.

SAM'S RULES FOR LIFE
1. Success in life requires self-knowledge, self-love, and pride. Know that by choosing the profession of Criminal, you are following in the proud tradition of

buccaneers, highwaymen, gunslingers, and robber barons who have made our country the interesting place that it is. Kiss yourself repeatedly every morning in the shower.

2. If you find yourself the object of frequent probes, investigations, or arrests, perhaps your crimes aren't big enough or your friends aren't important enough. Consider looting a national treasury. Give frequent contributions to members of legislative committees.

3. Lawmen do hard work for little pay. While a pat on the back and a big thank you are important, they are no substitute for fast cars and passionate women. See if you can help them out a little in this area.

4. If they want you to talk, they don't have a case.

I was working on rule 5 when Charley knocked softly on the door.

"Sam. You planning on getting up today?"

"Yeah, man." I let him in. "What you up to?"

"I've been busy this a.m. Got us another auto over at the garage, and I got started on the deathmobile. Figure if I work on it tonight I might be able to get it done tomorrow. I called Cavanaugh and told him I might repaint it while I was taking care of the family stuff, and he gave me an extra week's paid vacation to do it. I figured as long as I'm going to do it anyway, I might as well get some money for it."

"Smart."

"Lloyd and Bob picked up a dandy little video camera last night. They got the van fixed up real good for surveillance. Put some silver Mylar on the windows. Got themselves a couple of magnetic signs for the side. Bob got himself a hard hat with a green plastic face mask and an old weed whacker and a drill with a grinder to carry around as props. One of your better disguises. He looks like he could be anybody.

"They went on out to the airport to start scoping the

place, but I told them to head down to Stewart in the p.m. and run the camera on people coming in and out of Dong's place. Figure we might do the same thing on the developers and the lawyers if it's possible. Of course, if they are in a big building, it wouldn't be too practical. Be nice to get a nice collection of pictures of the players."

"Very good point. I know you've been chewing over our visit to Billy Dong Chandler last night," I said. "What are your conclusions?"

"Dong sure knows how to cook a pig. I'm tempted to join his gang just for the food. Other than that, I don't know if things are going all that well for Mr Dong.

"The news about Eldo made me wonder if someone might be whittling away at his mob."

"I wondered about that, too, but I can't imagine who it might be."

"Me neither. The Colombians ain't going to be interested in a business at his level and your local mobs are pretty much sorted out along your various ethnic and color lines. That's a good thing too, not all your crackers are as open minded about your racial groups as I am. Some of them think that if a man is born with black skin it means he wants to get lynched, and a lot of the brothers hate the crackers and neither one of them like the Mexicans. Your Vietnamese are off by themselves stealing from the Chinese.

"The guys at the top may not care about anything but money, but the ones at the bottom would just as soon shoot somebody who ain't of their race as do business with them. I can't see a black mob trying to muscle in on Dong's racket. What the fuck are they going to do with it? Can you picture them out selling crank to the hillbillies at your friend Vogel's place?"

"Not hardly," I said.

"That pretty much leaves some other white-boy gang or somebody on the inside. My guess is that he don't even know or the situation would have been over by now."

"Let's look at it from the other side. How do you think the Shirley business fits in with Dong's problem?" I asked.

"Well, we know Shirley was tied up with those other boys who were running the money laundry," Charley said. "Vogel connected the lawyer to Dong when you asked him about Shirley. The killings sure have Billy Chandler written all over them. Maybe the wife knew something and was going to go to the law."

"I don't think so. She didn't seem to have a clue when I spoke to her," I said. "Maybe she saw something and didn't understand what it meant."

"Then Dong told her old man he had to snuff her and when Shirley fucked it up, Dong killed both of them."

"What could she know that would frighten Dong that much?" I asked. "People know all sorts of things about him, but he's still on the loose. That's because they can't prove any of it."

"I guess that's just something we're going to have to work on," Charley said.

35

IT SEEMED THAT everyone was walking in Little Five Points. The early lunch crowd was drifting in along with all the many pointheads who didn't have anything else to do but enjoy a beautiful day.

"If you go in for leather jackets and funny-colored hair they got some pretty interesting ladies here," Charley said.

A young woman with a tie-dye t-shirt, jeans, and sandals with bright orange socks bustled past us.

"How's it going?" Charley asked her.

"Fuck off and die," she said.

"I need to find a new approach," Charley said.

"I've never seen anyone who had less luck with women," I said. "It's not a question of approach; it's a curse. I think you've been hit with a hoodoo root."

"Back when I was a kid, we had a saying, 'Unlucky at love, lucky at grand theft auto,'" Charley said.

I liked the neighborhood with its funky shops where you could buy anything from chapbooks of lesbian poetry and crystals that will cure mental illness to latex spank-magic ensembles.

The car, a conservative dark blue Chrysler, was parked in the garage, next to the deathmobile, since Bob and Lloyd were out in the van doing surveillance.

"I got one of those free-standing closets so our clothes won't get nasty," Charley said.

He had started taping the trim and windows of the hearse. He saw me looking at it.

"I worked in the body shop at the joint. Over in that part of Carolina, every prison guard's cousin and state flunky had the prettiest looking shit-bangers you ever saw."

We did the last of our shopping that morning, splurged on silk shirts at Nieman Marcus, picked up the altered suits, then Charley drove to the Indian Village section of Brookhaven, a nice enclave north of Buckhead.

"One last errand," he said.

We stopped in front of a small frame house surrounded by a chain-link fence. Motorcycles were parked in the front yard. A sign hung on the porch which read, "Harley's best, fuck the rest."

"Just stay here. I'm going to go in and check on something."

"You're going to spook them," I said. "This looks sort of like a cop car."

"I know. Just be cool. It'll be okay."

Charley was met at the front door by a man with long hair and a beard, blue jeans, and no shirt, but plenty of tattoos. They talked briefly, then Charley followed him inside. A few minutes later Charley came back on the porch. He spoke to the man who followed him through the door holding a small sack in his hand, then they both walked to the car.

The man looked inside the car from the driver's side then both of them walked to the passenger's side. The man gave me a hard look.

"He wants to make sure you're not a cop," Charley said.

The man rested his arms on the car door and bent close.

"How do I know you're not a cop?" he asked.

"I don't know," I said. "How do I know you're not an asshole?"

"He's not an asshole," Charley said.

"Alright, Charley, I'll take your word for it," I said.

Charley pointed at me. "He's not a cop."

The man laughed, then handed Charley the sack. Charley handed him some money.

"You're looking good, Charley. Good luck with whatever the fuck you got going."

"Don't let the pavement creep up on you, Ray Lee," Charley said.

As he climbed in the car he handed me the sack. I looked inside and saw two watches.

"That's the last part of our clever disguise," Charley said. "Two genuine Rolex two-tones."

I slid them out of the sack. He was right, they were real. I fastened one on my wrist and looked at it. It made me feel like someone who had made a lot of money in the drug trade. Hell, I was someone who had made a lot of money in the drug trade, I just didn't feel like it very often.

"We're going to pass, man. This is the finishing touch. All we've got to do now is help get Bug out of the crazy joint, and get our stories straight. We'll make up legends and tell them to each other until we believe them."

Charley looked at the watch on my wrist.

"I wonder what sort of asshole wears a watch you could get killed for."

"You're going to meet them on Friday," I said.

36

CHARLEY AND I holed up at the garage for the rest of the day. While he worked on the hearse, we got our stories straight. The secret of believable identity is not just having your story, but making people work to get it. If it's too easy, it sounds like you're trying to sell something.

The other challenge is remembering who you are when somebody calls your name. As a result Charley and I began calling each other by our cover names. I was Carter Sams and he was Dullard Gooch.

"I got a reason for that," he said. "I thought about it first time you hung me with that handle. It's a way I can establish myself real quick. My role is to be the dumb shit-kicker bodyguard, and so what I do is get introduced with this stupid name and give people the hard eyes, like I'm daring them to laugh. That way I set myself up from the get-go as a dangerous moron with an attitude and a short fuse. I don't have to wait for the chance to sell them on this, I pull it right out of the box at the how-do-you-do."

We worked at it till late that evening, till Bob and Lloyd came back from the airport and Chandler's. We broke for a while to look at their video, hooking up the camera to a little black-and-white television they bought at the pawn shop up the street.

They had done a good job of documenting the layout of Peachtree-DeKalb. A slow 360-degree pan from several key locations showed how the location of the Bice plane related to the various landmarks, hangars, buildings, and roads. There was also a series of static shots of the pad where the plane was parked, as well as likely spots for passengers to disembark short of that spot.

"We were looking to see what would be the best places to watch from," Lloyd explained. "We need to see if we can find a map of the airport and the surrounding streets. I can tell you right now the biggest problem is going to be that there's only one road into the place. We don't want to get caught on it."

"Maybe Elizabeth Martin would know about maps. That stuff's got to be on the county records," I said.

"This next stuff shows some people walking into Ding Dong's," Lloyd said.

There was a series of twenty or more clips of men walking from the parking lot to the front door of Chandler's Bar-B-Cue. I recognized four of them from the bar the previous night.

"I need to go down to the lounge and drink a few beers, see if I can connect some names with faces," Charley said. "Maybe I can let it out down there that I been doing some work under an alias for some out-of-town guy. That way if I ever get connected as running around with Bice and them, nobody will be surprised."

Charley and I kept working into the night. We repeated our stories to each other till we believed them. He sanded Bondo, and I laid on a pad and sleeping bag and listened to the saga of Dullard Gooch until I went to sleep.

The next morning Charley went out for coffee and sweet rolls, and we went at it again. We opened the garage door for ventilation. I parked the van on the street a few blocks away, and he spent the next four hours painting the hearse.

"Looks good," I said when he finished.

"Let's lock it in here and stay away till the paint hardens if we can. Don't want to stir up the dust."

We walked to the hotel so we could wash up and change clothes before lunch. Harold called to me as I walked past the clerk's desk.

"Sam, you got a letter." The envelope bore the familiar

warning that the enclosed correspondence was from a lunatic.

"Heard anything about the Jacksons?" Charley asked.

"Cops are still looking. Haven't found them."

I opened the letter.

> Sam
>
> Things are going well. I now know I can attain spiritual freedom. I have found the way. Thanks to my daily therapy sessions I have begun to examine my dependency on drugs. By hard work I can end the vicious cycle of drug dependency and helplessness.
>
> Confinement can be very hard to take. Luckily, I have a beautiful view from the window of my room. I am looking toward the sun setting over the green meadows and groves of trees. A mile from here, I can see an abandoned farm with an old barn whose roof is caving in and it is covered with vines. It is a truly inspiring sight.
>
> Please let me know your plans. I eagerly await your reply. I do need your help and support in the next phase of my spiritual journey.
>
> Sincerely,
>
> Bug Raiford

"Bug is ready to make his break. We better get over to Alabama. I know it isn't his cup of tea, but do you think your friend Ray Lee might be able to come up with a small motorbike real fast? Something very quiet?" I asked.

"I'll give him a call."

"I'm going to go to the computer place on Peachtree and print another pamphlet. When Lloyd and Bob check in, tell them we are going to need the van as soon as we get all this ready."

The same young woman was on duty at the desktop publishers. She smiled as I entered until she remembered who I was.

"Back to do more work for those who are imprisoned," I said. "Of course, all of us are imprisoned in our own way, aren't we?"

"I hadn't thought of it that way," she said.

I sat at one of the computers and typed. She left me alone.

GOOD NEWS
from
THE GOSPEL PRISON MINISTRY

Be assured that a path has been prepared for you!
Your clear vision has been rewarded.
If you go unto that place, you will know freedom.
But only if you look for guidance from the Cross.

This is the only sure way to paradise.

It was short, to the point, and hopefully inspirational. After I paid for the computer time, I slipped it into one of my official prison ministry envelopes and mailed it from a letter box with a late pick-up.

Back at the hotel, Harold stopped me again.

"Charley wanted me to tell you that he and the rest of the crew had run over to Brookhaven. He said you'd understand."

This morning I had been confident that we had everything under control, but now I felt that tremor of fear that there were too many factors I didn't know, that there was not enough time, that we were playing with monsters. It was good to be frightened, because over the years I have learned that fear is the one thing I can trust. It is the reason I am still alive.

37

"IF YOU GUYS keep talking like you're Carter and Dullard, I'm going to start thinking that's who you are," Lloyd said.

There wasn't any traffic on the rural highway. I doubted there were many places to go around here at midnight. The headlights cut the dark for hundreds of feet in front of us, but otherwise we might have been traveling in a tunnel. An overcast sky hid the stars and moon. An occasional porch light identified a farmhouse on a distant hill, but everywhere else anti-matter radiated from the Alabama void.

"I hope it ain't raining when we get there. Don't want to leave tracks in the mud," Charley said.

We were looking for an abandoned farm a mile due west of the hospital. Our map was only detailed enough to show secondary roads, and it could easily be at the end of an overgrown drive on a dirt road. It promised to be a long search.

"There's a sign to the damned crazy hospital," Charley said.

"Doesn't say how far it is. Keep looking to see if the road turns off," Lloyd said.

We all looked ahead toward the right shoulder. After ten minutes we saw another sign.

"Straight ahead. I bet it ain't far," Lloyd said.

"I think I see some light ahead. On the right," Charley said.

As we approached I saw the hospital sitting on a grassy, treeless hill. A four-story central building with small square windows was surrounded by clusters of low, round bungalows. Floodlights shone down the empty lawn to a chain-link fence.

"Alright, man. It's your basic 1960s-style progressive incarceration facility designed to give people the feeling that they are living in a rehabilitating community instead of an old-time dungeon. Very easy to bust out of. Reminds me of the county juvenile. All Bug has to do is paint himself the same color green as the grass and he can walk out. Look at that. They only got the one guard house at the entrance, and it doesn't look to me like he can see anything."

"I don't like the looks of it," I said. "Too much light and open space."

If it was a dope run, it would have worried me, although I might have done it. Sometimes you just have to go balls to the wall and hope the other side is having a bad day. I imagined breaking out of jail had one thing in common with smuggling. The watchers have to be everywhere; you just have to be in one place, and you can know that place so well that you own it.

"Well, maybe it's a little harder than I represented, but he's had plenty of time to think about it," Charley said.

He flipped on a little penlight with a thin tube of black construction paper taped to the end to contain the beam and lit a map.

"OK. We got a county road up here about three miles to the right. Turn on it and hit the odometer. See, this road cuts back at a sharp angle for about a half mile, then it straightens out. I'd say about a mile and a half past the turn we should start looking. This road should put us pretty close to it."

Lloyd made the turn then slowed at the mile-and-a-half point.

"Why don't you stop, Lloyd. You two can stay here. Sam and I will look on foot. We'll give you two blinks if we want you to come ahead. You guys sit tight and look innocent."

Our eyes adjusted to the darkness once the van lights were out. As we walked up the road, I couldn't see my feet at first, but after a few minutes, some places were not as dark as others, and I saw the bare outline of the road. We each carried powerful flashlights wrapped with black construction paper like the penlight. If pointed down, their beam couldn't be seen at a distance. We would walk a few feet, then quickly sweep the roadside for signs of a track, walk on, then repeat the process. After walking about a hundred feet we found an opening and followed it into the woods.

The path had recent tire marks. It was wide enough that we could walk briskly, and the brush at the sides was thick so we kept the flashlights on. After four or five minutes it ended in a clearing. At the center lay a dead dog. It looked like it was holding a point only it was lying on its back.

"Looks like old Rover is still hunting quail in doggy heaven," Charley said.

We turned back to the road and found another track a hundred yards later. This one was narrower and was only a few car lengths. At the end there wasn't even room for a Toyota to turn around. A pair of women's panties hung from a branch.

"OK. We've found the dog burial ground and the rustic rendez-vous. Now all we got to do is find the barn."

Once we returned to the road it wasn't far. We almost missed it.

"Is that a path or not?" Charley asked.

"I don't know. Let's give it a try."

It seemed like a path, then it disappeared, then we picked it up again. This happened several times before we hit an open field with brushy growth that looked like it might have been cultivated at one time. On the far side I thought I saw a shape. I pointed the flashlight toward it and flipped it on and off very fast.

"There's your barn," Charley said. "Why don't you check it out. I'll go back for the others."

I walked slowly across the field and noticed for the first time how lovely the night was. It reminded me of being out on the Gulf in late fall. A breeze with just a hint of coolness moved the moist air so it tickled the back of my neck, and I could almost smell the ocean.

Three of the sides of the barn were almost intact. The roof had collapsed in the center, and the entire structure was about to be swallowed by kudzu. I found a clear spot of wall for my art work and lost track of time as I enjoyed the darkness and silence till I heard Charley and Bob returning.

Bob was pushing the motorbike. Charley carried a nylon sack.

"Watch out when your messing around this place. It could have all sorts of nasty critters like wasps and hornets and snakes just waiting around to fuck us up," he said.

They covered the bike with black plastic and slid it under a spot where the vines climbed to the roof but the wall had fallen inward leaving a passage as wide as the handle bars. Charley unzipped the nylon bag and handed me a garden trowel, a can of white spray paint, and a small packet in a ziplock bag, then shut the bag again and slid it in beside the motor cycle.

I went to the open outside wall I had found and painted a large white cross with "I am the way," crudely lettered above it. The base of the cross held a more subtle arrow pointing to the ground.

While Charley held the light I drew a map showing the location of the motorcycle and a note telling Bug the bag contained road maps, clothes, cash, a jacket, and helmet then sealed it in the ziplock along with a small penlight and motorcycle keys.

Using the trowel, I buried the packet at the base of the cross, then pressed the earth till it was firm and spread mulch till it looked undisturbed. Finally, I leaned the trowel against the barn.

If Bug could make the first mile, we had given him his ticket to Atlanta.

38

We PULLED INTO town as the sun was rising. I was shot. I curled up on a pad on the floor while Charley pulled the masking tape and paper from the deathmobile.

Lloyd and Bob headed to the airport after they dropped us at the garage. Their plan was to take turns sleeping and watching for Bice's plane.

I was glad Charley's big ride was back in action. After the long night, I didn't feel like walking back to the hotel.

"Let's get some sleep. This evening we can hold a dress rehearsal, put on our Carter and Dullard outfits and go out to dinner."

I dozed as Charley drove but woke when he came to a stop in the parking lot. I felt like Sam Lead-Legs as I walked to my room.

"Any Jackson action?" Charley asked Harold.

"Nope. Haven't seen them. Haven't heard that they were picked up either," Harold said.

"I got to sleep," I said.

I drifted into a peaceful sleep, but along the path to sweet dreamland I made a wrong turn. I found myself being chased by a monster who thought I had taken something that belonged to him. It chased me through the streets of a city, and each time I thought I had found sanctuary, the monster was there again, and I ran. Finally I stopped at the edge of an ocean and there was no place left to go and the monster held a gun at my face.

"You aren't really going to do this, man?" I asked.

I looked at the monster's face and saw myself.

Then I was somehow in the air looking down at the scene. A man was standing on the beach looking at the ocean. I remembered him. I had known him years ago. I saw his face. It was Philip Negrone. He had worked for us as a mule.

Another man was walking down the beach toward Philip. I saw his face, and it was me. Only I had another name. It was the name I had been given at birth, which I never said and barely remembered. I was no longer in the air but walking down the beach toward Philip with a gun in my hand.

"What's happening, man? What's the gun for?" he asked.

I pointed it at his face.

"You aren't really going to do this, man?" he asked.

No speeches, no fucking around. I blew his brains out.

I woke up and put my bare feet on the cold tile floor.

We all tell ourselves lies to help us forget our pain and cover our failures and humiliations. The best lies are the ones you can't remember are lies.

I liked to remember the happy days that ended when the boat exploded, but the fact is that I had begun unraveling before that. I was drinking day and night, smoking dope, and powdering my nose. I was turning into a psycho; I was going completely nuts after killing the headneck bandits. Night after night I told myself that I didn't care about it. If I hadn't been drunk, I would have noticed that I was talking a lot about something that hadn't meant anything.

When I found Negrone had been stealing from us, I decided to prove that killing the hillbillies hadn't bothered me by shooting him too.

And when I finally escaped up the coast I was running as much from myself as from the Columbians. Now I'm on the same path again. I think maybe this means that I'm stupid.

I was ready when Charley knocked on the door. At the garage we dressed like swells, and a life of crime seemed much better to me. The main thing I needed to remember was that I didn't like shooting people.

Charley was a sight. The combination of the ducktail and the Oxford gray suit, the Bally slip-ons, the knit raw-silk shirt, and the expensive watch made him seem like he had come up fast and hard.

He adjusted his lapel, shot some cuff, and mugged self-consciously.

"I got to act like I'm used to wearing this," he said.

I wasn't sure that he could. "No, I wouldn't," I said. "It might work better if you act over-impressed with yourself."

"Good idea. I'll add that to my Dullard concept."

"You've known people like that. Just think of them. Fix them in your mind."

"I knew this guy named Rosco Booth. When we were kids he had him one of those windbreakers like the college students, only his was a cheap knock-off. He used to wear it with the collar up. Thought he was better than everyone else and the windbreaker proved it.

"One day this guy named Loyal Odum called him a sissy. Said if he was going to dress up like the college boys, he better learn to blow cock like they did. Rosco went nuts and lay into Loyal like he was going to kill him. Only problem was that Odum was this wiry little shit and he kicked Rosco's ass up and down the pavement. Ripped his fancy jacket up, too. I remember Rosco standing there crying, not because he got his nose broke, but because without that jacket he looked like cracker trash like the rest of us.

"You know what they say, 'Clothes make the man.'"

We decided to check into the Ritz-Carlton and eat at the cafe. We waited for seats in the bar and practiced our routines.

"I'm Dullard Gooch," Charley said.

"That's a really stupid name," I said. "Do you have ringworm?"

He practiced looking like he was going to kill me.

"We got a dandy little laundromat down in the Antilles.

Why don't you give us all your money?"

"Let me be frank with you. I hope you don't take this as a reflection on your operation. We can get money to the Netherlands Antilles without any problem, and from our perspective, that's the most difficult part of the operation. The people I represent simply can't set up pipelines into the US fast enough."

"We can flat lay that pipe, Bubba," Charley said. "As long as we don't all come down with the ringworm."

Aside from being surrounded by business swells, the bar was pretty much like any bar – most of the patrons were too drunk to notice or care about Dullard or Carter – but the dining room was a different matter.

As soon as we sat down Charley said, "These people are looking at me like I don't belong here."

"It's their way," I said. "These people don't beat you up with their fists; they use their eyes. This will give you good practice. Look at them and think this thought: I am going to pop your eyes out, eat your brains, then go to your home and kill your family."

I noticed that within several minutes the diners in our immediate area had their eyes locked firmly on their plates.

"It seems to be working," Charley said.

We'd left a note on the deathmobile telling Lloyd and Bob where we were. When we got back to the room Charley called for messages.

"Lloyd says they got video. Wants to meet us at the garage."

We drove back to the garage feeling full of food and ourselves after our stellar two-hour performance. It was a ten-minute drive. Lloyd and Bob were sitting in front of the television looking full of themselves, too.

"Look at you two. Feels like we're rich already. Bob and me are going to have to get outfits like that. Look at this video we got. We got real good pictures. Bob, turn it back to the good part."

Bob rewound the tape in the camera, then played it for us. The plane taxied beside the yellow hangar, cut the engines, and two men climbed from the cabin, one on the co-pilot's side and one from a back seat. They spoke for a moment, then unloaded luggage.

The pilot eventually emerged, waved to them and walked toward the hangar. The two men seemed to be telling jokes, occasionally glancing toward the road. Then one waved as a new black Camaro came into the frame on the road and drove toward the airplane. The driver got out and stretched his legs, then unlocked the trunk.

"The driver is one of the guys we taped going into the barbecue place," Lloyd said.

"That's right. I recognize him from the other night. He's the one who was sitting by the door," Charley said.

"You're right," I agreed.

The two men put their luggage in the trunk, slammed the lid, then got into the Camaro and drove off.

"We got the license plate," Lloyd said.

The tape started again as the pilot walked from the hangar. He climbed back in the pilot's seat and began arranging gear and wiping the interior with a rag. A dark blue Mercedes appeared on the road and drove on to the concrete pad and stopped near the plane. An attractive woman, maybe early thirties, got out of the car followed by two young children dressed like they had stepped out of the LL Bean catalog. The children were running around, obviously excited. The man climbed down from the plane, embraced the woman, then leaned over and hugged each of the children.

"It's just a guess, but we figured the two guys that left in the Camaro worked for Dong and this here is Henry Bice and his family," Lloyd said.

"I think you're probably right," I said.

For just a moment Bice stared right at me like he had seen the van but hadn't thought anything of it.

39

AT FIRST I had been surprised when I learned that Bice's office was located in DeKalb County along I-85 rather than in East Cobb or North Fulton. But as I thought about it, I saw that Dong's crew of unrepentant rednecks would stick out like two dogs humping at a polo match among the Northside new rich. It made sense to have it in a place where they could come and go without raising eyebrows.

Charley drove, since as the primary drug swell I wouldn't have lowered myself to the task. He also opened the door for me and told the receptionist, "Mr Carter Sams is here to see Mr Bice."

I was interested to see how the next part of the game played out. If we were American businessmen, we would probably be kept waiting a few minutes on principle just to demonstrate that Bice was an important man. On the other hand, if Bice was used to dealing with people who are likely to kill you if they think they haven't been shown proper respect, we would be at least shown into a private office and served coffee immediately.

Bice greeted us himself. I identified him at once as the pilot of the plane. He was flanked by a man whose body language suggested he was something between an assistant and an associate. Both men wore conservative suits but with loud print ties.

"Henry Bice," he said.

"Carter Sams."

We shook hands, and Bice gave me a subtle once-over to make sure everything fit. I saw him glance at my watch, and I also saw that he couldn't resist giving me a glimpse of his — solid gold rather than two-tone.

I put my left hand in my pocket to suggest I had left my really expensive watches at home and pushed against my jacket so he could see the outline of the revolver at my waist.

"This is my colleague, Jerry Winkler," he said.

I introduced Charley: "Dullard Gooch."

As I said the name, I saw a look of smug amusement on Winkler's face. Charley unbuttoned his suit coat, so as he shook Winkler's hand I saw both the hate pouring from his eyes and the 9-mm in its shoulder holster.

"It's a family name. Pretty common where I come from over in South Carolina."

Winkler knew he had fucked up and looked terrified. I had an intuitive flash that if we needed a weak link we had found it. No one who scares this easily should be in this business.

"That certainly is a beautiful part of the country." He was kissing butt as fast as he could.

"Got some of your more unusual schools over there," Charley said.

"Yes, I've heard that," Winkler agreed, "very unusual."

Bice seemed puzzled by the exchange but didn't make much of it. "Why don't we step into my office. Would you like some coffee? I know we'll have trouble topping what you're used to in Costa Rica, but we have some Sumatran that's quite nice."

"Thanks."

"Pastries?"

"None for me."

A secretary brought a tray that had four Limoges coffee cups, a silver pot, and a plate of pastries.

Jerry Winkler picked up the plate and offered it to Charley. "My favorites are the ones with the red in the middle," he offered.

Charley took one and seemed to soften up a little, like he might consider killing Winkler quickly rather than slowly and with a lot of pain.

"Pardon me for being abrupt," I said. "But I don't see any reason for extended tap dancing. I know the first question you're asking yourself is, Who is this guy, and is he blowing smoke out his ass?

"The answer to that question is that I represent a number of businessmen, most of them Spanish-speaking, who would like to move large amounts of money into this country. Who these gentlemen are, the source of the money, and its ultimate destination will remain unknown, and are not even known entirely to me.

"The second question I know you must be asking is, What if he is both full of shit and a representative of the federal government here to do me harm?"

I dug in my inside coat pocket and removed a piece of paper and handed it to Bice. My plan was to make this interview as short as possible, giving us less chance of shooting ourselves in the foot.

"That is a phone number in Costa Rica," I said. "The gentleman at that number should quickly be able to establish both his bona fides and mine.

"Until then, I don't think we should discuss any details, but in the meantime, let me give you a rough sketch of what we have in mind.

"I have a general understanding of the structure of your business. Let me be frank with you. I hope you don't take this as a reflection on your operation. We can get money to the Netherlands Antilles without any problem, and from our perspective, that's the most difficult part of the operation. The people I represent simply can't set up pipelines into the US fast enough.

"What we are looking for is an outside contractor to set up and manage these pipelines for a fixed percentage of the handle. Believe me, this works to your benefit. It's best to have things completely cut and dried. Some of our Colombian investors have a rather severe view of business misunder-standings."

I saw Winkler swallow although Bice's benign smile remained fixed.

"It should also be understood that while the funds are in your possession they are your complete responsibility. My suggestion is that in your estimation of your capacities you be very careful that the amount in the pipeline should never exceed your current liquid assets."

"How current?" Bice asked. "How long would we have to cover any losses? We've never had any, but it's something I'd like to know."

"I have a friend who lives in Cali, which is a very beautiful town," I said. "If my friend chose to visit Atlanta, it would probably take him a day or two to get here, and after several days he would miss his family and want to return home. I doubt he would want to wait."

"I see."

It was all totally appalling bullshit, but he seemed to be buying it.

"I will need to see an outline of your plan, and I want to meet the principals here and in the Netherlands Antilles."

"I'll arrange it."

"Mr Gooch and I are staying at the Ritz-Carlton. You can reach us there when you are ready to talk. This is very good coffee, by the way."

40

"I WAS WATCHING Bice real close while you were talking," Charley said. "I know he swallowed the whole thing. I wouldn't be surprised if he was on the phone as soon as we left."

"One way to find out," I said.

We were in our room at the Ritz-Carlton. I picked up the phone. "I'd like to make a calling-card call, please."

After a few moments of clicks and whirs I heard Jean-Paul's friendly voice in Costa Rica. I wished the connections were worse so it wouldn't sound like it was across town but actually in Costa Rica.

"Hello, Sam. Your friend called."

"I thought that he might. How did it go?"

"I dropped a few names. He seemed quite impressed."

"You think he bought it?"

"Yes. Although he may have sold himself. He seemed a bit anxious to believe."

"That's interesting. He was quite reserved when I saw him."

"You must have put visions of sugar plums dancing in his head."

"This was Bice that called?"

"Yes."

"I'll keep you posted."

I hung up the phone.

"What did he say?" Charley asked.

"He thinks Bice liked the bait so much that he hooked himself."

"I believe it."

"We should grab some lunch," I said.

"You know something? You know how they're always ordering room service in the movies? I've never stayed at a place that did that. I was thinking it might be nice to sit next to our window at our table here dressed up in our fancy clothes and eat ourselves some room service."

So there we were, sitting at our table next to the window wearing our fancy clothes finishing our room service lunch – salmon for me, steak for Charley – when the phone rang. Charley answered it since the primary drug swell never answers the phone when there are underlings around.

"Mr Sams' room," he said. "Mr Sams is eating his lunch. Let me see if he would like to come to the phone. Who should I say is calling?"

He held his hand over the receiver and mouthed, "Bice." I picked up the extension, and he continued to listen.

"There's somebody I'd like you to meet. Do you have this afternoon free?" Bice asked.

"Yes."

"We'll send a car for you. I'll have the driver tell the concierge to ring your room."

"Fine."

It was a rented limousine. Charley helped me into the back like I was the king of a country no one has ever heard of. I rolled down the front window and spoke to the driver.

"Do you work for Mr Bice often?"

"No. It was Mr Weatherby that hired the limo. I work for him often."

"Quite a well-respected attorney, isn't he?" I asked.

"Yes, Mr Weatherby is a great man."

"Seems like I heard he was working for this pro-life group that was in town."

"He's donating his time, actually. He's a champion of the rights of the unborn and the born."

"What about the born again?" Charley asked.

"Yes, the born again as well as the born and the unborn. He's a champion of the moral reformation of America."

"I bet he's a Republican, too," Charley said.

"Yes, of course."

"I heard he was at that demonstration they had on the other day at that abortion clinic on Ponce," Charley said.

"Yes, he was there observing it. He made sure that none of the demonstrators' civil rights were being violated, and after the arrests, he saw that their rights were respected at the jail as well. My wife had the honor of being arrested at that demonstration."

"That's OK, man, I went out with a couple of lady jailbirds. It's nothing to be ashamed of," Charley said.

"No, you don't understand. I'm proud of her for being arrested."

"No. I do understand. Same thing happened to me. First time I got busted for B&E as a juvenile, my father said, 'Son, I'm proud of you. At last you're setting your mind to learning a trade.'"

"You still don't understand. It wasn't like that. My wife's got principles. Her case was different," the driver said.

"You're the one that doesn't understand, man. Everyone thinks their bust was different, and everyone's got principles. Maybe my principles say I don't take shit off anybody, and I get busted for brawling in a bar room. Maybe her principles say something else, and she gets busted for brawling in front of a hospital. A bust is a bust. Sooner she realizes this, the sooner she can turn her life around, and you can get her on the straight and narrow."

The driver shook his head and looked ahead. "You still don't understand. She did what was right. I'm proud of her."

"Don't worry about it, man," Charley said. "I know it's a rough break. Your old lady has got an arrest record so now she's going to be a suspect every time there's a sex crime in the neighborhood. You're shook up, and your thinking isn't right. We all like to think we're special, only none of us are. Now, if you'll excuse me, I got to do some work with my boss."

He rolled up the window so if the driver responded we couldn't hear it. Charley opened the bar and poured a Jack Black on ice.

Jerry Winkler was waiting for us in front of the building. Lucky Jerry had been chosen to be humiliated by being the curbside door–opener and butt-kisser.

"Mr Sams, Mr Gooch, welcome. It's good to see you again."

Charley stepped out of the limo and handed Winkler his half-finished drink.

"Take care of this for me, Jerry," he said. He gently shouldered Winkler aside and held the door for me.

"Yes, of course." He shifted the glass from one hand to the other then finally handed it to the driver. "Mr Weatherby is anxious to meet you."

What an idiot. Jerry Winkler reminded me of James Shirley. I wondered if there was a profile they looked for in their junior associate: "Must be well groomed and stupid."

We followed him through a rose-marble lobby. A young woman who could have been an attorney was holding an elevator for us. She pressed 8.

"Our offices are on the top floor," she said. "We have a lovely view of the skyline. I'm sure you'll notice it from Mr Weatherby's office."

"Thank you for mentioning it," I said.

Bice met us at the elevator door. "Mr Weatherby is waiting for you in his office."

I could see they had established a rough pecking order by their relative assignments. Winkler was an idiot, so he met me at the curb. The woman probably served some important function in the firm they would go bankrupt without, but since she was a woman, they wanted to let her know who was really in charge by making her ride down in the elevator, and Bice was too important to ride the elevator, but not important enough to wait in the office. I was being set up for a game of who can step on whose dick as we progressed to the throne room of the Emperor of Ice Cream.

Weatherby paused the mandatory beat before looking up from his papers. He was the man we had seen at the demonstration, alright. I looked past him like I hadn't noticed he was there.

"It is a beautiful view," I said.

He was pissed that I had stepped on his line, but he delivered it anyway.

"I understand that you want to see me," he said. He gave the impression he didn't have much time. He had a haircut like a model I had seen in a Ralph Lauren ad. Long in front and short in back, worn to the side, he pushed it away from his eye.

"No. If you want to work with us, I need to see you," I said. "What I want or don't want has nothing to do with it."

"I'm not sure exactly what you want to evaluate, since I'm not going to show you my books."

"I'm going to evaluate you," I said.

He smiled, and I saw a crazy excitement in his eyes that was almost sexual. I looked at Bice but he didn't seem to be saying, "Shit, the man who's running this operation is out of his fucking mind." He didn't seem to be reacting to that crazy glow at all.

"All right," Weatherby said.

"Don't take this personally, but have you seen the news from Colombia lately? There are people there who kill policemen, prosecutors, judges, ministers, even presidential candidates. Working with these people requires a special talent. Not everyone has it. It's no reflection on them."

"I see," he said.

His demeanor was calm and collected, almost languid; the madness was entirely in his eyes. It was as if I had poured gasoline on an already raging fire. He wanted what I was offering and I understood why. It wasn't the money. He loved standing next to the flames, and I was offering him the inferno.

I could know this in less time than it took me to know anything I have ever known because, in fact, he was me at my worst, when I had fallen over the edge, when I had pointed the pistol at Philip Negrone's head and blown his brains across the sand.

Only, in the wreckage of my own life, I had heard the faint voice of my humanity calling me back from the abyss. Weatherby's eyes looked at me from a spiritual free-fall. All that was left of the human were insatiable appetites, and they were feeding on themselves.

I understood him better than he understood himself and I was going to use that knowledge to skin this motherfucker and take him for all he was worth.

41

THE MEETING DIDN'T last much longer.

"We'll outline a proposal for you," Weatherby promised. "Henry is planning a trip to the Antilles next week. Perhaps you can fly with him and he can introduce you to the people down there."

"We were thinking about having a get-together at my house Saturday evening," Bice said. "It will give us a chance to get to know each other away from the office. Bring any of your associates you want. I can send a car about six."

"We'd love to come."

The limo driver seemed to want to explain something to Charley, but Charley rolled up the window. Mostly we made small talk in character for the ride back to the hotel since the car could easily have been bugged.

"Are you going to want me to fly south with you?" he asked.

"I think I might have you stay here to stay in contact with the local people and set someone else up as a liaison down south."

"Makes sense. I can handle this end."

"Right."

We went on like that until we were dropped off at the Ritz-Carlton and entered the lobby.

"What a fucking idiot," Charley said. "Weatherby is crazier than bat shit."

"Why do you think it was so obvious to us and they couldn't see it?" I asked.

"I don't know. I guess we know what that sort of craziness looks like. Maybe it happened by degrees and they got used to it. Maybe they don't want to see it. Maybe they figure they can't pull off the hustle without him, and they just make believe.

"I don't know how that works. My old man was an alcoholic and my mother lived with him almost thirty years and couldn't admit it. It was about the most obvious thing in her life. I guess most people don't see anything unless it doesn't matter."

"My pick for the weak point in their operation is Jerry Winkler," I said.

"Yeah man, I agree on that. So far we got what we came for. We're going to know exactly when the next flight leaves, and we know who to squeeze if we need to know anything more. You organized one of your better cons, my man."

"I think I'm going to celebrate by going to bed. I'm still beat from last night."

"You go sleep. I think I'm going to head down to Dong's and drink some beer with the barbecue boys."

As I lay in the bed, I decided to spend a few minutes sorting through the last few days' developments but went to sleep instead. It was deep and restful but my eyes sprang open at seven the next morning, and I realized Charley hadn't come in during the night.

"Shit." I picked up the phone. "Any messages?"

"Yes sir. One from Mr Gooch, delivered at 2:45 this morning. He asked that we not disturb you. Would you like me to read it?"

"Yes."

"The shit has hit the fan."

"Is that what the note says?"

"Yes."

"Is that all there is to it?"

"Yes, although the box is checked which indicates that Mr Gooch will call back."

"Thanks."

I hung up the phone and dressed quickly. Since he hadn't indicated which direction the shit was flying after it hit the fan, I thought it prudent to wear the Kevlar vest. But I didn't like the bulge of the 9-mm and carried the little .38 instead. There wasn't any point in going overboard with paranoia, so I decided the best approach was to exhibit the level of caution you might have going to a large drug deal where you could be arrested by the law or murdered by rogue cops, rip-off gangs, your partners, your customers, or some neighborhood what-not who wanted your shoes.

I rode to the garage, parked the Chrysler, and since the deathmobile was gone, walked to the Fairmont.

"Hey, Sam," Harold said.

"Any messages?"

"Lloyd and Half-Moon wanted you to know they are here."

"Anything else?"

"Nope."

"Nothing from Charley?"

"Nope."

"If he calls, will you let me know?"

"Sure. You don't think the Jacksons found him."

"No. I don't think so. It's nothing. I just want to get in touch with him."

I walked into the lobby and, just out of sight around the corner, sitting on a plastic-covered sofa pretty as you please was someone I should have expected but was surprised to see. Sporting a motorcycle helmet and a shit-eating grin was Bug Raiford, the Destroyer of Worlds.

42

"How's it hangin'," Bug asked.

"I'm doing good, but one of our crew seems to be MIA. How are you feeling?" I asked.

"I'm feeling free. Other than still hearing the road hum, this is a very fine day. Man, the outside looks good. I'm sorry to hear about your amigo."

We walked to my room. It had the musty smell of having been closed for several days, and it wasn't all that clean to begin with. I watched Bug for clues of his mental state. He seemed what passed for normal, for him, at least. There weren't any obvious signs of his medication.

His hair was cut very short, instead of its usual shoulder length. Confinement hadn't changed his lean quickness. He had never been very impressive physically, so his strength was always a surprise. It was his speed, though, that really made him deadly. He could put his fist on your jaw before you saw it move.

I figured that if he had broken out of the hospital and rode the little motorbike from Alabama, it was a good competency test.

I sat on the bed and gave him the chair.

"There's a lot to catch you up with. How did your break-out go?"

"Smooth. It was very smooth." He paused a bit as if he'd heard an echo.

"They cut back the staff over there. What I did is get some of the other fellows acting up, so they were paying attention to them. They watch you pretty good to see that you take your medicine. I practiced palming it. The hard part was getting all this organized when they still had me strung out.

Once I got clean, it got easier.

"I still feel it a little bit. It doesn't make everything slow. I just feel disconnected.

"I managed to find some pliers that had some wire cutters on them. Made some little extensions out of pipe for leverage. With the staff cut back there were some blind spots on the lawn and the fence. They'd have people watching from the building, who'd get called away to help handle someone who wanted to buck dance and cry at the same time.

"Cut me a little crawl hole at the bottom of the fence. They're going to have a hell of a time finding it. I imagine they just figured out I'm not there. Wasn't much of an organization they got over there. They got all sorts of crazy people like me in the general population. The cottages were sort of grouped.

"There was some pretty interesting fellows in that place. One guy likes to write words to songs. He wrote words to the 'All Things Considered' theme song, you know that one they keep playing all the time? dah–duh dah–duh dah–duh-di-dah–duh?"

"Right. It's burned forever into my consciousness," I said.

"This guy also wrote words to all the Brandenburg Concertos. I don't see how he remembered all the damn things. All those baroque grace notes and everything. He'd sing them all day long.

"Then, of course, you had the dancers. There were these two guys that used to do something they called a story dance. They named it 'The Free Willy.' It was about their willies yearning to be free. The dance ended when they took their pants off, and the attendants would come and get them and take them off to discipline.

"Then you had your religious. For a while, they were worshipping me, because they said I was the Fire God of the Andes, but after you sent that brochure with the code they got into Christianity. Liked to drive the staff nuts. All day long they repeated all that Scripture over and over. When the staff tried to put them on discipline, they sent for the chaplain, and he said it was fine, they should be allowed to do it, freedom of religion and everything. They got together with the guy who sang the words to the Brandenburg Concertos, and they'd have all-day church services.

"This drove the staff so crazy that about three of them quit. Made the staff even smaller so it was easier to break out. They might as well have fired the whole lot of them. I never saw any patient get better. Couldn't hardly see a doctor. Most of group meeting was taken up with people dancing around and shit so they'd have to be led off. End of group there wasn't anybody left. About all the staff could do was keep everyone blasted. That wasn't so bad, unless you developed other plans. It was sort of hard thinking your way out of that condition.

"The whole thing gave me a chance to think about things, though. I'm not saying that the open-casket surrealist funerals with animal parts grafted on the dead was necessarily a bad idea, but I recognize now that the market for it may have been more limited than I suspected."

"You may have put your finger on the flaw of the plan," I agreed. "And from the sounds of it, you're going to feel right at home on Ponce de Leon."

There was a soft knock at the door.

"Sam?" It was Harold.

"Yeah, just a minute." I opened the door.

"Charley called."

"Good."

"He wants you to stay put. He says he's coming over here."

"Thanks. I appreciate you coming up to tell me."

"No problem, man. Well, got to get back to reading. Just started *The Trial*."

"He's a Kafka fan," I explained.

"I wonder if he'd be interested in the funeral business?"

"Maybe so."

"This Charley the one who was MIA?"

"Right. I thought he might have got his shit blown away."

"And who might have wanted to do that?"

"The cops, a couple crazy white Rastafarians from Hoboken, a psychotic lawyer, some real estate developers, Dong Chandler, God knows who else."

"Good. I was hoping you had something crazy like this going," Bug said. "What are we up to?"

"We're going to knock over a courier taking some of Chandler's money down to the Netherlands Antilles. We're also thinking about taking down his bank."

"Great. Man, this is wonderful. I needed a little lift. Was it Dong that got Jimmy?"

"I don't know, man. A couple days ago I would have said yes for sure, but the situation has gotten cloudier. I don't know well enough to want to pop him yet," I said.

"Sort of hard hating somebody this much and not knowing who it is," Bug said.

"I agree."

"Why don't you give me the rundown?"

"I'm afraid I got Jimmy caught in the middle of something I didn't see coming. This yuppie jerk gave me thirty thousand to kill his wife. I told her instead."

"That's funny."

"I knew he was going to be pissed so I planned on leaving town for a while. I gave Jimmy my old trailer. Next thing I know this yuppie asshole and his wife are dead, and Jimmy is burned up in my trailer house."

"That's the pits for sure. Jimmy was probably the sweetest man I ever met in my life, and he's got to be the most screwed over too. It really burns my butt," Bug said.

"I came down here to hide. We got a crew together, went up to Vogel's, and scared the shit out of him."

"What's Vogel got to do with it?" Bug asked.

"Not much, but he's the one that sent the yup over to see

me. I had a heavy suspicion toward Vogel, since the yuppie shitass called me Samuel Fuller, you know, that stupid formal way Vogel has of talking business. I figured that's where he got the name."

"Right."

"Vogel said the guy used Dong and this lawyer of his as references. So we figured out they had a laundry going and decided to hit it. I figured killing whoever got Jimmy would be letting him off too easy, I wanted him to know we had screwed him first."

"Shit yes, man," Bug said. "Let him know you're going to fuck his livestock and barbecue his wife."

Another knock at the door interrupted the litany for revenge.

"Sam."

"Charley?"

"Yeah."

I opened the door and saw Bob and Lloyd standing behind him.

"Good to see you alive."

"Good to be alive. I had quite an adventure during the night."

"Come on in and tell us about it."

Bug stood up as they came through the doorway.

"These are the three guys who set up your deal over in Alabama," I said to Bug.

"In that case, I'm most happy to meet you. The name's Lester Raiford, but people call me Bug, or the Destroyer of Worlds."

"How you doing, Mr Destroyer?" Lloyd asked.

43

"ASIDE FROM ALMOST getting the old tape on the mouth and bullet in the brain pan, I learned a lot last night," Charley said.

"I got there and drank a beer and everything was proceeding very delightfully, and then this guy comes in, tells Dong something, and the next thing I know it is a very bad situation. There's this dude very politely saying I might like to go for a ride with him, only he has the bad manners to point a gun at me."

"That's shocking," Bug said. "If I'd known people were acting like that over here in Atlanta, I would have stayed in Alabama."

"What happened next?" Lloyd asked.

"DID THEY KILL YOU?" Bob wrote.

"Very funny, Bob. With the benefit of hindsight, I can tell you, no, they didn't kill me. But it seemed like they might be about to. I ended up sitting on a bench in the back of this van being interviewed by Billy Dong himself.

"Basically, he wanted to know why I had just happened to show up on the worst night of his whole fucking life and why he shouldn't kill me, and what the fuck could I tell him?

"It wasn't hard to convince him I didn't know what he was talking about, because I didn't. I told him my cover story. I was working as a bodyguard and so forth for the fellow I took to the restaurant. He was connected – in the drug business on the money side instead of the product side. I didn't represent myself as being somebody that was particularly important, but I did point out that if this financial man representing some guys that talk Spanish with Colombian accents comes to town and the first thing happens is Dong kills his bodyguard, they might start wondering why he's going out of the way to piss on their shoes.

"He saw my point. I guess he figured he didn't need any more problems. Asked me more about people I done time with and where. I just told him the truth. Gave him selections from my life story including the school where you had to fuck the teachers and pretty soon we were the best of pals. I said if they're short-handed, I can help them out, drive some guys or something if they got a problem.

"And they sure as shit got a problem. Seems like somebody has grabbed Billy Chandler Jr, Dong's boy."

"I never heard anything about Billy Jr." Bug said.

"Me neither," Charley agreed. "Turns out the reason is that he isn't involved in the family business. Dong keeps him at a distance. The mother left Dong a long time ago because she doesn't approve and all that. Wouldn't take any of his money on account of where it came from. Billy Jr went to college and became an accountant."

"You're saying Chandler cares about the kid?" I asked.

"Sure, he's torn up about it."

"Sort of hard imagining him caring about anybody," I said.

"I've known some hard men whose deepest secret was that they loved somebody. Some of your worst outlaws have got this place in their brain that wants some small part of their life to have been decent. They can get very romantic about their families," Charley said.

"Caring is what gets you in trouble," Bug agreed. "Letting people know about it is even worse. Could be the reason Billy Chandler acts like he doesn't give a damn about anybody is he doesn't want anybody to figure out who he does care about."

"But who would have grabbed the kid? Is it for ransom money?" I asked.

"No, man. This's the interesting part. I go out and ride around in a car with some of the barbecue crowd. We're looking for people who might know something. Anyway, they get to talking.

"They say there's something going on that Dong doesn't understand. As soon as old Eldo got burned up, he knew it was a hit. His first suspicion was it was the north Georgia crowd.

"You know in the old days they'd make shine and the people down here would buy it and distribute it to your shot houses and filling stations, then they took to growing reefer between the rows of corn and that was still cool, but back in the seventies they couldn't grow it fast enough and those guys got into trafficking."

"I remember," I said. "Back then the Black Tuna was probably the biggest dope gang in the Southeast."

"Right. After all those Black Tuna boys went to the joint or run off and hid, the younger generation came up and got back to old tricks. They got connections in Florida and run stuff up into North Carolina, Tennessee, and over into South Carolina. That's where I got to know some of them. Most of the transactions take place in counties where your law enforcement element has an understanding attitude because they see it as being like moonshine. Part of a grand old tradition.

"Dong and these boys stay out of each other's way, but the old relationship has been changed, instead of one supplying they're both trafficking, and Dong wondered if they were wanting to edge south.

"Now get this . . . they say the next thing happens is this old boy in real estate and his wife who were working with Dong's lawyer get killed up in North Fulton. They're all tied up with silver tape and shot in the head . . . all professional and everything. Remind you of anyone you may have known?"

"Has a familiar ring to it," I said. "What did they think about it?"

"They said Dong can't figure this one out at all. He can't

see why these mountain boys are going to want to come down to Atlanta and execute a real estate salesman and his very lovely wife," Charley said.

"Which means Dong is either playing his cards very close, or he didn't do the Shirleys, and since they're connected, he didn't do Jimmy Cooley either," I said.

"If it wasn't Dong, who are we supposed to kill?" Bug asked.

"I don't know, Bug. We're working on it."

"We'd better find out fast," Bug said. "I'm getting impatient."

"I like this guy," Charley said. "He's been out of the joint eight hours and he's mad because he hasn't killed anybody."

Bug laughed. "It isn't anyone in general, it's that special someone."

"I can't see any of the north Georgia crowd grabbing Billy Jr, not if he's not in the business," I said.

"Hell no, those people have got their own families spread all over the mountains. That's the reason it isn't in the rule book. You start hurting families and nobody is going to want to have anything to do with you."

"So you don't think Dong has a clue?"

"No, but he's definitely starting to hunker down."

"What does he think about Weatherby?" I asked.

"He thinks he's a pencil dick," Charley said. "Wishes he didn't need him, but there's no question Weatherby can set up this off-shore money business that your basic cracker hood couldn't figure out with a guide book. The problem is there's too much money to wash through places like the barbecue.

"He thought Weatherby was wacko to start with but he knows he's been tooting the marching powder, and it hasn't helped his personality profile much. Dong was about to make him go to a treatment center to dry out before this came up."

"I know how that goes," Bug said. "I lost my mind to nose powder. It made me do impulsive things."

"Yeah, I heard about that, man. But it's good that you're out now, and doing so good. What time did you get here?"

"I got here a little before six," Bug said. "It gave me a couple hours before Sam arrived to sit in the lobby, relax, and worship Satan."

"No shit? I used to be in a robbery ring with a guy that worshipped Satan," Charley said. "One time before we did a job he drew this star on the floor and said since we were about to do the devil's work, we should get down on our knees and worship the devil.

"I told him, 'Forget it, I'll rob a bank with you, but I'm not going to worship Satan with you because I'm a Christian.' Of course, right now I don't have any faith, but when I think about it, his point of view made a lot more sense than mine. At least he knew who he was serving. You serious about that? You really worship Satan?"

"No, it's just a joke," Bug said. "I don't have any faith either, but I guess if I was going to build an altar and bow down to somebody it would be Jerry Lee Lewis."

"Sam," Charley said, "I really like this guy."

44

"I'M ABOUT TO starve," Bug said. "Could we go get some breakfast? You can work up a serious appetite breaking out of the loony bin."

It was probably the presence of Bug that made our attention wander, but when we walked out the front door of the hotel onto Ponce I heard a familiar voice with a Hoboken accent.

"You fucked up, Charley. Now you're dead."

The Jacksons were standing flush against the wall on either side of the door. One of them pointed a gun at us.

"You fucked around with us two times too many, and now we're going to teach you to stop disrespecting by making you dead," the other one said.

"Right now you're going to be dead."

"Who are you?" Bug asked as if it were only a matter of mild passing interest.

"We're your worse nightmare," the Jackson said.

I thought Bug was going to get plugged for sure because he moved so slow. He walked toward the man with the gun looking as vacant-eyed as a man in the suburbs still half asleep, getting the newspaper out of the driveway in the morning .

He grabbed the hand with the gun and pushed it away, then head-butted the man's face and broke his nose. The Jackson looked like he was passing out. He was slumping forward.

"What you doing with my brother?" the other Jackson yelled.

Bob caught him and held him in a bear hug so all he could do was yell and watch.

Very deliberately Bug squared himself in front of the man

who was slumping over and aimed a powerful kick between his legs to his groin, lifting him two feet from the pavement. The air rushed from his lungs to form a breathy groan. As he settled back to earth, Bug put his weight into an uppercut which changed the shape of the Jackson's jaw, then let him crumple to the ground.

He reached into his overall pocket and pulled out a lock-blade knife and flicked it open.

"What you doing? What you doing to my brother?" the standing Jackson screamed and struggled against Bob.

Bug bent over the man on the ground and cut his ear in half. Then he wiped the blood on the man's shirt, folded the knife, put it in his pocket, and diverted his attention to the man in Bob's arms.

"What you doing? What you doing?" the man screamed.

"I don't like people talking about my nightmares," Bug said.

Calmly he took the man's arm and broke it over his shoulder against the elbow. The Jackson was unconscious before he could scream. As he hit the asphalt, Bug kicked him once in the solar plexus.

"I see why you wanted to bring this guy along," Charley said.

"Let's go get some breakfast," Bug said. "I'm starving."

"Charley, why don't you tell Bug where you work?" I said.

"I work up at Cavanaugh's Funeral Home," Charley said.

"No shit?" As we walked to the deathmobile Bug leaned his arm on Charley's shoulder. "Listen, I got this business plan I want to talk over with you."

We decided to eat at the Majestic since being seen in public on Ponce was safe again. Bug was cutting into a double order of pancakes like it was a Jackson ear.

"What sort of animal parts would you attach to the bodies at these surrealist funerals?" Charley asked.

"It could be something that made up for a physical short-coming, like bald men could have squirrel tails sewed on their heads, but I was thinking it mostly would be decorative. A good example is the jackalope. You ever seen one of those?"

"Can't say that I have," Charley said.

"They got them in the bars out west," Lloyd said. "They put something like antelope horns on a bunny head."

"Now that you mention it, I think I've seen them," Charley said.

"Let's say somebody wanted to have elk antlers on their head," Bug said.

"You'd have to have a special casket," Charley said. "Regular caskets wouldn't fit."

"Right, I figured there could be a couple ways around that. If people wanted a regular burial, you could come out with a special line of caskets that would accommodate things like antler heads and buffalo butts, or else for a guy with antlers you could just cut off his legs and scoot him down so the head would fit. Maybe you could have him holding his feet in his hands. But I figure the real deal would be having the funeral be a form of performance art.

"You could have the dead guy nude except for a Day-Glo orange jock strap and elk antlers. Have him propped up with a wooden platform, and everyone could get drunk and dance around and sing songs about how he was a great guy and then they could burn the son of a bitch down. After that they could scatter the ashes over a crowd of weeping naked women."

"We should talk to Cavanaugh about this. See what he thinks," Charley said.

"THE BAPTISTS WON'T GO FOR IT," Bob wrote.

A man at the next table cleared his throat. "'Scuse me folks," he said. "I'm trying to eat my breakfast. Think you can change the subject away from dead bodies and goat heads for a while?"

"Good idea," I said. "You never finished telling us about last night, Charley."

He spoke in a more subdued tone so his voice wouldn't carry to the next table.

"Mostly I drove around in cars. I got to make that one phone call to the Ritz so you'd know I was alive but something was shaking. I couldn't really talk because I was being overheard. We'd go someplace and say, 'You heard anything about Billy Jr.?' and they'd say, 'No,' then we'd go someplace else and do the same thing.

"Main thing I got out of it was a good idea of who some of the major people are with the barbecue and some of Chandler's places where he's running things. I met the two guys we saw on the videotape getting out of Bice's plane. If there was ever a question about it, there ain't one now. They belong to Dong. One is Earl Otis. The other is called Wheezer Keener. I take that first name to be a handle. They were at a warehouse over on Northside that might be worth checking out."

"Definitely. It isn't necessarily true, but they could be coming from the bank when they arrive at the airport. I imagine they are going to be covering their tracks pretty carefully. Be interesting to see some of the places they go," I said.

"We need to put the first thing first," Charley said. "It's the bird in the hand."

"You're right about that," I agreed. "I suggest we meet after the first deal and put it to a vote. If we got enough people interested who want to proceed, then we can go and do it. Everyone OK on that?"

Charley, Bob, Lloyd, and Bug all nodded.

"We need to get Bug fixed up to look like one of the swells," I said. "I'd like him to go to this party tonight so he can get a look at the laundromat crowd."

"I can run him around," Charley said. "It'll give me a chance to window shop."

"You need any more video on the airport?"

"Not now," Charley said. "I called Elizabeth Martin about getting a map, and she's bringing one over. Then we're going to need more tape. I feel a lot better now that we got Bug. There's a lot more we can do with Bob being able to either help us by holding people down or being a second close-in driver. We can have more cut-off cars and fall-backs."

"It's a pleasure to work with somebody that knows his business," Bug said.

"Likewise," Charley said. "I've never seen anybody put away quite as neat as you did those boys in front of the hotel."

"That?" Bug seemed surprised. "That wasn't nothing. I didn't hold any grudge against them. I do my best work when I'm pissed. Although I do get a little extreme."

An understatement if I've ever heard one.

We took the deathmobile to the garage, gave Bug his vest and personal arsenal, then they dropped me at the Ritz. While Charley and Bug shopped, I ate a room-service lunch, read the Saturday Atlanta Constitution and New York Times, and watched CNN. Sometimes I worry that my life of crime is hastening the collapse of western civilization, but after several hours spent catching up with the news I decided that if this were indeed the case, it was something to be proud of.

At 4:00 Charley returned with the renovated Bug Raiford looking positively elegant in a pearl-gray double-breasted suit, soft cotton white on white shirt, and expensive haircut.

"Charley and me dropped by Cavanaugh's on the way back," Bug said. "I talked to him about the funeral plan. He was definitely interested. Said he would do them if I could sell them. Have to keep it quiet, though."

I think this was further proof of my growing conviction that you could convince people of almost anything as long as your clothes were expensive enough.

"Bug picked the cover name of Arlo Pierce. I guess we better get cranked on knowing his story."

By the time the limo arrived at 6:00, Bug was a convincing Arlo Pierce. We had the same driver who had taken us to Weatherby's office.

Charley introduced him to Bug. "This man's married to a jailbird," he said.

"She got any friends?" Bug asked. "I go in for women who know how to be bad."

"It's not like that," the driver said. "You don't understand."

"He says his wife's bust was different," Charley said. "He says she's innocent."

"You should wise up, buddy," Bug said. "Everybody says they're innocent."

45

As THE LIMOUSINE drove closer to the Chatahoochee River, I recognized some of the same neighborhoods I had passed on the way to warn Anne Marie Shirley. The driver made a call on the car phone, and we turned down a private asphalt road that wound through a stand of hardwoods. After a hundred feet, I realized it was Bice's driveway. The house was a three-story cube of dark stained wood and glass on a bluff overlooking the river. It was nestled in the trees and seemed to fit.

Laundering drug money had been very good to Henry Bice. While the place was grand for my tastes, there was no question that Bice had spent his money well. We stopped in a turn-around on the side of the house padded with pine straw, and Bice walked out to meet us and opened the car door. He gave Bug a hard look as he unfolded from the back seat. You had to look to see the weapon, but Bice had seen it as Bug slid past him.

Both Bug and Charley looked like hard cases. Charley intentionally acted half-moronic; Bug had a natural crazy brilliance. Charley gave the impression he might kill you without thinking; Bug, that he might actually enjoy doing it.

"You haven't met my associate Arlo Pierce," I said.

Bice and Bug shook hands, and Bice's icy mask failed him for an instant as he eyed the three of us. All was not well in this woodland paradise. I saw fear in his eyes.

The kidnapping of Billy Chandler Jr had unhinged Dong. God only knew what that had meant to his money men, who could juggle books with criminal intent, but wouldn't have a clue what to do in the middle of an ass-kicking drug war. And now three well-dressed, well-armed punks were standing in his driveway.

I imagined that for the first time Bice might be putting together what he had gotten himself into. It wasn't all profits and bribes and intrigue; it could also be bowel-freeing fear and a bullet in the brain.

"The others are in the house," he said.

We entered a huge open room three stories high, glass on one side, the opposite wall opened to second- and third-floor galleries, a huge fireplace centered in the far wall. The furniture was traditional, overstuffed leather chairs and sofas, grouped into three areas: one by the fireplace, one under the gallery overhang, and the third in front of the window wall. Weatherby and Winkler sat by the window.

An attractive woman in her late thirties was placing a silver tray of sandwiches on a butler's table. She surveyed the results, then allowed herself to notice us, crossed the room to meet us, and shook my hand.

"I'm Barbara Bice," she said. She was the same brunette who had met Bice at the airport, only now she was dressed like a Phipps Plaza Mexican peasant instead of an LL Bean camper. The two children who had run around the airplane in the video entered the big room from a hall, ran around the furniture, then stopped by their mother. The boy appeared to be seven or so, the girl five.

"This is Timmy and Alice," Bice said.

"Carter Sams and my associates Dullard Gooch and Arlo Pierce," I said to Barbara Bice.

She tried to look pleased to see us but the smile was brittle.

"Is your name really Arlo?" the small boy asked.

"Is your name really Timmy?" Bug countered.

"Yes."

Bug bent over and looked at the side of the boy's head closely.

"I think I see something," he said.

"What's that?"

A coin appeared magically in his hand.

"Look at this."

It was nice to know Bug had spent his time in confinement wisely. He could now pull quarters from young boys' ears.

"How did you do that, Arlo?" the young boy asked.

"Just reached in and grabbed it. You need to keep track of your money." He handed the boy the quarter.

"I want one in my ear too," the girl said.

He repeated the trick for the girl, only she didn't look too sure that the quarter hadn't actually been there.

Barbara Bice seemed to be relaxing, as though she believed that someone who did close-up magic for children couldn't be all bad.

I wish that people were that simple.

The window where Weatherby and Winkler sat opened to an amazing view of the river turned to gold by the setting sun. A second woman was bringing them drinks. She wore an off-the-shoulder blouse and long skirt, was ten years younger than Barbara Bice and blonde.

"You know Don and Jerry. I'd like you to meet Kathy Winkler."

Like Barbara, Kathy was doing her best to smile, but she was clearly terrified. In her case, she seemed to wear the terror so naturally that I wondered if it might be due to acute shyness as much as anything more specific.

"You and Jerry certainly married well," I said to Bice.

Kathy Winkler blushed. It had been a long time since I had seen anyone do that.

"I don't know why they put up with us," Winkler said.

I couldn't understand it either. Barbara Bice was lucky enough to have a beautiful house, and her asshole husband was gone often, but the only attraction I could see for Jerry Winkler was that his wife probably had such a low opinion of herself that he seemed like a good deal.

"Don't give them any ideas," Weatherby said.

Everyone laughed, but when he said it, it didn't sound like a joke.

"Mr Weatherby was just telling us about the moral reformation of America," Kathy Winkler said.

"I don't think they would be interested," Weatherby said.

"Not at all, I find the subject fascinating," I said.

Barbara Bice led the children to a babysitter who took them from the room.

"I'd like to hear about it too. It's one of your more interesting subjects," Charley said.

The fire in Weatherby's eyes burned brighter. It seemed to make his face glow like a man possessed of divine light, but it was only the gold reflecting from the river. I suspected that his reform rap was more than a cover, that he was one of those lunatics whose life was so compartmentalized that he could both hate what he was and be what he was with equal intensity.

"I was just saying that the spiritual core of this country has been perverted by unwed mothers, promiscuous abortions, and drug addicts," he said.

There was something deliciously insane about watching a group of people whose sole source of income was drug money talk about sin.

"I used to be one of those people, so I know what you're talking about," Bug said. "I was a hopeless drug addict, until I turned my life around. I was caught in a life of sin and degradation. I used to lie in bed all day and night having sex with women. I was insatiable."

"At least you got your life straightened out," Kathy Winkler said.

"That's right. I can see you're doing better now," Jerry Winkler said.

Bice's reaction was similar to most of his reactions, nothing at all, but his wife seemed to think it was a terribly embarrassing faux pas.

Weatherby was the only one who understood that Bug was making fun of him. Hate streamed from his eyes. He looked at Bug. I'm not sure what reaction he usually got when he glared at people like this – probably either fear or embarrassment – but I could see he was taken back by Bug's reaction. Bug's cool gaze looked a lot like a death sentence.

Then I saw it again – that peculiar, almost sexual excitement on Weatherby's face. This was it for him. Fear and hate were his drug of choice. He was in paradise. He loved this shit.

After an hour and a half, the party had become progressively more drunken and had broken into smaller groups scattered across the room. Winkler and Weatherby had moved to an outside patio and were talking about real estate developments, Charley was in the kitchen telling Bice what it was like to do time, and a horny Bug Raiford had his hand most of the way up Kathy Winkler's skirt. Having temporarily forgotten about the moral reformation of America, she seemed to enjoy having it there.

For the first time since I had met Bice, he showed an unguarded emotion – panic, indicating that Charley's instructions on the best method to keep from being a fancy boy were making an impression on him. From the look of Kathy Winkler, in just a few minutes she and Bug would begin looking for a place where they could take their clothes off.

I asked Barbara Bice for a bathroom, and she led me down a short hall to one, but followed me inside and shut the door. I didn't know if she was going to strip off her clothes or ask me if I thought Al Jolson was prettier than Jesus.

"My husband would kill me if he knew I was doing this, but I have to know what's going on," she said.

She slurred her words. I imagined she had needed to get drunk to say what she had said. She was terrified of the question and even more terrified of the answer.

"Explain to me what you mean, and I'll see if I can help you out," I said.

"I don't know what I mean. I'm just frightened. A couple was murdered. He worked with my husband. They think it was done by gangsters ... I'm sorry, that was the wrong word, I meant to say professionals. My husband ... I've had my suspicions but it seems like he may have gotten into something. I'm not making myself clear."

"I understand what you're saying. I'm not in a position to tell you anything, but I don't want to mislead you either. This may surprise you, but I believe that people should always understand the risks. There's a saying: Don't do the crime if you can't do the time."

"I've never heard it."

"I'm speaking figuratively, but are you ready for you and your children to do the time?"

"No, I'm not."

"Then your husband made a serious mistake by expecting you to share risks you weren't willing to take."

"Thank you," she said. "I think you've explained the situation." She seemed to be gathering her strength. "I need to talk to him about it."

"Can I be blunt?" I asked.

"Please do."

"I don't think you do entirely understand the situation. I wouldn't bother talking to him. I don't think he's in a position to change anything. The only person who can make a decision is you, and you're the only one who can get out."

When I left her in the bathroom, she was maybe beginning to grasp that her marriage was gone, and her husband was probably as good as dead.

I still hadn't done what I had gone to the bathroom for. I

find it hard to urinate and tell a woman that her life is ruined at the same time. Bug and Kathy weren't in the living room, but everyone else was where I had left them.

I walked outside, away from the light of the house and peed on a tree. A short distance away I heard the sound of a woman trying to be quiet but moaning from the pleasure of sex. I was glad someone was having fun tonight.

By the time we left, the two ladies had restored themselves, the one behaving as though she hadn't received devastating personal news, and the other as though she hadn't been committing adultery in the bushes. Jerry Winkler proclaimed to Henry Bice that tonight ranked as one of the best of his life, and Bug enthusiastically agreed. Kathy blushed again.

Bug and Charley had climbed in the limousine when Bice took me aside for a confidence.

"We'll be leaving for the Antilles next Thursday at 10:00 in the morning from Peachtree-DeKalb Airport. If you call my office Tuesday or Wednesday, they'll give you the details."

"I'm looking forward to it."

As I slid into the limo, Bice slammed the door.

"I'll be going down to the islands on Thursday morning," I said to Bug and Charley.

Four days to get smooth or get dead.

46

IN CHARLEY'S ROOM on Sunday we had a what-are-we-going-to-do-next meeting that lasted all morning. We were tense, but it felt like the right amount of tense. I'm always suspicious of people who seem too serene before a job; I don't know if they're psychos who don't feel anything at all or beginners who don't have any idea how frightening a job can be. Either type can get you in big trouble. The right amount of fear can make you smart, but it's best felt when you're considering what might happen, then pushed aside for dead calm when the deal goes down.

Since the Jacksons seemed to be out of the picture, we relaxed our vigilance at the Fairmont — and Harold did too. As a result, we weren't surprised when Elizabeth Martin turned up. She had her sister in tow, who may have possessed Glenda Martin's body but only recognized the late Janis Joplin as its current occupant.

"I got my lawyer here," Janis said. "We're going to go out to lunch. We got to go over contracts. Isn't that right?"

"That's right, Janis," Elizabeth Martin said. She handed a thin file folder to Charley. "Here's the map of the DeKalb-Peachtree area," she said. "I don't want to know anything more about it."

"You haven't met my man, Bug," Charley said.

Bug was leaning back in a straight chair with his feet propped against the dresser. He sat up, stood up, and shook her hand.

"Pleased to meet you, lawyer woman," he said.

She gave a quick involuntary laugh that was almost like a cough. If she had been drinking a glass of water, she would have choked.

"You boys certainly have colorful names," she said. "We've got Half-Moon Bob who's the Poet, Stinky Lloyd the philosopher . . ."

"My new handle is Wheels, ma'am," Lloyd interrupted.

"I like that better. OK, Wheels is the philosopher, Charley drives the hearse, Mr Money Bags is the financier, and what's your role in this merry band, Mr Bug?" she asked.

"I'm the hoochee-coochee man," he said.

There was an unmistakable spark of interest that passed between Bug and Elizabeth.

"He's also one of your better religious mystics, and he's developed this plan for surrealist funerals as performance art," Charley said.

"Surrealist funerals?" she asked.

"I don't know what they are, but I might like to get me one of them," Janis said.

"It's like this, Janis," Lloyd said. "You get this dead guy with the blue balls and glue a goat head on him and everyone gets drunk and dances and sings with a bunch of naked ladies and then they burn him up."

"How very bizarre," Elizabeth said.

"I think I like the sound of that," Janis said. "That's it for me. That's what I want."

"We already got a funeral home that's agreed to do it," Charley said.

"You're kidding?"

"No."

"You might be interested in my current theory. It concerns Dadaism and the law," Bug said.

"Where are you going to try the cases? A squash court?" Elizabeth asked.

"No. Everything would have to stand up in a regular court. The legal reality would provide the tension that would reinforce the effect of the absurd gesture. Imagine this. After attending a relaxing surrealist funeral, the family would consult their melting watches and realize it was time to rush home for the reading of the will.

"Once home the family assembles in the study. The bespectacled family solicitor begins reading a perfectly legal and reasonable will and at the same time throws potato salad at the bereaved."

She laughed again. "I don't know how much call you'd have for that sort of thing."

"Precisely the point," Bug said. "If it were common practice, it would have no value. There are those, however, who would insist on this approach, if they only knew it was available. Why, just this morning I spoke to someone who was interested."

"You've got to be kidding," she said. "Is he kidding?"

"No ma'am. He isn't kidding," Lloyd said. "It's some professor fellow."

"WANTS TO BE BURNED AT THE STAKE," Bob wrote.

"That's correct," Bug agreed. "He's a professor of comparative literature. Lived in Paris in the twenties, boxed with Hemingway and got paranoid with Ezra Pound. He's over at Emory hospital connected to about 200 tubes. Says he thinks our whole culture has fallen into the shit-can of euphemism. He wants his corpse to be publicly burned wear-ing an ensemble which cannot be revealed at the moment."

"You are serious."

"Absolutely. The only question is whether you're willing to give him the legal representation he needs to ensure that his wishes are carried out," Bug said.

"Why me?" she asked.

"Because not only are you an attorney but you are a woman. You understand that life is not only reason but passion."

"Passion isn't one of my strong points," she said.

"And because of your diligent representation of Janis, you understand that life is not always what it appears to be," Bug said.

"See, I got you some more work," Janis said.

"I'll think about it," she said.

"Give me your phone number so I can keep in touch," Bug said.

She dug into her purse and handed him a business card.

"And what am I supposed to do if the potential surreal dead need legal representation after office hours?"

"I have an answering service."

"It might not be quick enough. Things proceed at a different pace in the world of warped watches."

She took the card back and wrote a phone number on it.

"Are you two going on a date?" Janis asked.

"No," Elizabeth said a little too quickly not to have been thinking about it.

"Ooee! You are going on a date. I can tell. Bug and Elizabeth sitting in a tree. K-I-S-S-I-N-G. First comes love, then comes marriage, then comes Elizabeth with a baby carriage."

After Janis and Elizabeth left, Charley unfolded the map. It was actually a number of small photocopies which had been taped together.

"Now let's get back to work."

He pointed at it but seemed distracted.

"But before we go any further, I need to have Bug explain why he's so lucky with the ladies."

"Really, Bug. Charley needs some advice on the subject," Lloyd said.

"I don't know, man," Bug said. "I guess I just let my love light shine."

"That's it Charley," Lloyd said. "Just do what Bug says and shine your love light."

"MIGHT TRY A LAVA LAMP, TOO," Bob wrote.

"I'm going to have to think awhile on that one," Charley said.

47

"WHAT WORRIES ME is that we got only one way out," Charley said. "All sorts of things can happen and it might not be too good, but if our way out gets blocked, we are truly absolutely fucked.

"Only thing I can think is we have a car parked near the place. If the shit hits the fan and the road is blocked we all take off running in different directions. If we can't hook up with Wheels, we try to work our way back to the car, alright?"

"Sounds good to me," Bug said.

"I figure over the next couple days we need to rip off four cars. Nothing that would stand out. Get four plates. Pull the old switcheroo.

"One car we use to go to the job, one we leave for a close-in escape, the other two are cut-outs. We have one close cut-out, the other farther away. These are here." He pointed to the spots on the map.

"OK, Lloyd. You're going to watch the deal outside the airport in the van and warn us on the radio if anybody is coming we need to know about. If we can't get out, you cruise along the fence. Otherwise you watch until we're close enough to the gate that warning us won't do any good, got that?"

"Right."

"This is no punk job. Covering our asses depends on you being cool, warning us if there is a problem, and not running if we get in trouble. There's no way anybody out there can connect you with us until we're in the van, so stay cool."

"Don't worry, Charley. I'll be cool," Lloyd said. "I'll be sitting out in the van laughing at those doctors that thought

I was stupid and hope one of them walks in front of me so I can run over him and chop his legs off too."

"Once we get out of there, you drive to one of the pick-up points," Charley said. "After we clear, the only clicks we make are going to be for you, one for pick-up point one, two for two, and so on, no clicks and you get your ass out of town. Got it?"

"Got it."

"OK. Bob, same thing is true for you. You drive us into the airport and you're our way out, so you stick with the car no matter what, unless you get the signal that we need you at the plane. We're only going to do that if things seriously fuck up. If we need you, and you come to the plane, the car is still your responsibility. Understand?" Charley asked.

"UNDERSTOOD."

"We don't want to come out of a tight spot at the plane and find the car has been ripped off by teenagers, or find a policeman sitting on the hood."

He held the sign up again. "UNDERSTOOD."

"As long as you're in the car, you can be a lookout and give the sign if anyone is coming, but once you come to the plane we don't have a lookout up close. Lloyd is going to have to cover us from the outside, and he may not be able to see everything."

"Got it," Lloyd said.

"UNDERSTOOD."

I thought Bob might be on to something. I had to get a sign that said, "Understood."

"Now we come to the part for me, Sam, and Bug," Charley said. "Assuming it's the same guys who are carrying the money each time, and I think that's a safe bet, I can tell you something about these guys. I spent the night riding around with them asking every cracker criminal in the metro area if they knew where Billy Jr was. If you say, 'Stop or I'll shoot,' these guys are going to take it as a promise, not a threat. The only serious regret they got is they were born too late for the OK Corral. They are going to pick up their artillery and quicker than you can say, 'Oh fuck,' you got a shoot-out on your hands. I don't think this is what we want."

"That isn't what I want," Bug said. "I want to see the lion lie down with the lamb after the lamb beats the hell out of it and gets all the lion's money."

"It's good to see a man with strong religious convictions, even if they don't make any sense," Lloyd said.

"This means we are going to have to work fast to overwhelm them or create some sort of diversion or con," Charley said.

"We could drive a Winnebago down there and tell them there was a woman inside giving blow jobs. Once they were inside we could lock the door and fill the thing with carbon monoxide," Bug suggested.

"I don't think that would work because I think they already probably got blow jobs waiting for them in the Antilles," Charley said.

"What if we asked for some help for something?" I said.

"Like if somebody was hurt?" Lloyd asked.

"They might walk over to look at somebody that was hurt because they wanted to laugh," Charley said. "I can't see them wanting to help anybody."

"What if it was in their interest to help?" I asked.

"How so?"

"What if something was going on that might attract the cops, disrupt their schedule, cause them to get busted. Something along those lines," I said.

"We need to work on that idea," Charley said. "It's a good one, but there's a problem, too. These guys have never seen Bug. Wheezer and Earl have never seen Sam, but some of Dong's crowd saw him down at the Bar-B-Cue, and they know me. We can fix you up so they can't recognize you with a glue-on mustache and some makeup. But I think they're going to make me, unless I got a ski mask on. I spent too much time with them. So that means when we set the hook, it's just you and Bug. That's one on one if we can hit them before Bice gets there. You'll be out-numbered if he's there."

"Might make it seem more like we need their help," I said.

"True, but it also makes it riskier. But let's say we lure them out of eyesight. We may be able to do that, but we also may not. The point is we might be doing this whole thing in front of people. If that's so, all we got going for us is reaction time. We got to drop these guys hard and fast. Tape their hands, feet and mouths, get the money, and get out fast.

"If somebody sees us, they aren't going to believe it's really happening at first. That buys us a minute. Maybe they come over to see what's going on. We show them some gun. Then they really aren't going to believe their eyes. They are going to freeze. They don't want to get killed. That gives us some more minutes. Then we get the hell out. They wait till it's safe, walk to a phone, and call the cops. That buys us a couple more minutes.

"That's the best we can hope for, and if we aren't too lucky it means the cops are fast on our ass about a minute and a half after we leave the gate. We got to get to the first cut-out fast and switch cars. That buys us a little bit of time because they don't know what car they are looking for. The second cut-out buys even more time because they don't know that car either and they're dealing with a much bigger search area. By the time we get to Lloyd we're home free. Main thing we need to worry about then is getting hit by a meteor or a bolt of lightning."

"I knew somebody who got killed by lightning," Lloyd said.

"Then you got more reason to worry than the rest of us," Bug said.

"Another possibility is this," Charley said. "Let's say we don't see some guy, but he sees us, and he's standing next to a phone. He's a cool son of a bitch. He knows the score and calls the cops immediately. Let's say the cops don't fuck up the call and have a car close where the officer isn't asleep or playing with his dick. If he catches us inside the airport, we're fucked. In the neighborhood outside, we can get lost in the streets real quick. You see how important a couple seconds can be."

"No kidding," Bug said.

"Now let's talk about the really worst thing that could happen. Let's say we got a citizen out there who is concerned about big bad criminals, he bought himself a gun, he took some shooting lessons, and now he dreams of the day he's going to head the posse and round up the wild bunch.

"He hasn't ever seen anybody that's been gut-shot, puking up blood and crying for their mommy. On television everyone gets to compose stupid heroic speeches before they die. In other words, he's a dumb peckerwood who don't know shit from good apple butter.

"If we run into a member of that species, I want you to feel real sorry for him. I want you to try to scare the fresh-air fart out of him and dissuade him by speech, thought, and deed not to get involved.

"But if the simple motherfucker draws down on you, you better blow his shit away. Because if you don't, and he shoots me, I'm going to be extremely pissed. People like that need to learn not to become so involved in another man's business. A few perforations from a 9-mm should make the point in a very handy fashion."

We had the beginning of a plan. Of course a plan is always modified by the chaos you impose it on.

We took a break. Lloyd and Bob went back to the airport area to tape some locations Charley had pinpointed on the map. Bug, Charley, and I decided to return to the Ritz-Carlton.

"On the way back to the hotel, if you got the time do you think we could stop off and make another one of those brochures with the Bible verses? I think the guys back at the crazy hospital would like to have some new assignments."

Before we stopped at the garage to change cars and clothes, we took the deathmobile to the desktop publishers on Peachtree.

The same young woman was behind the counter. She didn't look pleased to see me, even less happy that I had brought friends.

"I want to make some more of them brochures for the convicts," Bug said. "Only I think I might change religions on them and get them worshipping the fire god."

We went back at it that night. Looking at the map, looking at video, talking. We did this for days. I woke up at 6:00 Thursday morning. It was time to steal some money.

48

THE HANGAR WAS deserted. We hid behind the front wall, beside the open door. Our radios were on, the little earphone in my ear.

I picked up the black Camaro while it was still on the entry road – three men inside.

It stopped on the concrete pad about fifty feet from the airplane. The driver got out of the car followed by Earl Otis and Wheezer Keener. I could see why they called him Wheezer. His enormous square shoulders moved up and down as he struggled for breath. It was probably emphysema.

The driver opened the trunk and Otis leaned over and grabbed two large suitcases, then carried them to the plane.

"Got to get back to the restaurant. Chandler wants me back on account of Billy Jr. You guys be okay here?" he asked.

"Go on back. We got it under control," Keener wheezed.

Keener walked toward the plane. The driver turned the Camaro around and waved as he took off.

Still no sign of Bice. The Camaro was on the road out of the airport, then I couldn't see it anymore. We were in the time zone where seconds meant you were rich or dead.

I nodded to Bug and grabbed him.

"I seen that angel, and he talked to me," Bug yelled.

I was trying to restrain him. We wrestled through the doorway toward the two men next to the plane.

"Just take it easy, man. What did you see?"

Bug continued to struggle as I put my arms around him from behind and held him in a bear hug. I guess we looked pretty odd; with our paste-on moustaches and wigs we could have been Geraldo Rivera and his twin brother.

"I seen an angel, and it talked to me," he yelled.

"I didn't see no angel," I insisted.

"That's 'cause he didn't talk to you. He talked to me," he shrieked.

"I didn't hear nothing either."

"He told me I was going to give birth to the Messiah," Bug yelled.

"You can't give birth to nothing, Leroy. You're a man."

"He said a woman had to do it last time, now it was a man's turn."

We were struggling to a spot right in front of Earl and Wheezer. I pretended to notice them.

"You guys think you can give me a hand? My friend here went crazy. Seems to be having some sort of religious vision."

They looked at me like I was the one who was crazy.

"He's on probation. I'm afraid if the cops come they'll lock him up."

To emphasize the point I let Bug break loose from the bear hug. I grabbed him by the right wrist, and we had a tug of war.

"Only problem is, I ain't a virgin," Bug yelled.

Earl looked at Wheezer, who gave him a nod. He grabbed Bug's left wrist.

"Let's walk him into the hangar, so nobody can see him, maybe we can calm him down."

"I had a great-aunt who had religious visions," Earl said. "She ended up going to Central State. They made her sit on a bench till she died of old age."

"Thanks for pointing that out," I said.

We pulled Bug into the hangar about halfway down the side wall, and I let go of Bug's hand. Earl realized he had the lunatic all to himself and concentrated his attention on trying not to get punched. He didn't see my hands going into my coverall pockets.

I sprayed the mace into his eyes. He was blind but was reaching for his gun. I laid the sap along the back of his head as Bug punched him in the jaw.

He went down hard.

Bug taped Earl's mouth shut and put a burlap bag loosely around his head as Charley broke from the bathroom door a few feet away. He handed me a roll of duct tape and I wrapped the ankles as he fastened the hands behind Earl's back.

Done.

Charley pulled him up against the wall and threw a tarp over him as Bug followed me to the door. I walked by myself to Wheezer.

He looked at me like, "What the fuck is going on?"

"You're not going to believe this. This is weird, but my friend was right. There is an angel back there."

His attention slipped into a black hole as he tried to figure out what I was talking about.

I maced his face and hit the tip of his jaw with the sap. It rocked him, but he didn't go down. He reached across his chest for a shoulder holster.

Bug was racing from the building. I took a full swing with the blackjack and hit the reaching arm. I heard it crack. It slowed him down but he was still going for it.

Bug was behind him, grabbed him by his hair and pulled his head back, flipped open his lock-blade and held it at Wheezer's throat.

"You don't want me to fuck up this nice suit of yours with bloodstains, do you buddy?"

"Uhh," Wheezer said, but he put his arm down. Bug kicked the back of his knees and he dropped to the cement.

His eyes were red and tearing, but he looked at me as I taped his mouth and slid the burlap bag over his head.

Charley ran from the hangar and taped his wrists, while Bug secured his legs. The two of them carried him to the hangar and covered him with the tarp. I clicked the radio for Bob to pick us up.

In the struggle, my earphone had fallen from my ear. I put

it back in time to hear the nine clicks of an SOS. We had a serious problem.

Looking around I saw a security guard in a car on the entry road. I signaled "acknowledged" and "come ahead anyway" to Bob. He started our car rolling.

The security guard turned toward us on the road. No blue light. No indication he was talking on his radio. He might have been daydreaming. Bob stopped the car up so it blocked the view of the suitcases. I strolled casually over to them, picked them up, and put them in the back seat, then walked to the hangar.

"I heard the signal," Charley said. "What's happening?"

"Security guard might be on his way over here. Doesn't act like he saw anything."

Bug had a hard hat on. He handed Charley and me our hats as well.

"We better get on to that next job site," Bug said. "We don't get paid for sitting around."

"Good idea," Charley said. "After all, time is money."

"Hell, we got funerals to sell."

"If I never see Wheezer again, I'll be a happy man," I said.

"Ditto on that," Bug said.

The security vehicle was turning onto the concrete pad.

We got into the car and rolled past it. Bob gave the universal southern salute, the index finger raised from the steering wheel as a wave.

The security guard raised his finger also, and smiled.

As we cleared the gate you could feel the tension melt. We made the first cut-out, and switched cars without a hitch.

On the way to the second car Charley said, "I don't think anyone saw us. It didn't have that feel. I didn't hear any sirens or nothing."

"I think you're right," Bug said.

I relaxed even more.

When we were in the second car, it felt like a party.

"This one went smooth," Charley said. "I would have liked to have duked it out with that second boy out of sight in the hangar, but it worked out real good how we got them separated like that. One of your better jobs."

We gave Lloyd the signal to meet us at the first pick-up point. He was waiting when we got there.

"Good to see everyone is still alive," Lloyd said. "I got worried when I saw that security car, but you came through it real good."

"See any signs of cops, hear any sounds of sirens or anything?" Bug asked.

"No," Lloyd said.

"I guess we ought to have a burnt offering to Jerry Lee Lewis," Bug said.

"What you want to burn?" Lloyd asked.

"How about an ox?" Bug asked.

"Don't rightly know where you could find them," Lloyd said.

"Maybe we should settle on some steaks," Charley suggested.

Back at the garage we counted the haul and voted on what to do next. The results were $322,000.00, three nice suits that looked like they would fit Bob, and a definite yes from all on hitting Dong's bank.

As Charley said, "It looks like we're in the robbery business."

49

"HELLO JEAN-PAUL."

"Sam. I have the feeling you've been very naughty."

"I was wondering if you'd heard anything more from Atlanta?"

"Yes. I received two calls this morning."

"Two?"

"Yes. The first was from your friend Bice."

"What did he say?"

"That they had experienced a security problem. He wondered if it was the sort of thing you might be involved with."

"And what did you tell him?" I asked.

"I told him it was unlikely."

"And the second call?"

"That one was less pleasant. It was from an attorney named Weatherby."

"How was it unpleasant?" I asked.

"He was less impressed with my assurances, and he made some uncomplimentary references to my veracity," Jean-Paul said.

"How shocking," I said.

"He even threatened me." Jean-Paul sounded very formal and precise, which meant he was mad.

"No shit?"

"He threatened to tear my head off and piss down my throat."

"Did he, now?"

"We were not amused. Is there someone in Atlanta who can advise him on protocol?"

"I'll speak to them."

"Let me know how your adventure turns out, Sam."

Jean-Paul was a funny bird. He could tolerate all manner of sin from gun-running to subornation of perjury, but he considered rudeness an outrage. It reminded me of the outline of moral regression described by another French wag. It goes like this: first you begin by committing murder, then you steal, then, eventually, you become impolite.

Charley was curled up on the bed reading *The Art of the Deal*.

"What did your buddy South of the Border have to say?" he asked.

"Bice suspects. Weatherby is convinced it's us," I said.

"I guess in spite of the fact he's nuts, he's pretty smart," Charley said.

"We may have underestimated him. He seems to be very perceptive. I'm sure he's capable, in his own way, but he has one serious disadvantage," I said.

"What's that?"

"I believe he's out of control."

"I think you're right," Charley said. "I've seen guys like this before. Did some time with a couple of them. They use what they sell, and they probably have delusions of grandeur to start with. It makes one of your more peculiar personalities, someone who's got bad paranoia and also thinks they're God.

"Sort of a crazy mix because if you're God, why do you care who's out to get you?"

"Good point. How's that book, by the way?"

"Very interesting. This guy's got some of your better ideas. You definitely got me thinking on this. There was this article in this old magazine I borrowed from Half-Moon. It was about that savings and loan rip-off you were telling me about. It said that when that S&L out in Colorado went down, the one they called Desperado, there was something like $200 million lost, which is better than three times the total losses from all the bank robberies done in the whole country that year.

"This is the one the president's son, what's his name, Neil, was involved in. You got to admire that guy. It makes me realize I've been on the wrong track all my life. Of course, it wasn't necessarily my fault. I grew up a dumb, ignorant cracker without much education other than teacher fucking, so I never heard of white-collar crime. The only career path open for us was knocking over filling stations and so forth.

"But I tell you something, man. That's definitely the way to go. It's the field of the future. That's what I decided I'm going to do with this money I got out of this job we just done. I'm going to go to school and learn how to become a white-collar criminal."

"That's great, Charley," I said. "I'm glad to know I've been a good influence on you like that."

"So, what you think we need to do next?" he asked.

"I'm going to call Bice and see if we are burnt with those guys," I said. "After we get some rest, I think we should hit the streets. See if we can pick up Wheezer and Earl and see if they lead us to the bank. It might be a little while before they are feeling good enough to wander, so maybe we should check out that warehouse too. We need to be very careful until we see how this settles down."

"Bice here," the voice said.

"What the fuck is going on?" I asked.

"I was about to ask you the same thing," he said.

"You got serious problems."

"Tell me about it," he said.

"I got to the airport a little early this morning so my men Arlo and Dullard could check out the situation," I said. "Make sure we weren't being observed by the Federales. Next thing I know this black Camaro comes driving up. It leaves off these two guys. Then there's this work crew in blue overalls and hard hats that beats the shit out of them. That's when I left. I figured you got a little security problem here that you got to work on before we can talk any more business."

"We're trying to solve it," he said. "It's part of something bigger that should get sorted out very soon. Bear with us."

"I'm trying to," I said. "Only that isn't your only problem. It seems your friend Weatherby called that number I gave you down south. He said some unpleasant things and threatened to kill the party on the other end."

There was a protracted silence that made me wonder if the connection had been broken. Finally Bice said, "He threatened him?"

"Yes. I'd say judging by my friend's tone of voice that an abject apology might be the best plan. Either that or try not to be anywhere near Weatherby when he starts his car."

Another long silence followed by, "I see. That bad?"

"Yes. I'd look for another lawyer if I were you."

"I need to get back to you," he said.

"I'll tell the desk to put further calls through to my room. Don't try coming up here, though, or sending any of your little friends. My colleagues are feeling a bit nervous after seeing this morning's events, and they have a better idea of the cast of players in town than you may think. If any of them show up unexpected, we're going to end up with some bad PR. A gun fight in the Ritz-Carlton would be big news."

"Don't worry about that, I'm going to talk to everyone and calm down the situation."

"We'll wait and see," I said.

Bug had gotten a room down the hall from us, and I tried to call it several times but he wasn't in. Charley was still reading his book. I watched CNN for a while, then turned to the first local evening news show.

The teaser tightened my gut. Charley looked up from his book.

"Two bodies were discovered this afternoon in a field adjoining Peachtree-DeKalb Airport. Both men, described as white males, were the victims of apparent execution-style slayings . . ."

I dialed Bug's room. The phone was picked up by the desk on the fourth ring.

"I'm afraid Mr Pierce isn't in," the operator said.

"Could you tell him our business arrangement has hit a serious snag, and he needs to call me as soon as possible," I said.

"What went wrong?" Charley said. "Think they suffocated on those bags?"

I thought about Wheezer Keener's eyes looking at me as I covered his head.

"I don't think so. It said that they were found in a field next to the airport. It means somebody came along after we did. But it also could mean we're being looked for on a murder charge."

After a few lighthearted jokes, the news anchor read a story about a sex scandal involving several members of the General Assembly, a representative of the Archdiocese of Atlanta, a television kids-show clown, and a half dozen members of a Bulgarian female contortionist stage act who were marooned in town when their minibus blew a head gasket.

Next the anchor affected a suitably sad face and explained what was known about the murder. The men were shot in the head and they wouldn't be identified pending notification of next of kin. Since I doubted anyone would admit to being related to either Earl or Wheezer, I wondered if that meant they would never be publicly identified.

Charley got up and walked toward the door.

"Where you going, man?" I asked.

"Thought I'd call the cops and tell them I heard about the

killing, and I saw a couple of white Rastafarians, one of them with his arm in a sling out in a field by the airport this afternoon."

"Wear your vest," I said. "Call from a pay phone."

"Sure would be nice if something about this was easy," he said.

"If it was easy then anyone could do it."

50

We CALLED BUG'S room several more times without any luck and left a message at the Fairmont for Lloyd and Bob to sit tight. Room service seemed like a good idea since we didn't know how many people liked us out on the street.

Charley had a gun in his hand under a pillow when the food and an evening paper were delivered, in case we encountered the old assassin-in-a-white-jacket trick. I didn't think it likely. Generally, the police will go through the motions when one asshole kills another asshole if the surviving asshole is connected, but you can only buy so much protection. When it comes to a shoot-out in a major downtown hotel in a city with as much convention business as Atlanta, there isn't enough protection available anywhere to keep the cops from coming after you in a big way.

The murders were noted in a small story on the bottom of the front page of the local section. There wasn't much information that we hadn't already seen on the evening news. The bodies were discovered by small boys playing in the area. They were bound hand and foot with tape, and shot in the forehead, like the Shirleys. No mention of the burlap sacks we'd put on their heads to keep them from seeing Charley.

It sounded like more death magic. The murderer looks in the victim's eyes and steals his soul at the moment it leaves his body.

"I'm going to call down at Dong's," Charley said.

"Good idea. You can let on you heard through the grapevine it was his guys that got popped."

He dialed the number.

"Chandler there? Right, this is Dullard. No, I heard they

was popped. No. OK, just a minute."

Charley held his hand over the mouthpiece.

"He's going to get Chandler," he said. "Hello, Mr Chandler?" He paused. "No sir, Uh uh. Wasn't us. No. Just a minute."

Charley covered the mouthpiece again.

"He says we killed Wheezer and Earl, and we got his kid, and he's going to cut our guts out and laugh as he feeds 'em to his dogs."

"Let me talk to him," I said.

"I'm going to let you talk to Carter Sams," he said.

I took the phone.

"This better be fucking good," Chandler said. "Otherwise, you're dead."

"Listen to what I'm going to say." I spoke with an affected calm which didn't reflect how I felt. "I didn't kill your men, and I don't have your son. I don't have any terms to dictate to you other than these. I can leave this city any time I want and you will never find me. I also know where I can find you any time I want. You will be right here in Atlanta, Georgia, being Billy Chandler. I will be someplace you don't know using a name you've never heard of. If you really want to play this game with me, we can go ahead and do it, but it will waste my time and money and you will end up dead.

"If I had your son, I would tell you right now what I wanted from you, but I have nothing to say. I don't want anything from you. I don't have your son. This has been going on long before I came to this town. It involves the death of Eldo and James and Anne Marie Shirley.

"Do you understand what I'm saying?" I asked.

There was a long pause. I imagined he was thinking it over and considering a response, trying to become rational amidst the pain and anger of having a missing son. The pause was a good sign.

"Yes. I understand. I'll call my boys off for now."

"Just so there's no confusion, if I see someone following me, I'm going to assume they don't belong to you. That way you won't have any problems if I kill them."

"No."

"We need to stay in touch," I said.

"If you find out anything call me," he said.

"You might consider who gave you the idea I did it, and ask yourself why," I said.

"I'm turning that over in my mind as we speak," he said.

"You were very convincing," Charley said.

"The situation was convincing," I said. "He knew that if I had his kid I would ask for something."

I called Bug's room again, no response.

"I don't see any reason to stay at the Ritz," I said. "They know we're here. We need to fade into Ponce as soon as we can find Bug."

The phone rang, and I picked it up.

"Hello."

"You're a dead man."

It was Weatherby's voice.

"Sorry, I think you have the wrong number," I said.

"Sams?"

"Oh, now I know who you are. You're that pencil-dick punk lawyer."

"You're a dead man," he repeated.

"What a fucking idiot." I hung up the phone.

"Who was that?" Charley asked

"Weatherby with a death threat," I said.

"We seem to be collecting those tonight. Why did he make the phone call?"

"Either because he's stupid, or he wants to flush us from the hotel, or he's stupid and wants to flush us from the hotel."

"I'll go for the last one," Charley said. "Actually, getting the hell out of here as soon as possible might be one of your better plans."

"Let's see if Bug is in his room and just isn't answering messages," I said.

We put on our vests; ankle holsters for the .38 specials and I even wore my shoulder holster and the 9-mm, and topped it all off with a silk white-on-white shirt and a light gray tropical-weight wool suit with a relaxed drape.

Charley raised his eyes when he saw this.

"You must be expecting some serious shit," he said.

"I think we'll pick them up when we try to leave," I said.

I walked toward Bug's room. Charley was a pace behind, watching my back. There was some sort of commotion inside. I put my ear to the door, and put my hand inside the suit coat with my palm on the pistol grip.

Charley tensed and touched his gun, looking toward me then back and forth on the hall. I strained to sort out the noises and heard the sound of lunatic, bed-breaking sex.

"Some kind woman is giving Bug the fuck of a lifetime," I said.

"I need to talk to him about that," Charley said, but he still glanced cautiously up and down the hall.

I knocked hard three times with no response other than excited moans and more mattress pounding. I knocked again.

"Bug," I said. There was nothing but quicker cries of ecstasy.

"They sound like a couple of happy monkeys," I said.

"That's one good thing about never getting any," Charley said. "I never sound that stupid."

"While old Bug is in there doing his dick dance, we're liable to get our ass shot off in the hall," I said.

Charley reached for the door and knocked. I joined him.

The frequency of gasps decreased, then I heard the floor vibrate as Bug walked to the door.

"At last," Charley said.

Bug opened the door a crack.

"Sam, Charley, what's happening?"

We pushed through and walked into the room. I handed Bug the paper with the story circled.

"Things aren't going well. We need to get the hell out of here."

Beyond him, on the bed, sat an obviously nude Elizabeth Martin holding the sheet in front of her, barely covering her breasts. Her hair was tussled and her features were softened by the love hangover.

"You boys look like gangsters," she said.

"We are gangsters," I answered.

51

BUG AND ELIZABETH joined us in our room. She was wearing one of her lawyer suits, but with flats.

"Dong said he was going to call his boys off. I believe him, but not enough to bet my life on it. Weatherby's convinced we hit the courier. He said he's going to kill us," I said.

"Donald Weatherby, the attorney, said he was going to kill you?" she asked.

"He's up to his ass in the drug business, and he's crazy as shit," I explained.

"Wheels and Half-Moon are going to meet us at the garage," Charley said.

"I figure if Weatherby's got any people on the street they'll be looking for us outside. They'll probably follow us and try to pick a place to kill us," I said.

"Which means we got to pick the place first," Bug said.

"Best thing for you is to stay here," I said to Elizabeth. "Go down to the lobby alone. Nobody's going to place you with us. Wait till we clear the building, then get the bell captain to find you a cab."

"I'm going with you," she said.

"I thought you just worked your way through law school and you didn't want to get in trouble," Charley said.

She glanced at Bug.

"Well, there's trouble and then there's trouble," she said.

"Why do you want to go?" I asked.

"Let's cut the crap," she said. "You aren't in this just for the money. I guess I'm a lot more like you boys than I care to admit. I get bored easily."

"Think you could drive through a shit storm?" I asked.

"I think so," she said.

"OK, you're the driver. We got three shotguns in the trunk of the car. If you drive, it means we can use all three of them. That alright with everyone?"

I didn't hear any objections.

"My plan is to lead them to that park by McGill Place. The street is deserted over there at this time of night. You know the way?"

"Yes."

"Then let's get the fuck out of here."

The parking deck was deserted. I didn't think it was likely we would be ambushed here, but there were a hundred places to hide and I didn't like the look of it one bit. Charley walked first. He passed well beyond our car, did a full 360, looked between the cars, then waved for us to come ahead.

Quickly, he retrieved the nylon zip bags with the disassembled shotguns from the trunk, unlocked the car doors, and slid in the back.

We walked briskly. Elizabeth slid in the front and Charley handed her the keys.

"Go ahead. Start it and pull out," he said. "But hang in the garage till we get these things together so we can use the light."

Bug and Charlie slid the barrels on, replaced the slides, and screwed back the magazine caps. Then they worked the slides a few times and stuffed shells in the bottom.

"We're going to give you the one with deer slugs, Sam. You work on the engine area. If nothing else, we can fuck up their car so they can't follow. Bug and me will work on the passengers with the buckshot."

"See if you recognize anybody," I said to Charley. "You know the guys who work for Dong. I'm wondering if any of them are here."

We exited on a side road off Peachtree. Elizabeth had the

brights on and their beam raked the black Camaro from the airport parked across the street. One man stood next to the car on the sidewalk talking on a portable phone. Three more sat in it. He opened the passenger side door and jumped in.

The driver turned on the car light and quickly pulled into traffic to follow.

"They aren't trying to be too subtle," Elizabeth said.

"I think they want us to see them. They're trying to scare us. They're talking to another car on the phone. Once they figure out where we're going, they'll call ahead. The other car will set up an ambush. They'll run us into it," I said.

"An ambush, huh?" she said.

"Right. Only problem is that we're going to ambush them first."

"You talk like somebody who used to be a smuggler," Bug said. He glanced around, then handed me a shotgun over the seat. "Remember to go for the engine," he said. "And hold tight. Those slugs kick pretty bad."

"You want to make a turn at every block you can. That will keep the second car at a distance," I said.

Slowly we worked our way toward the nearly deserted park. There were a half dozen people sleeping on the grass, but that was it.

"OK, slow down and stop," I said.

She did. The car behind us stopped also. I could imagine the conversation they must be having.

"What the fuck are those guys doing?"

"I don't know what the fuck they are doing. What the fuck you think they're doing?"

"I don't know what the fuck they're doing either."

"Be fucked if I know."

I touched Elizabeth on the shoulder.

"OK now, slip it in reverse, I want you to gun it till we're under that streetlight about a hundred feet from them. Then stop sharp. Put it in drive and get ready to run. Understand?"

"Yes."

"Go."

We raced backwards with tires squealing. As she stopped we piled out. First thing, Charley raised the pump and shot out the street light. I fired the shotgun at the front of the car till it was empty then drew the 9-mm and fired a half dozen rounds. Charley and Bug did the same. I couldn't see any signs of return fire.

It sounded like a war. The street people had jerked up and were scrambling past the tennis courts. A few had grabbed their belongings, but most had simply run in terror. It wouldn't take long for the cops to show. We jumped back in the car and raced off. She peeled right for two blocks then took another left. Bug and Charley lay on the floor of the back seat.

We made another eight blocks before we were passed by a cop car going the opposite direction. He slowed but when he saw an obviously prosperous white couple in an obviously prosperous automobile, he blew on past.

I watched for tails, but didn't pick anything up.

The garage was open; we pulled in and shut the door behind us.

"What happened to you guys?" Lloyd asked. "You look like you been smoking weed and taking go-juice, your eyes are so wide."

"We just been in one of your better shoot-outs," Charley said.

"What was so good about it?" Lloyd asked.

"We were the ones who did all of the shooting," Charley said.

"Those two-door cars like those boys had aren't worth a shit in a tight spot, are they? Everybody jumps on top of each other trying to get out," Bug said. "I wish I'd had me a fire bomb."

"Don't worry. The night's young. You may get to use one

yet. You recognize anybody, Charley?"

"The man with the portable phone was one of Dong's men. Name of Tombo Willis."

"I'm going to make a call," I said.

I slipped out of the suit jacket, shoulder holster, and fancy shirt, slipped a black t-shirt over the Kevlar vest and left the .38 in the ankle holster, then walked five blocks to a pay phone.

It was shaping up to be a typical Thursday night in Little Five. The drummers were wailing away and dancing their special twisting dance, hoping that the Dead would go on tour soon. Hungry intowners were wandering toward the Bridgetown Grill, La Fonda Latina, and Fellini's, beer drinkers were converging on the Yacht Club, radical lesbians were reading poetry at Charis, skinheads were snarling, junkies were nodding out, and a certain cult-film mogul was holding forth at Blast Off Video. Some people were here to try to be different, most couldn't be normal if they worked at it all day.

Chandler answered the phone.

"Yuhellow, this is Chandler."

"We had a little problem with some of your men," I said.

"My men?"

"Tombo Willis and three guys in a black Camaro. I think they had another car they were talking to on the phone."

"What happened?" Dong said.

"They were following with intent to do bodily harm. So there was an exchange of fire," I said.

"Where abouts?"

"Up by McGill Place."

"I heard it on the scanner. Didn't know it was them."

"Some of them may come wandering in with buckshot in their ass," I said. "I thought you were calling them off."

"I did," Dong said.

"Maybe they didn't hear," I said.

"They heard," he said.

"Makes you wonder who they're taking orders from," I said.

"Thanks."

He hung up the phone.

52

"DONG SAYS HE called his people off," I explained. "They knew they weren't supposed to follow us, but they did anyway."

"Sounds like he might not be in control of his own crew," Bug said.

"I think he's beginning to figure that out," I agreed. "This might be a good time to place ourselves in the middle of the chaos. I thought we might cruise on over to that warehouse on Northside."

"Right. Aside from the fact that Earl and Wheezer were there, there was a feel to it I can't explain exactly," Charley said. "I think it was the way the guys I was with acted when we were driving there. The rest of the places they were off-handed, but this place they were pretty uptight about, had a peephole in the door, and the man inside checked them out pretty good before he opened up. I thought maybe it was gambling or a pussy parlor, but there wasn't nothing there but an empty warehouse and some office rooms I couldn't see into."

"How's the place secured?" Bug asked.

"When I was there they had a guard at the door, aside from Wheezer and Earl," Charley said. "The only lock I saw was a big padlock on a hasp, they close it with a bolt from the inside. I suspect they would have three men there, the guard plus two to replace the dead guys."

"Think we could force our way in?"

"It would be hard."

"Fake our way in?"

"Possible."

"What about setting the place on fire?" Bug asked. "That

way the guys gather up the money and run before the firemen get there. We get them on the way out."

"Might work if nothing else does," Charley said. "A lot could go wrong, though. Like they could panic or miscalculate and get burnt up with the money, firemen could get there too fast. I'd say we leave that plan for last. We ought to take along the bolt cutter and the pry bar just in case there's nobody there."

"Would you leave the bank without anybody there?" Bug asked.

"No, but could be everything is going to hell out there with Dong's crew, or they could have moved the money, but we can get an idea where they went if we toss the place."

Lloyd and Bob sat up front. The back of the van was crowded with Lloyd's wheelchair, shotguns, Charley, Bug, Elizabeth, myself, and six Molotov cocktails mixed to incendiary perfection in extra fragile bottles.

We were no more than eight blocks from the garage on an unfinished road near the Carter Center when a car's headlights lit the front of the van. We came to an abrupt stop. Lloyd leaned over and stuck his head through the window.

"What you think you're doing there, Mister?"

Bug grabbed a shotgun and stood hunched on his feet next to the sliding door and began opening it very slowly and quietly, then stepped outside.

"You tell that Mr Charley we going to make him dead."

"Shit. It's the Jacksons," Charley whispered.

"You got him in there. Maybe we going to make him dead right now."

I hadn't noticed the .38 in Lloyd's lap until he put it in the man's face.

"I'm sick of being pushed around by you and the damned doctors," Lloyd said. "Maybe I should blow your fucking brains out."

"I ain't no doctor. What I got to do with the doctor?" the Jackson asked.

I heard Bug's voice from the street. "Get out of the car, asshole."

"Hermann, Hermann … it's that buck what broke my arm and swelled up your balls. You better do what he want, Hermann," the Jackson in the car said.

Charley leaned forward and looked out of the window next to Lloyd.

"You never told me your name was Hermann," he said.

I stepped out of the van and walked around the front. The other man had climbed out of the car.

"Both you boys take off your clothes, now," Bug snarled. He looked very scary. "Charley, bring me two of them handcuffs and a cocktail. Throw those clothes in the car," he said to the Jacksons.

Both men were naked.

"Now I need to explain something to you boys. The reason you been acting so casual to me is that you don't know who I am. I'm the physical incarnation of the god of pain. I have been sent to this planet by my father, the sun god, for one purpose only, and that is in the event you ever give Charley a hard time again, I'm going to pull out your fingernails and your teeth and cut off your nose and ears and eyelids and dick and balls and pound a tent peg up your ass, and then you know what I'm going to do?"

"No, sir."

"I'm going to do some even worse shit you can't even imagine. Now take these two handcuffs from Mr Charley and I want you to fasten yourselves together. Wrist to wrist and ankle to ankle. That's right. Now take off. Get out of here."

They were walking away trying to coordinate their motions with their wrist and ankle attached. They weren't having much luck but were making some headway.

"Now everybody get in the van and pull it up a ways; leave the back door open so I can jump in."

We pulled the van around the Jacksons' car. Through the back I saw Bug toss the cocktail into the car. It exploded into a ball of fire.

The Jacksons seemed to have gotten their movements together and were hauling ass through an empty lot.

On Boulevard Charley said he wanted to stop at a pay phone.

"Who you want to call?" Bug asked.

"The cops," Charley said. "I want to tell them I saw these two white guys that looked like Rastafarians up by the Carter Center. They took their clothes off, fastened themselves together, and set their car on fire."

"Good idea," Bug said.

Elizabeth Martin, attorney at law, looked like she was enjoying herself.

The warehouse was dark, no signs of Dong's crew inside or out. The only sound was the scuttling of rats. Lloyd backed the van to the loading dock, and Charley and I checked the door. It was padlocked from the outside. He worked at it with the bolt cutters while I held one of the penlights. After several tries he found the necessary leverage, and the lock snapped loudly and fell to the ground. In the silence it sounded like a pistol shot.

I pushed the door open and searched the room with a large flashlight. Nothing to see but a half dozen long empty tables.

I signaled for the others to follow. Bug and Elizabeth came first followed by Bob pushing Lloyd. Once we were all inside I pushed the door shut, shot the bolt, and turned the light on.

"Look at the money," Charley said.

Scattered randomly across the floor were several thousand dollars worth of twenties.

"Looks like this used to be the place," I said.

"They left in a hurry," Charley said.

"Let's check the offices," Bug said.

There were two doors near us to the left and a small framed cube at the far end of the building. I walked toward it while the others checked the closer ones.

"More loose money," I heard Charley say.

I don't know why, but the plain cube-shaped office looked like a mausoleum. Maybe I sensed something before I opened the door and smelled the fresh blood and guts.

I turned on the overhead light and saw what might have been — except for all the blood on his face — a young Dong Chandler. I imagined it was Billy Jr. He had fallen forward on his side. His arms were taped behind him, his ankles and mouth taped too. He had been on his knees looking at the man who killed him. Pleading with his eyes. Both loving and hating the father who had gotten him into this, who might save him. The bullet had entered the top front of the head down and traveled toward the brain stem. The worst part was the way the blood had run over the open, confused eyes. I heard a sharp rap on the warehouse door.

In the large open room, I signaled to the others that they should spread out and take defensive positions. At the door, I found a second light switch which I guessed was for the loading dock. I flipped it on and cracked the peephole open.

Outside stood Dong Chandler and two of his henchmen. I knew it could be a terrible mistake, but I unlatched the bolt and let them in.

53

DONG LOOKED LIKE he didn't have a care, but the guys that stood on either side of him were clearly nervous. Finding us in the warehouse wasn't high on their list of things they wanted to do at this moment.

"Surprise, surprise, motherfucker," Dong said. "What are you doing here?"

"Following a hunch," I said.

"How did it turn out?"

"About like I thought it might," I said.

"Is that good or bad?" he asked. It seemed like he was trying to size something up. Since we had him outgunned, I didn't think he was wondering if he could take us.

"It's as bad as it gets," I said.

"Tell me," he said. He dropped his eyelids like a snake. Aside from the tension in his brow, I wouldn't have thought he felt a thing.

"I haven't had a chance to tell the others, I just found him in that back office. I've got very bad news. I'm afraid your son is dead," I said.

He looked past me, towards the others to see if they showed any surprise or if it was more than a coincidence finding me in the same location with his dead son. Finally he spoke.

"Billy?"

"I'm afraid so," I said.

"What a bunch of shit," Charley said angrily. "Bringing a man's family into a business situation is about as fucked up as you can get."

"I'm going to introduce the man who did this to the world of pain," Bug said.

"Billy." Dong said it again softer. Very slowly he reached inside his jacket for a pistol. At this distance I didn't have to do much aiming with the shotgun. It was pointed at his chest from my waist.

"Watch it," I said.

"I don't have a problem with you over this," he said.

What he meant sunk in, although the men standing on either side of him still didn't have a clue. He drew the gun slowly. Both men watched him curiously, looking at the gun as if it were an item that had fallen from a distant star – looks nice but what is it for.

He busted a cap in the brain of the man standing next to him. Blood, gray matter, and bone flew out on the floor and the man collapsed backwards. His arms flew up in an odd position, almost like he was signaling a touchdown.

"Oh God." Elizabeth Martin sounded like she might throw up. It seemed like a good idea, maybe I would join her. Dong pointed the gun squarely at the second man's face.

"You brought me here to kill me, didn't you?" he said.

"What you talking about, boss?" the man said. I could see Dong didn't believe him for shit.

Blam! He fired the pistol a second time, and the second man went down. Elizabeth turned away. Bug put his left arm around her while he held the shotgun with the right.

"They brought me here to kill me," Dong said. He seemed to be repeating it because it seemed so incredible.

"I thought they might have that in mind when we left the Bar-B-Cue, but I decided to ride along and see how it played out."

The unspoken logic was that if members of his crew had sold him out and were going to kill him, it might be safer in a lonely warehouse where he knew the enemy, rather than back at the restaurant where he wasn't sure who he could trust.

"I think you got some serious problems. Is there anybody

in your outfit you know you can turn to without question?"
I asked.

"There's a couple," he said.

"I think you better lock yourself in here and be damned careful about who you let in. My guess is that they were going to hold you here and call someone else to do the killing. I think our boy likes people to look at him when he kills them."

He clenched his jaw in suppressed rage. He understood that there are people who kill because they must and those who kill because they like it. The thought of someone getting pleasure from killing his son and having those same designs on him was too awful to consider.

"Are you going to kill him?"

"Of course," I said.

"Are you going to make it hurt?" he asked.

"You can count on it," Bug said.

"So, lets talk grits and groceries," I said. "The way I see it, you want the guy who got your son to be dead but you aren't in a position to do it yourself, because you don't know who you can count on. Am I right?"

"That's about the size of it," he said.

"When we find the guy you want dead, we're also going to find the money that used to be in this warehouse. When we find it, we're planning on keeping it. You understand?"

"Yes."

"I'm not going to kill you because I don't have any reason to, but I want to know if we are going to have a problem next time we meet if I take the money." I said.

He thought for a minute. I was about to save his ass in a major way, and give him revenge which he couldn't get himself. I imagined both of those would be worth a lot to him, but then again, he didn't get rich giving it away.

"I know how much money should be there, and it's a hell of a lot to pay for a hit," he said.

"You know it's a special situation," I said. "As a percentage of the business you're about to lose, it can't be spit. Plus how much is the revenge worth?"

"If you want the money why the hell don't you just kill me? Why the hell bargain?" I could tell he asked the question with the certainty that he already knew the answer.

"I'm always looking down the road," I said. "In the long run, I think we'll do each other more good if we're alive."

"You're just slicker than snot," he said. "Who the hell are you guys, really?" he asked.

"We're a collection of dedicated criminals," Bug said.

"We consider outlawing one of your better professions," Charley said.

"He killed a friend of ours, too," I said.

"So you'd do this for nothing?" Dong asked.

"Fuckin' A," Bug said. "We'd pay to do it."

"You guys drive a hard bargain," Dong said. "You know who it is for sure? As I see it, could be one of three or four people."

"Yes."

"Tell me."

I shook my head.

"That phone in the office turned on?" Bug asked.

"Yes."

"We'll call you when it's done," I said.

"We're going to leave now. You better lock yourself in and call somebody you can trust. Once this guy goes down, you'll find your crew is more loyal. You can weed through them when the time's more suited. You son's in that back office. It's not pretty. I'll be happy to go back there and fix him up for you," I said.

"No. I'll do it myself."

"OK. You've had as much time to think as we've got. I want an answer."

"There's about two and a half million," Dong said. "You

can have it all with my blessing. Only you got to do one thing. You got to make sure when he dies, it's got to hurt."

"You got it," I said.

"As a matter of personal pride, I wouldn't have it any other way," Bug agreed.

54

WE WERE DRIVING toward the river in the van.

"Oh God. That was the worst thing I've ever seen. I thought I was going to throw up," Elizabeth said.

"I know. It was fucking awful," I said.

"Thing about your criminal line of work is the courts ain't going to give you any justice. It's a do-it-yourself operation," Charley said. "Thing about your citizens in the general public is they get all worked up over somebody wants to charge them fifty cents more a gallon on their gas, and they send the army over to blow hell out of some guy in the desert, and the preachers come on the television and tell everybody it's alright with God because He loves Americans more than anyone else and wants them to have the gasoline real cheap so they can drive to their churches and synagogues and put money in the collection basket. Only thing is, up-close, it's pretty much like what we saw in the warehouse.

"One guy pops another guy because he's afraid of him or he wants what he has. It's fucked up, but it's the way it goes."

"I understand that, Charley, but I guess I hadn't thought through what it meant to me," she said. "It's a lot more comfortable living in that bullshit zone where you feel clean because other people are willing to get dirty for you."

"I don't think any of us are prepared for it," I said. "I know I wasn't and probably am not still."

"Pull over please," she said.

Lloyd pulled over sharply. She threw open the sliding door, stumbled to the curb, leaned over and vomited.

"You doing OK?" Bug asked.

"Yes, better," she said.

"We can leave you off someplace safe," Bug said.

"I might as well stick around," she said. "How much worse could it get?"

"A lot worse," Bug said. "In a little while we aren't just going to be watching it, we're going to be doing it."

"This is the guy that's been killing all these people?"

"Yes."

"I guess I'm in for the bitter end," she said.

Bob handed her a gallon jug of water he'd saved to pour on his clothes if they felt like they were on fire.

"Thanks." She rinsed out her mouth and climbed back into the back of the van.

"So who is it?" she asked.

"I think we all know, or think we know anyway," Bug said. "But we want to be certain. That's why we're going to grab Winkler. You want to be sure before you do something like this."

"After what I just saw, you don't have to explain that. What makes you think Winkler is going to talk?"

"Sam and Charley have got him down as the weak link, and I have to say I agree with them."

Bob was sitting next to Lloyd with an Atlanta street map. At intervals following some unspoken command he would flip on a penlight and point to the map. Lloyd would slow, look, and make a turn.

As it turned out, the Winklers only lived a mile or so from the late James and Anne Marie Shirley.

"This is his street," Lloyd said.

He slowed to look at a mailbox.

"Judging from the house numbers I'd make it to be that place about half way up the block with all the lights on."

It was the same gothic dollhouse architecture as the Shirley house. Three stories of pink gingerbread stucco in the middle of a treeless lot. It stood out like a dog with a hard-on.

"Looks like every light in the place must be turned on," Lloyd said.

"You might want to park at the curb, just in case he ain't feeling too social," Charley said.

Lloyd brought the van to a stop and killed the lights. It didn't make much difference. With the outside floods on there wasn't going to be any sneaking up on the place.

"Let's hope he's scared enough to talk but not scared enough to shoot," I said.

From deep within the house I heard an argument between two people whom I took to be Jerry and Kathy Winkler. It was a man and a woman, anyway. I couldn't understand the words, but the sounds were of a woman's voice, angry, then pleading, and a man's deeper tones starting with speech then degenerating to a disorganized, hysterical barking.

I rang the bell – silence, then frantic arguing, then silence again, then the sound of footsteps, then the door opening slowly to reveal Kathy Winkler.

"Could I help you?" she asked. It was a stupid thing to say, but then what the hell can you say when the world is ending.

"We need to talk to your husband," I said.

I pushed the door softly, and she stood aside letting me in. Charley waved to the van then followed me inside. We left the door standing wide open.

"Jerry, Carter and Dullard are here to see you."

"I'm coming right down," he said.

"He has to slip something on," she explained.

I heard a sound on the front porch and looked back and saw Bob and Bug lifting Lloyd in his chair over the front steps.

"Nobody ever has any damned ramps on houses," Lloyd was muttering.

"Oh, there's more of you," Kathy said. She walked to the door. "Won't you come in. Hello, Arlo. Oh." She saw Bob and fell silent.

"My friend here needs to take a shower," Lloyd said.

"A shower, yes, of course, I'll take you to a downstairs

bathroom. Just follow me." She acted like having strangers show up in the middle of the night to take showers was a matter of routine. Given her husband's co-workers, I imagined the demented could have become the usual.

As Bob followed her, he twisted uncomfortably and flashed a note reading, "CLOTHES ON FIRE."

Jerry Winkler tentatively descended the staircase.

"Time to talk," I said.

"Yes," he agreed. "Time to talk."

He led us to a formal living room. It was the sort of space that was kept spotless and never used except for ceremonial occasions when visiting dignitaries dropped in unexpectedly, and you didn't want to let on there were human beings living in the house.

"Where do you want to start?" Winkler asked.

"It's your story," I said.

"Can you save my wife?" he asked.

"Yes."

"What about me?"

"I don't know. Maybe. We'll work that out as we go along," I said.

"I just found most of this out," he said.

"From whom?" I asked.

"Bice. They were playing me for a fucking idiot right under my nose."

"If that's the case, I'd say things should go better for you," I said.

"You could put in a word to Chandler?" he asked.

"Yes."

"Would he listen?"

"Yes."

He leaned back in the chair and breathed a deep sigh. "Thank God," he said.

Kathy Winkler walked into the room. "I'm sorry," she said. "I don't want to interrupt, but I'm afraid, um, your friend is.

. . he's taking a shower with his clothes on."

"Nothing to worry about. He thought his clothes were catching on fire," Lloyd said.

"Oh," Kathy Winkler said.

Jerry nodded as if he knew there was a logical explanation.

"Why don't you start at the beginning," I asked.

"At the beginning, yes," Winkler said.

"Start with Eldo Justus," Charley prodded.

"I remember Eldo," Winkler said. "That's when things started to get out of hand."

55

"THIS WAS NEVER a plan. It was something we all stumbled into. At first, Weatherby represented a few of Chandler's men who had minor scrapes with the law. As he started doing more work for Chandler, he began to have an idea of how much money Chandler was pulling in running coke through the clubs and so forth.

"The problem Chandler was having was they couldn't wash their money fast enough. He still thought in terms of operating a few businesses and stuffing money in the tills. Weatherby set up the pipeline for him. Smuggling the money to the Netherlands Antilles, setting up dummy corporations which were untraceable, then moving the money back to the US through real estate investments. These were investments you could borrow against, so you could have squeaky-clean money from American banks."

Winkler spoke with a slow, almost hypnotic cadence. The insight bought with so much pain gave him a dignity he hadn't possessed before the fall. I am always amazed at the surprises of a cataclysm. The tough guy whines and cries while the dipshit dashes through the flames to save the baby, the Chihuahua, and the china.

Kathy Winkler seemed to be responding to the change in her husband, too. She sat on the arm of his chair and put her arm around his shoulder.

"It was a dream deal," Winkler said. "The US Customs are set up to catch people coming in, not going out. The bankers in the Antilles didn't care where the money was coming from. They would have given us a fucking parade if we had asked for it. Chandler had limitless amounts of cash and would buy anything. We were even making money for him on the investments we were laundering the money through. It was unbelievable. You have to understand. Aside from a few suspicions, this was all I knew about the operation until Bice talked to me yesterday."

"What did you learn then?" Elizabeth Martin asked gently. I was glad that she did. I knew her cross-examination skills had to be better than all of ours put together. And somehow the question seemed less frightening coming from a woman. It was less like being asked to give an accounting for which you would be judged, by which you would live or die, and more an opportunity to let the guilt escape, to grow light with innocence, to bury your head in the soft flesh of her lap and be a child again.

"It went to Weatherby's head. He'd always had a weakness for the shortcut and a belief that nobody else would notice. He was right most of the time. Everyone thought he was wonderful. It only got him in trouble once, when he was working for the DA's office.

"At first he started skimming. He'd set aside a little bit of the handle each trip for himself. He purposely made the paper trail so tangled that nobody could figure it out. Chandler seemed pretty happy at the way things were going. No questions asked.

"Then he got this idea that people like Billy Chandler were the dinosaurs of crime. That in the future the best crime would be done on computers, with the help of governments. Crime would be traded like any other commodity. It wasn't a bad idea, as far as they go. Only he got crazy with it. He saw Chandler as an insect and decided he could be dispensed with. With the right help he figured the tail could wag the dog. He could run the whole show, get all the profits for a while, then kiss off the drug operation entirely. He would have so much money he wouldn't need it."

"How did he plan on doing that?" Elizabeth asked. "He didn't have any of Chandler's contacts."

"His plan was to break Chandler's operation into smaller franchises," Winkler said. "He would make the big buys, then Chandler's boys would distribute for a much bigger cut than they had now. The point was to do it gradually. If he just knocked over Chandler, a war would break out, but if he won over the people a few at a time, it could be done smoothly because everybody would have known what their deal was. No surprises."

"But it didn't work out that way, did it?" Elizabeth asked.

"No. It almost did. The problem wasn't so much the plan as the personalities. Bice was in it at this point. He began making the trips to the Antilles with Wheezer and Earl. He romanced them pretty good down there. They had fancy suites, clothes, women. After a while they got used to being treated like royalty and resented Chandler treating them like stooges. It wasn't too long before Bice had them."

"What about Eldo Justus?" she asked.

"Eldo was the next one they tried to turn. Only problem was Eldo was a loyal son of a bitch. I think he may have figured Weatherby for a maniac, too. He was going to tell Chandler."

"Eldo always was a good old boy," Charley said.

"What happened to him?" Elizabeth asked.

"Burned up in a cabin fire," Winkler said. "At the time we thought it was an accident. Turned out it was Wheezer and Earl that did it, Weatherby that told them to. Bice didn't know anything about it. He just thought it was a fortunate accident. Afterward, recruiting Chandler's crew became a lot easier. I guess they figured they could either go down to the islands and have a good time or get burnt alive. There wasn't much of a choice."

"Those sons of bitches. I had them and let them slip through my fingers," Bug said.

"It ain't like they got to enjoy themselves much after you finished with them," Lloyd pointed out.

"That's some consolation," Bug agreed.

Bob drifted silently into the room. His head, his torso, and his legs were all wrapped in towels but he dripped on the carpet anyway. Neither of the Winklers seemed to notice or care about the spreading puddle.

"FIRE OUT," Bob wrote.

"Good news," I said. Elizabeth drew us back on track.

"Then there were the Shirleys," she said.

"Yes . . . James and Anne Marie . . ." he mumbled.

Kathy Winkler sobbed quietly. Her husband looked at her.

"You've got to believe I didn't know anything about it. If I had I wouldn't have stood for it. No matter what the consequences," he said.

"I'm sure that's the reason you weren't told." Elizabeth held out the moral shelter, and he scrambled to it.

"Yes. If I'd known I would have done something. I mean I obviously knew they were killed, and it had something to do with us. Weatherby told me that Chandler did it. He caught Shirley skimming. He said as long as I played it straight I would have nothing to worry about."

"But that wasn't what really happened, was it?" she asked.

"No." He muffled a sob of his own, leaned forward, and held his head, trying to gain composure. His wife silently stroked his hair. After a moment he leaned back and spoke again.

"Bice didn't know at the time, so this is pieced together after the fact. It may not be a hundred percent . . ."

"We understand," she said. "Just tell it as well as you can."

"James was an asshole and a fuck up," he said bitterly. "He took some papers home, and his wife saw them. They wouldn't have meant a thing to her, but they made it clear what the various legs of the laundry were. Weatherby said he had to have her killed. He gave James the name of this guy who could find somebody to set it up."

"Oh God," Kathy Winkler said. "He didn't do it."

"I'm afraid he did, baby. He gave this guy thirty thousand to kill her. The guy told her instead. She was furious and told her husband. Weatherby called her. She didn't know he was involved and made the mistake of letting him know that she hadn't told anybody else. She was ashamed about it and just didn't want to tell anybody. He told her he would work it out if she let him. Wheezer and Earl were there when he killed them. They got drunk and told Bice on the next trip."

"They killed the guy that was supposed to shoot Mrs. Shirley, too, didn't they?" I asked.

"Yes. That was Wheezer and Earl. That's when Bice figured out they had gotten Eldo, too. The spooky thing about it is when Weatherby killed the Shirleys, they said it looked like he enjoyed it. They felt like maybe he told Shirley to do it in the first place as much to screw around with him as anything else. She wouldn't have put anything together.

"It was like he got the first taste of a drug, and he couldn't stop using it. Like he couldn't get enough of seeing the fear in others, smelling it, whatever."

"The kidnapping of Billy Jr. How did that fit in? I can't see Chandler's men going for that, even if they had turned on him. He didn't have anything to do with the business," she said.

"He was supposed to be a hostage. Weatherby was getting ready to move. The plan was that they would use the kid to coax Chandler into retirement. The guys thought it was a good idea. A lot of them liked Chandler; they just figured he wasn't any more use."

"And what about the men at the airport?" she asked.
"Bice found them tied up and called Weatherby. Weatherby thought they had turned on him. That they were in on it. The guy's gone paranoid. Too much cocaine and death. He said they'd thrown in with you, and you had robbed us. Did you?" he asked.

"Sure as shit," I said.

He made a humorless laugh. "You fooled me. Fooled Bice, too. He figured you were what you claimed to be. So you aren't connected to the cartel?" he asked.

"No."

"What about that guy in Costa Rica?"

"You want to live long and prosper, you'll forget about him."

"OK."

"What did Weatherby do next?" Elizabeth prodded.

"Bice thought he was nuts. Weatherby killed Wheezer and Earl right in front of him. Put out the hit on you, too. Said he thought the secret was blown. He was going to kill Billy Jr and Chandler. This scared the shit out of Bice. He knew Weatherby was completely out of control at this point. He tried to slow him down. Bice's wife was almost comatose."

He leaned forward again, held his head in his hands, and stared at the floor, looking for a long-lost secret.

"Then comes the worst part. Bice was frantic. He thought that, as bad as it was, the only alternative was to go to Chandler, tell him Weatherby had lost his mind and hope for the best. So Weatherby grabbed his family."

"Oh shit," I said.

"He made Bice come to him."

Kathy Winkler was sobbing again, her husband joined her. Bug nodded with sadness. The Bice children that he had entertained with magic tricks were in the hands of a lunatic.

"Where are they?" Charley asked.

"They might be where the money is," Winkler said. "He has a little house out by the river."

"I know where it is. I turned it up on that asset search," Elizabeth said.

"We best get there," Lloyd said.

"Get the van ready. I'm going to call Chandler."

Dong picked up the phone.

"Chandler," he said.

"You got anyone with you?" I asked.

"Yes. Two boys I can count on."

"Good. I've just been talking to Winkler."

"And?"

"You can back off him. He didn't know anything till Bice told him."

"Bice."

"Right. He and Weatherby were going to rip you off, but it was Weatherby that did all the killing."

"That asshole."

"He's grabbed Bice's family."

"He's got a couple little kids, doesn't he?"

"Right. We think he took them to a place out by the river. We're on our way now. In an hour or so, you should find some of your people running for cover. They'll probably want to make peace."

"That damned punk. These yuppies don't know when to stop. They can't just take their piece of the pie, they want everything. They screw it up for everybody. They screw up everything. Listen to me. You skin that punk. I want you to skin him."

"I'll let you know when it's over." I said.

56

THE LOWER CHATTAHOOCHEE River feeds from the frigid floor of Lake Lanier. The water is still teeth-chattering cold by the time its banks rub against Cobb County. It's as if the Clark Fork River had been airmailed from Montana to the Atlanta suburbs.

In the late-night hours, when the cold rolling water meets the warm moist air, together they form a cotton fog that obscures the river and drifts across the flood plain over damp clay soil and twisted vegetation.

Under Elizabeth's guidance we circled the roadside border of Weatherby's property until we found a dirt drive with recent tire tracks.

"This has to be the road to the house," she said. "There's nothing else around here that could be it."

"This place is spooky," Bug said.

"Notice how sounds are muffled," I said. "That plus the lack of visibility should lend itself to surprise. Only problem is we don't know who it is that's going to be surprised."

"We just need to spread out on the road so nobody can see all of us at once," Charley said. "That way even if we're ambushed, most of us will be able to take cover."

"How far is the house from here?" I asked.

"I'd guess about a fifteen-minute walk," Elizabeth said.

"OK. Here's a plan. Charley and I will take point. Once we get a little farther up the road, we'll work our way around to the back of the house. If there aren't any sentries outside the house, you guys spread out, open fire, make it sound like the Chinese army is outside. Charley and I will get them as they run out the back. Just don't shoot inside till we know who's in there.

"If they've got outside sentries, then we make another plan, but this way we don't have to talk and make a commotion if there aren't any. Another thing – Bug, I know you're anxious to employ those Molotov cocktails, but if you burn up all the money, we are going to be very pissed."

"Got you covered on that," Bug said.

The others gave Charley and me a two-minute head start. It wasn't hard walking quietly. We stuck to the center of the track and the damp, moss-covered soil, walking toward the river and the thickest mist. You couldn't see the moon, although I knew it was bright. As it filtered through the fog, I could see our vague shadows once my eyes became accustomed to the darkness.

I heard men talking, moving down the road toward us, and I reached out and touched Charley on the shoulder. We had a problem, and we both knew it. If we took cover now, there was a chance the others would walk past us and run into the men on the road. All we could do was keep walking and break for cover at the last possible moment.

The men were carrying on back and forth. I couldn't hear what they were saying but they sounded angry. They were walking fast, making good time, and not caring much who heard them. It sounded like there were three or four of them.

They were getting close. As we walked forward, I put my hand on Charley's shoulder. When they were less than a hundred feet away I pushed him gently to the side of the path, walked forward another fifteen feet, and stepped off the road. Then they were on top of me.

"Hold it right there, fuck-face," I said.

"Freeze," Charley said from farther down the road. I heard footsteps that could have been Bug and Bob running toward us.

"No problem, man. All we want to do is get out of here," one of the men said.

"We're supposed to be guarding the sick piece of garbage,

but I don't want anything to do with him," another said.

"He's up there by himself. Do us a favor and go kill him."

"I'm going to do that for you," I said. "Here's another favor, some news. Dong knows you been fucking out on him. If I were you I'd take off running till you hit Idaho."

"Thanks buddy, we appreciate the warning."

"How far to the house?"

"Five or ten minutes."

"Are the Bices up there?"

"We don't know nothing about that."

Bug strolled into view, saw us talking to the men, and held his hand out to let the others know it was alright. Bob trotted up pushing Lloyd in the chair. Elizabeth was running behind, still in her lawyer suit carrying an arm full of Molotov cocktails.

The men looked them over.

"You got quite a crew here," one of them said.

Bob looked him in the eye and gave a laugh that sounded more like he was crying.

"It sure tore an extra asshole in your operation," Bug said. "You best get gone."

"No problem, man. We're out of here."

"What did they say?" Bug asked.

"Weatherby is a sick piece of garbage. They are supposed to be guarding him but they aren't. He's up at the house by himself. They hope we kill him."

"We got him," Bug said.

"It doesn't sound too good for the Bices," Charley said.

"No it doesn't," I agreed. "I asked if they were there. They didn't want to talk about it."

"I take it alone means alone," Elizabeth said.

"I don't know, maybe it's a figure of speech," I said. "Maybe the Bices are there but nobody wanted to cop to a kidnapping."

"Or worse," Charley said.

"I'm thinking we may want to force the issue at the house," Bug said. "Not give him any time to waste them. What if we do it like before, but I kick the door down. He doesn't know he isn't guarded. Maybe he panics and takes off through the back. You two can be either side of the back door. If he shoots at me in the front, you can kick down the back."

"We can do it that way," I said. "Let's just get this thing over."

In all the running around we'd forgotten to bring the radios we'd used at the airport. We could see the house, lights showing from every window, blinds pulled so you couldn't see in. Bug gave us another five minutes to get in place in back, and it was plenty of time. We stooped under the windows, just in case he was looking out, and positioned ourselves on either side of the door. We would have had time to smoke half a cigarette before Bug kicked in the door.

Smash. It flew open and splintered.

"I've come for you, and I'm going to burn you alive like you burned Jimmy Cooley," Bug snarled. It scared the crap out of me and it wasn't me he was after.

"Uh." It was Weatherby's voice making a guttural grunt of surprise.

He broke through the back door. It was like he knew we were there. Without looking he shot Charley and Charley stumbled backward and fell over. I definitely blew it. I was looking at Charley instead of shooting Weatherby.

He shot me in the center of my chest, and it felt like a stake was driven through my heart. I couldn't breathe, lurched forward and dropped my gun, stumbled to the ground and grabbed it. He was about to pump a round in my head when Charley rolled over and put four or five rounds in his shoulder, turning it to pulp.

I bobbled the 9-mm, gave up, pulled out the little .38, and shot him twice high on the inside of his right leg.

The tan pants turned dark below the wound. Weatherby held it with his good arm and lurched away.

"Oh God, no." Bug spoke from inside the house, then he stumbled through the back door.

"You two OK?" Bug asked.

"Oh no." I heard Elizabeth Martin inside the house now. It must be bad.

"Got me in the Kevlar. Just knocked the wind out and broke some ribs," I said.

"Same here." Charley panted.

"Which way?"

We heard a car start.

"Bug. Charley practically took off his arm and I tore open his femoral artery. He's bleeding to death. You don't have to rush it."

"I want the satisfaction," Bug said.

Elizabeth looked demented as she leaned out the door with the cocktails in her arms. They ran toward the sound of the car.

"We got to get up, Charley."

"Right." He struggled to his feet.

"In here, you get the money together and I'll go see if Bug needs help."

Charley followed me into the house.

"Oh man. This is your worst situation," he moaned.

The little house was essentially one room, because the interior walls had been knocked out with a sledge hammer. Old wiring hung next to smashed plumbing and shattered studs.

The money was here alright. I could see it in a half dozen open suitcases, but the Bices were here, too, at least what was left of them. The whole family had been slaughtered. I couldn't make myself look at it long enough to understand the whole story, but it was clear it had been a long horrible spectacle starting with the children and ending with Henry Bice.

Charley and I couldn't talk. We quickly fastened the suitcases and carried them outside. Bob was wheeling Lloyd toward us.

"They got him cornered in his car," Lloyd said. "We didn't want to watch."

"Do yourself a favor and don't go inside the house either," I said.

"The Bices?"

"Yes."

"Bad?"

"Worse than that."

"I'm truly sorry to hear that," Lloyd said.

"Don't be too hard on Bug or the rest of us," Charley said. "We did see the inside. And right now I want to go and watch that miserable piece of pus die."

"We understand, Charley," Lloyd said. "Believe me. We understand."

We walked toward the sound of Bug's taunting. I had the feeling I was watching a ritual as ancient as the part of my brain that dreams. A demon was being driven out by the liturgy of fire.

Weatherby was sitting quietly in his car in the middle of a soggy clearing. He wasn't resisting. There wasn't anything left to do but drift into eternity. A Molotov cocktail arced through the air and ignited in Weatherby's lap. He began to jerk and struggle to escape with the arm that wouldn't work, the leg that was paralyzed and the body that was weak from loss of blood.

"Die, motherfucker. Die!" Bug screamed at him.

Elizabeth and Bug were illuminated by the burning gasoline. I could see their faces. Both of them were crying.

"You got him, Bug."

"Actually it was Elizabeth. She's the one who threw the bomb," Bug said.

"You've been a bad influence, man," I said. "Before she met

you she was a mild-mannered lawyer."

"I know." The two of them started laughing, punchy from moral exhaustion and near hysteria.

"Sam. Inside that house. I've never seen anything like that. That was the worst thing ever."

"You're right, Bug. But at least it's over now."

I heard a half dozen gunshots from the direction of the road.

"It may not be as over as we want," Charley said.

57

"IF IT'S THE Jacksons I'm going to be pissed," Charley said.

"I don't care who it is," Bug said. "I'm in a shitty mood. They better not get in my way."

We had begun drifting away from the car because of the smell. The combination of burning gasoline, seat cushions, and human flesh was unbearable.

The fire was dying, producing more smoke than flames. Weatherby was a human cinder drawn forward on the remains of the steering wheel. His hands were black claws.

"I'm afraid it's Dong," I said. "I told him we were coming out here. I didn't think it was possible he'd regroup so fast."

"Don't worry about it," Charley said. "If he isn't going to stick with the deal, we might as well get it over with right now."

Our drift had become a purposeful walk to the front of the house. Bob had arranged the six suitcases in a neat line, like they were about to be loaded on a bus.

"We heard some gunshots and it sounds like a pickup truck is coming down the road," Lloyd said.

"Let's get the bags out of sight," I said. "Then spread out. If it turns to a fight, we might have to bushwack back to the van."

The truck was running without lights. It reminded me that Dong had started his career running shine. It wouldn't be new to him.

I stood in the middle of the road and watched the others creeping behind a covering of shrubs.

The pickup truck was an old dark Ford. It stopped in front of me. Dong was behind the wheel wearing work khakis and a straw hat. A man sat beside him in the front, and another stood in the bed holding on to the top of the cab, a pump shotgun in his other hand.

Dong opened the door and I walked to his side of the road to join him. The corpses of the men we had seen earlier on the road were stacked roughly in the bed of the pickup wrapped in a clear plastic tarp.

"I didn't expect to see you here," I said.

"I wanted to see for myself," he said. "Did you get him?"

"Yes."

"How?"

"We shot him up, then burnt him up," I said.

"Was he alive when you burnt him?" he asked.

"Yes."

"Good. Where is he?"

"I'll show you. But you better tell your boys to be careful. Some of my people are feeling aggressive tonight," I said.

"You heard him," he said.

The man in the pickup put down his shotgun. Chandler followed me to the clearing at the side of the house. The flames inside the car were flickering, silhouetting Weatherby's charred corpse. Dong picked up a handful of dirt and threw it at him.

"You sorry son of a bitch," he said. Then, after a pause, "Those two guys back there are about all that's left of my crew."

"Maybe you should retire," I said.

"Maybe so," he said. "I wonder what it would be like?"

"I've tried it. It's very safe and very boring."

"I don't know if I could do it."

"We found the money," I said.

"Then you better get out of here with it before I change my mind," he said. "We'll clean this up like it never happened. It'll be like everyone went on a long vacation."

I walked back to the front of the house.

"Let's get out of here," I said.

"Sounds like one of your better plans," Charley said.

58

I HAD TO run someplace, so I went to Mexico Beach, where a young widow and I had walked on the beach and tried to cast our grief away with a sad imitation of love.

I couldn't find the old motel. The place had changed. I couldn't recognize any of it.

We had found a dozen computer disks in one of the suitcases with the money. I didn't think much about it at the time, but I took them to Florida with me anyway.

I was walking along the beach one day and remembered what Jerry Winkler had said about Weatherby's skimming from the money shipments. When I called Jean-Paul, he thought the disks might be worth looking at, so he flew up from Costa Rica with his laptop.

They were the key to twenty different offshore bank accounts which Jean-Paul help me discreetly loot. We were all very rich.

Bug is in deep hiding. I suspect he is somewhere around Atlanta, because I recently received an envelope which contained two news clippings and a photograph of Elizabeth Martin. She had an enigmatic smile on her face.

One news clip reported that the home of the doctor who had run down Lloyd with his Mercedes-Benz had mysteriously burned to the ground. The other detailed the bizarre funeral of a comparative literature professor.

Bob had a cosmetic prosthesis made for his face which he reports looks funny but doesn't scare people. He published a book of poetry called Clothes on Fire, and he is touring university campuses with Lloyd, who reads the poems. Bob says he's had twenty-five signs printed which contain his favorite answers to questions. Lloyd assures me that he frequently feels even better than the man who sits at the top of the building filled with a billion dollars worth of pussy.

Charley is buying clothes. He also thinks that some of Bug's magic must have rubbed off because now he has a girlfriend. She's the nice young lady with pink and green hair who came by the garage looking for the band which used to practice there – Gregor and the Roaches.

And as for myself, I am given to the favorite occupation of many a rich old fart, lying on the beach, day-dreaming, and constructing fantasies.

My favorite one goes like this. I am taking a walk one day, and I finally find the motel I stayed in many years ago, owned by the woman whose husband was killed in Vietnam who knew me through a haze of alcohol.

I go inside the office and see a kindly old gent behind the counter.

"Do you know what happened to the woman who used to own this place?" I ask.

"Things got very bad for her for a while," he says. "You know her husband was killed in the Vietnam War. She took to the bottle real hard, ended up losing the motel. But we heard she moved to California and cleaned up. Married a nice man, has a family and everything now."

I guess I'm a sucker for sad stories with happy endings.